CECE SLOAN IS SWOONING

JAMEY MOODY

CeCe Sloan is Swooning

©2023 by Jamey Moody. All rights reserved

Edited: Kat Jackson

Cover: Cath Grace Designs Instagram: @cathgracedesigns

This is a work of fiction. Names, characters, places, and incidents are the product of the author's imagination or are used fictitiously. Any resemblance to an actual person, living or dead, business establishments, events, or locales is entirely coincidental. This book, or part thereof, may not be reproduced in any form without permission.

If you'd like to stay updated on future releases, you can visit my website or sign up for my mailing list here: www.jameymoodyauthor.com.

As an independent author, reviews are greatly appreciated.

❋ Created with Vellum

CONTENTS

Also by Jamey Moody	v
Prologue	1
Chapter 1	7
Chapter 2	16
Chapter 3	25
Chapter 4	34
Chapter 5	44
Chapter 6	53
Chapter 7	61
Chapter 8	71
Chapter 9	79
Chapter 10	87
Chapter 11	96
Chapter 12	104
Chapter 13	113
Chapter 14	122
Chapter 15	130
Chapter 16	139
Chapter 17	147
Chapter 18	156
Chapter 19	165
Chapter 20	173
Chapter 21	181
Chapter 22	188
Chapter 23	198
Chapter 24	207
Chapter 25	216
Chapter 26	225
Chapter 27	233
Chapter 28	242
Chapter 29	250

Chapter 30	259
Six Months Later	267
About The Author	273
Also by Jamey Moody	275
Cory Sloan is Swearing	277

ALSO BY JAMEY MOODY

Stand Alones

Live This Love

One Little Yes

Who I Believe

What Now

The Your Way Series:

* Finding Home

*Finding Family

*Finding Forever

The Lovers Landing Series

*Where Secrets Are Safe

*No More Secrets

*And The Truth Is ...

*Instead Of Happy

The Second Chance Series

The Woman at the Top of the Stairs

The Woman Who Climbed A Mountain

The Woman I Found In Me

Christmas Novellas

*It Takes A Miracle

The Great Christmas Tree Mystery

With One Look

*Also available as an audiobook

PROLOGUE

"What are we looking at?"

"It looks like a shopping center to me."

"Oh, it's not just any shopping center," Cory replied. "It's ours. You are gazing upon the Sloan Sisters' Shopping Extravaganza."

At forty-four years old, Corrine Sloan was the oldest sister. She had thick blond hair and clear blue eyes that saw a vision of what this property could be.

"What are you talking about? I think I would remember buying a shopping center," CeCe remarked.

Cecilia was the quintessential middle sister of the Sloan siblings. Her fiery red hair and crystal blue eyes matched her personality. She was a forty-two-year-old good time ready to happen and was usually responsible for the fun.

"We didn't buy it," Cat Sloan said. "Explain yourself, Cory."

The youngest and therefore the baby sister, Catarina was thirty-seven. Her rich dark chocolate hair set off her blue eyes that matched her big sisters'. She was the quiet, reserved one, but not to be overlooked.

"Do you remember when Dad's rich uncle died and gave us all that money?"

"Of course I remember," CeCe scoffed. "He took us out to dinner and told us not to get any ideas about spending it."

"Yeah, as far as I can remember that's the only time he spent any of it," Cat added.

"Well, Daddy set aside part of that money for us," Cory said. "He left explicit instructions for us to do something with it together. This shopping center includes three stores, one for each of us."

"Why are we just now finding out about this?" CeCe asked, giving her sister a measured look. "And why isn't Mom telling us about it?"

"You know since Dad died Mom gave over all the financial stuff to me," Cory said.

"Yeah, Dad's been gone a year, Cory. What took so long for us to find out about this?" CeCe demanded.

"Dad had this in an investment that didn't mature until now. Mom told me about it last month," Cory replied.

"Why didn't you tell us!" Cat exclaimed.

"Because I had to be sure there was plenty of money for Mom to live comfortably going forward," Cory said defensively.

"I thought Dad made sure of that with his life insurance," CeCe said.

Cory nodded. "He did, but there were other things we had to do to get the money. It was all documentation bullshit and as you've both told me numerous times, neither one of you cared to be bothered with that. Right?"

CeCe and Cat looked at each other and smirked. "So, tell us what happened," CeCe said with a dramatic sigh.

"Mom told me about the investment. I contacted the company and they gave us an option of monthly disburse-

CeCe Sloan is Swooning 3

ments or a lump sum." Cory took an envelope out of her pocket and handed it to CeCe. "This is what Dad wanted."

CeCe opened the envelope and held it so Cat could read over her shoulder. Tears welled in both their eyes as they scanned the handwritten letter.

CeCe looked up at her sisters with fire in her eyes. "I don't know why he couldn't have enjoyed this money instead of saving it for us! He kept working at that damn factory, building planes, when he could've retired and spent time with Mom or us!"

Cat put her arm around her sister. "He loved building those airplanes. Can you imagine him sitting around? No, that wasn't who he was. The man was always building something. And did you ever hear Mom complain? Did any of us ever really want for anything growing up?"

CeCe sighed loudly. "We weren't poor, but we damn sure weren't well-off either!"

"This is what Dad wanted," Cory said, taking the letter from CeCe's hands. "Can you imagine how proud he would be if we owned our own stores, side by side? This is the place!"

"It's not even finished yet," CeCe observed.

"That's the beauty of it. CeCe, you have always wanted to open your own salon. You can customize this space and make it yours. How many chairs do you want?" Cory asked.

"Hmm." A smile grew on CeCe's face. "I can see three on each side as you walk in and then two or three stations in the back to do nails and facials."

"Okay, so CeCe gets her salon. What kind of store are you going to open, Cory?" Cat asked.

"There's not a liquor store within ten miles of this area. Look at the storefront at the end. That's about to become The Liquor Box," Cory said proudly.

"What!" Cat laughed.

"That's right," Cory replied with a laugh. "I'm a lesbian and that's what we do. We lick—"

"Stop!" CeCe and Cat yelled in unison.

"We know what you do. You've told us over and over," CeCe said.

"We get it. The Liquor Box," Cat added.

"I've already lined up my first big customer."

"Who?" CeCe asked.

"You know that sapphic resort at the lake where the Hollywood gays go?"

"Yeah, Krista Kyle owns it with Julia Lansing. I've done their hair and they've brought several of their clients in over the last couple of years," CeCe said.

"Didn't you go out there for a party last summer?" Cat asked.

CeCe wiggled her eyebrows. "I certainly did. Those Hollywood folks know how to have a good time."

Cory and Cat both chuckled.

"So CeCe opens a salon and you're opening a liquor store. What do you have in mind for me?" Cat asked.

"Well, little sister. I have an idea, but if you could open any store you wanted, what would it be?"

"Hmm," Cat murmured as she stared at the building.

"Oh, I know!" CeCe exclaimed. "It has to have something to do with books. You love to read!"

"That's what I was thinking." Cory nodded.

Cat glanced at her sisters with a sly smile on her face. "I'd love to open a bookstore, and in the back I'd have an exclusive toy store."

Cory and CeCe gazed at their little sister with confused looks on their faces.

"A private, clandestine adult toy store," Cat stated.

CeCe Sloan is Swooning

"Oh!" CeCe exclaimed as her eyes widened.

Laughter bubbled from Cory as she said, "Oh my God, Cat. That's perfect!"

The three sisters gazed at the building as ideas flowed through their heads.

"What do you think? Will you join The Liquor Box?" Cory asked.

"I can see it now," CeCe said, holding her arms out wide. "Salon 411. You'll not only get the perfect hairstyle, but you'll know everything that's going on in town."

"Oh, I like it," Cory said. She turned to Cat. "Your turn."

"Hmm, let's see. How about Your Next Great Read?"

"Yes!" CeCe exclaimed.

"Do you have a name for the room in the back?" Cory asked Cat.

"Yeah, I think I'll call it The Bottom Shelf." Cat grinned. "But let's not tell Mom about that part."

Cory chuckled. "You have to watch out for the quiet ones."

"So, little sister. Do we get a discount?" CeCe asked.

Cat laughed. "Do you think this is what Dad had in mind?"

"I can see it now!" Cory exclaimed. "Our clients can stop by and get a drink, a book, and get their hair done."

CeCe held out her hand. "I'm in."

"I'm in," Cat said, placing her hand on top of CeCe's.

"Watch out," Cory said, placing her hand on top. "Here come the Sloan Sisters!"

1

———

Three Months Later

"Are you ready?" Cory asked her sisters.

"Hold it!" CeCe exclaimed. She went over to a table where glasses of champagne were poured and waiting. She balanced three flutes in her hands and held them so each of her sisters could take one. "We should have a toast to kick off this open house."

"To the Sloan Sisters," Cory said, holding up her glass.

"May we bring joy to this little piece of our city." Cat held her glass next to Cory's and looked at CeCe.

"And...may we live happily ever after." CeCe chuckled and clinked her glass to her sisters'.

"What?" Cory laughed.

"I couldn't think of anything and I want us all to live happily ever after, so why not drink to that?" CeCe shrugged.

"How can we not? We'll be working side by side most days and doing something we love. Drink up," Cory said, "it's time to unlock the doors."

"Wait," Cat said. "Let's drink to Dad. This may not be what he had in mind, but he'd still be proud."

They clinked their glasses together again and drank.

"I think this is exactly what he wanted. We're together, doing our own thing, but still supporting each other," CeCe said.

"Remember to encourage people to walk through to the other stores," Cory said.

"It was a good idea to build these extra large openings in the walls so clients can move easily from store to store," CeCe said.

"We've got plenty of champagne in each store and other drinks if anyone prefers. Okay?" Cory looked at her sisters.

"Got it. I'll come by later to see you both. Now, get out of here. Salon 411 is ready to open," CeCe said, unlocking her front door.

Cory and Cat went to their respective stores and CeCe turned to face the other stylists.

"Everyone is going to come here to get their hair and nails done," Amber said, smiling at CeCe.

"Oh, I hope so." CeCe was barely able to contain her excitement. "I want to thank each of you once again for taking a chance and coming with me."

"It was a no-brainer," Ryan said. "We have brand new equipment, reasonable booth rent, and the best group of coworkers anywhere."

"And you let me put up my Nails by Nora sign," Nora said, clapping her hands. "Kerry wouldn't let me at my other shop."

CeCe laughed. "It's fine, Nora. I know we are all self-employed, but I hope we can be a team and help spread the word about *our* salon."

"We're more than a team." Heather gestured at everyone. "Everyone come closer." She put her arm around CeCe and the rest of them formed a circle, arm in arm. "We're a family," Heather said, smiling at everyone.

"Let's welcome our clients, family. Here they come," Ryan said, nodding towards the door.

For an hour a steady stream of customers came in the front door as well as through each entrance to the adjoining stores. CeCe and her stylists showed off the new salon and encouraged people to check out the other stores. The champagne and wine flowed along with snacks offered in each store.

"I love how this turned out," Marina Summit said, walking up to CeCe.

"Hey, if it isn't the best realtor in town." CeCe grinned. "Thank you again for helping us get such a good deal on the property. I know you're in residential real estate now, so I appreciate you looking into this as a favor to us."

"It's the least I could do for the best stylist in the entire metroplex," Marina said.

CeCe beamed. "Where's that beautiful wife of yours? I want to show her how the shampoo area turned out. She had the best suggestions to give us more room and stage the area."

"Dru is on her way."

"Have you been next door to Cat's bookstore?"

"Not yet. I stopped by to say hello to Cory before I came in here," Marina said, taking a sip of champagne.

CeCe leaned in and quietly said, "Be sure and ask Cat to show you the bottom shelf. Tell her I sent you." CeCe winked.

"Okay." Marina drew the word out. "That sounds deliciously secretive."

CeCe grinned. "Oh, it is. Take Dru with you. And tell Cat whatever you choose is on me."

Marina raised her brows and clinked her glass to CeCe's. "Okay, thank you. Congratulations, CeCe. I know you'll be very successful here."

"Thanks, Marina."

CeCe watched as Marina made her way through the entrance to the bookstore. Her attention was quickly drawn to the front door of the salon. A beautiful woman with rich brown hair the color of dark chocolate and sparkling chestnut eyes sauntered just inside the doorway and stopped.

CeCe couldn't stop the smile that grew on her face. This was one of her favorite clients and she was surprised she'd taken the time to come to the open house. She snagged a flute of champagne and met the woman as she started her way through the salon.

"Doc! I'm so glad you made it." CeCe handed the woman the glass of champagne.

"I couldn't miss this. You're one of my favorite people, CeCe Sloan," the woman said.

CeCe smiled shyly. "You say that because I make you look even more gorgeous while you're fighting off all the doctors and nurses and probably a few patients."

Doctor Alexis Reed was one of the premier, most sought after surgeons in the area. Her schedule was jam-packed and CeCe knew her free time was precious. For her to take time out and come to the salon's opening warmed CeCe's heart.

"Oh, I don't fight off all of them." Alexis smiled seductively and sipped her champagne.

CeCe Sloan is Swooning

CeCe raised her eyebrows and looked into Alexis's eyes. "Is there something you need to share with me?"

Alexis chuckled. "You're the one I've heard stories about."

"Oh, please!" CeCe scoffed. "Those were from a decade ago and have been greatly embellished."

"Hmm, I'm not so sure," Alexis said, raising one eyebrow. "Show me around your new place and I'll be the judge of that."

CeCe shook her head. "I'm telling you, Doc. They aren't true. Right this way."

They strolled around the salon and CeCe pointed out each of the new stylist stations. Towards the back on one side were several shampoo bowls and on the other side was CeCe's station which was separate from the others.

"Oh, I like this," Alexis said, walking over to CeCe's chair. There were strands of shiny silver beads hanging vertically from the ceiling to the floor, creating a wall of sorts. It gave the space a bit of seclusion from the rest of the shop.

Alexis sat down in the chair and spun around to face CeCe. "This gives us a little privacy for you to catch me up on all your shenanigans... Or are they dalliances?" She crossed her legs and stared up at CeCe.

"Could you be any sexier?" CeCe asked, putting one hand on her hip and looking Alexis up and down. She paused for a moment, hoping to deflect the attention away from her, but Alexis's stare never wavered. "What in the world are these stories you've heard?"

Alexis giggled and took another sip of her champagne. "Is this the end of the tour or is there a back room? I heard that's where the fun happens."

CeCe laughed. "How long have I been doing your hair?

You know there's always a back room. You've *been* to the back room."

Alexis got up and followed CeCe down a hallway where the restrooms were located along with a supply room. A door opened into a larger area that was mainly for storage. But in one corner, CeCe had arranged a little seating area complete with a couch, several chairs, a coffee table and a rug that gave it a homey feel. Over to one side was a refrigerator with a small table beside it. There was also a larger table with chairs around it where the stylists could eat and gather.

"Isn't this cute." Alexis walked over and ran her hand along the back of the couch. She looked around the room then nodded towards the back door. "Is that where you park your cars or is it for sneaking in?"

"What is with you? All of a sudden you act like I have all these trysts in some secret room," CeCe said, walking over next to Alexis. "This is the break area. You've had a glass of wine with me in the back room of the other salon. This isn't any different."

Alexis walked around and sat down on the couch. She looked up at CeCe and raised her eyebrows, silently inviting CeCe to join her.

"I heard that you may have fooled around a time or two in the back room of the shop when you needed to be discreet."

CeCe narrowed her gaze. "Is someone talking shit about me since I opened my own salon?"

Alexis smiled. "No. I ran into Krista Kyle and her wife, Melanie. We got to talking about the shopping center and they told me Cory was their new supplier for spirits. They particularly loved the name."

CeCe laughed. "Cory is quite proud of The Liquor Box."

CeCe Sloan is Swooning 13

"I mentioned that you were the talented stylist that keeps me looking my best."

CeCe smiled. "It doesn't take much."

Alexis returned CeCe's smile. "Thank you," she said softly. "But they mentioned you'd been to a party or two at their place at the lake."

"I have. They needed a hairstylist for a photo shoot they were doing. At the last minute, the stylist who was supposed to come with the photographer couldn't make it, so I helped out. They asked me to stay for the party afterwards."

"Those women know how to party," Alexis commented.

"They take karaoke and dancing to another level." Wide-eyed, CeCe laughed. "Have you been to one of their parties?"

"I've been to a couple."

"Why, Doc. I didn't know you have a soft spot for the ladies," CeCe teased. "Or is it just those Hollywood starlets?"

"You should know me better than that by now, CeCe. Much like you, I never walk the straight and narrow. Why do you think we get along so well?" Alexis chuckled.

CeCe grinned. "That leads me to believe my little back room, as you like to call it," she said in a low, deep voice, "must be a lot like the supply rooms or doctor's respite rooms at the hospital."

"I never kiss and tell." Alexis winked at her.

CeCe studied Alexis as she finished her glass of champagne. She'd harbored a little crush on Alexis since the first time she'd done her hair. There could never be anything between them because Alexis was way out of CeCe's league and CeCe never messed around with her clients. That had been a hard and fast rule from the beginning. But a little harmless flirting never hurt anyone, did it?

Alexis gave CeCe a genuine smile. "Do you have any idea how much I value my appointments with you?"

"I think so. I know how busy your days are," CeCe said earnestly. She tried to make all her clients feel special, but she took extra time with Alexis. There were times when she could feel the stress leave Alexis's body as she massaged her scalp or gently rubbed her shoulders.

"I can come here and put everything aside. You not only take good care of my hair, but you also ease my mind when I need it. Plus, you entertain me with all the craziness that surrounds a good salon."

CeCe laughed. "I don't know how it happens, but you're right. Craziness abounds at times."

"I love it and most of the time I need it!"

"I'm glad, Doc. I do have one other place I need to show you," CeCe said with a twinkle in her eyes.

"Oh?"

"Yeah, we can pick you up another glass on the way. You'll need it." CeCe winked.

CeCe led them back inside the salon and waved to a couple of clients as they walked through the threshold to Cat's bookstore.

"I love the name!" Alexis exclaimed. "If only I had time to read anything other than medical journals."

CeCe handed Alexis another glass of champagne as she waved to her sister.

"Are you going to drive me home?" Alexis asked as she took the drink from CeCe.

"Nah, I'm going to insist you hang around with me until you can drive yourself." CeCe grinned.

"Hey," Cat said, walking over to them.

"Hi, sis. I'd like you to meet...probably my favorite client." CeCe smiled at Alexis. "This is Doctor Alexis Reed."

CeCe Sloan is Swooning 15

"Oh, CeCe," Alexis scoffed. "It's nice to meet you," she said, holding out her hand to Cat, who took it and smiled.

"Listen Doc, you've worked hard and earned your title. Everybody would be calling me doctor if I'd gone to school that long and accomplished the things you have. You're a big deal," CeCe said.

Alexis shook her head and smirked, but CeCe could see her praise was appreciated.

"This is Cat, my little sister," CeCe said, finishing the introduction.

"Hi, Alexis. It's nice to meet you," Cat said. "I've heard CeCe mention you."

"Uh oh. Am I one of her problem clients?" Alexis asked.

"Not at all. She's always happy after your appointments," Cat explained.

CeCe looked over at Alexis and shrugged. "What can I say, I'm glad I'm your stylist."

Alexis smiled at CeCe and sipped her champagne.

"I gave Alexis a tour of the salon, but I saved the best for last. Do you mind?" CeCe asked, nodding towards the back of the store.

2

"It's all yours." Cat winked. "Mom has already been by so you don't have to worry about her seeing you come and go."

"Thanks for the warning. I haven't seen her yet."

Amused, Alexis gave CeCe a look then looked back at Cat. "It was nice to meet you."

"Thank you for coming out today. It means a lot to CeCe." Cat nodded then walked over to welcome a group of people entering the store.

"It does mean a lot to me, Alexis. I know how busy you are and I appreciate you taking the time."

"I'm happy to be here. Are you dodging your mom?"

"No. We just haven't told her about this particular room in Cat's bookstore."

They walked down a hall similar to the one in CeCe's salon. Once they passed the restrooms, CeCe stopped at a closed door. Before she opened it she turned to Alexis. "This particular room is only for special clients who we know can practice discretion."

CeCe Sloan is Swooning 17

Alexis smiled then made a motion across her lips as if zipping them closed.

CeCe giggled and opened the door. "Welcome to The Bottom Shelf or, as Cat likes to refer to it, The Toy Box."

Alexis walked into the room and gasped. "Oh. My. God." Wide-eyed, She turned to CeCe. "You've got to be kidding me!"

CeCe laughed. "Does this look like a joke to you, Doc?"

Alexis giggled and began to walk around the room. There were shelves with soft pink backlighting tastefully displaying all shapes and sizes of vibrators and other sex toys. She raised one eyebrow and looked over at CeCe. "This is impressive."

CeCe chuckled. "It was Cat's idea. Do you see anything that interests you?"

Alexis smirked. "Maybe a couple of things." She met CeCe's gaze and said, "Do they come with a demonstration?"

CeCe laughed. "I don't know. I guess it could be arranged," she stuttered.

"You Sloan sisters are full of surprises." Alexis walked over to another display and eyed a small vibrator. "Do you have a favorite?"

When CeCe didn't immediately answer, Alexis turned to look at her. The shy look CeCe gave her made her heart flutter in her chest. "You know, I don't have much experience with sex toys," Alexis said, hoping to ease the tension she saw on CeCe's brow.

"You don't?" CeCe said, her voice laced with relief. "Me neither."

Alexis smiled. "Maybe we should try these out and share our findings."

CeCe drew a breath in. "Together?"

Alexis had a feeling she wasn't hiding the surprise on her face. Finding her voice she said, "Are you asking?"

CeCe shrugged. "It was your idea."

Alexis pulled her gaze away from CeCe's penetrating blue eyes. CeCe's shyness was replaced by a sudden confidence Alexis wasn't sure she was ready to face.

"Take your pick, Doc. Consider it a gift from me for coming to the open house today."

Alexis made another pass around the room then turned to CeCe. "Can we touch them?"

CeCe nodded.

Alexis picked up a small aquamarine vibrator and held it in her hand.

CeCe raised her brows. "I like the color."

"It's the color that has your attention?"

CeCe shrugged.

Alexis pushed one of the small buttons and the vibrator began to hum. "Hmm, feel this," she said, reaching for CeCe's hand and pressing the vibrator to her palm.

CeCe's cheeks began to pinken as her face brightened.

"You're not saying anything," Alexis said.

"Neither are you," CeCe replied.

Just then there was a knock on the door and they jumped apart. Alexis pushed the button several times until the vibrator finally went silent. When the door opened they were both giggling.

"Excuse me, ladies," Cory said, giving them a curious look. "I didn't mean to interrupt."

"You didn't," CeCe said, trying to stifle another giggle.

"This thing keeps going and going," Alexis said, holding the vibrator in her open palm.

"Uh, there are so many things I could say." Cory chuckled.

CeCe Sloan is Swooning   19

"Oh, I'm sure there are. Doc, this is my big sister, Cory, the proud owner of The Liquor Box," CeCe said, making the introduction.

"It's nice to meet you," Alexis said, holding out the hand that still held the vibrator. She quickly emptied her hand and offered it to Cory.

"You're the doctor CeCe speaks so highly of," Cory said, shaking Alexis's hand.

Alexis glanced at CeCe and could see her face flaming from the awkwardness of the entire scene.

"What?" Cory said innocently. "I didn't say you have a crush on her."

"Oh my God," CeCe muttered. "Cory! Alexis is my client. Be respectful."

"I didn't mean any disrespect," Cory said, turning to Alexis. "I'm happy to meet you and glad you could come to our open house. Come by the store and I'll send you home with a nice bottle of wine."

"Wow, you Sloan sisters know how to show a girl a good time. First a little toy," Alexis said, holding up the vibrator, "and now a bottle of wine to go with it. Thank you."

"Is that the one you want?" CeCe asked quietly.

"I'll let you know how I like it," Alexis said, wiggling her eyebrows.

"Oh my God! Kill me now," CeCe said, looking up at the ceiling.

Alexis and Cory both laughed.

"Come on," CeCe said to Alexis. "We'll let you have the room, Cory." CeCe took the vibrator from Alexis and put it into a box then walked to the door.

Once in the hall Alexis bumped her shoulder against CeCe's. "You're awfully cute when you get flustered."

CeCe put her hands over her cheeks and groaned.

They walked back over to the salon and Alexis got her purse. "Why don't you walk me out?" she said, and CeCe nodded. Once the door closed behind them Alexis slowly led them to her car. "So, what about this crush?"

CeCe sighed. "It's just a little crush," she said, holding her finger and thumb close together while singing the line from the Jennifer Paige song.

Alexis watched as CeCe got her swagger back. "I see."

"A little crush makes for some fun flirting. Don't you think so?"

Alexis looked into CeCe's eyes and held her gaze. A smirk turned into a smile and she nodded. "This has been fun, CeCe. But I always have a good time with you."

"Me too, Doc."

Alexis patted the side of CeCe's face and got into her car. "Tell Cory I'll come by and get that bottle of wine another time."

CeCe stood there smiling as Alexis backed out of her parking space. She hit the brakes when CeCe motioned for her to stop.

"You have to think of me when you use your new toy." CeCe winked and walked back to the curb.

"You've definitely got your swagger back," she mumbled to herself.

* * *

It had been a while since a woman had grabbed Alexis's attention, but whatever that was between her and CeCe at the open house was still on her mind.

At forty-five, Alexis wasn't looking for anything. She'd been married for a short time in her twenties and although it was an amicable split, the sense of failure still stung. Every

CeCe Sloan is Swooning

so often she would indulge herself and have a fling. She was attracted to both men and women, but in the last few years only women had seemed to catch her eye.

"What's on your mind? I can tell it isn't the surgery you have scheduled later this morning," Donna Nall said, standing in the doorway to Alexis's office.

Donna had been the office manager at the clinic where Alexis practiced for nearly as long as Alexis had been there. They were more than colleagues; Alexis trusted her as she would an older sister.

Alexis furrowed her brow. "And how do you know that?"

Donna gave her a knowing smile. "You have a hint of a smile on your face and your eyes are a warm brown. You only get that look when—"

"Okay, okay. I wasn't thinking about surgery. You caught me." Alexis shrugged. "But I am about to leave for the hospital. What do you need?"

"Is there something or someone you need to tell me about?"

Alexis grinned. "No. I was just thinking about my hairdresser. She opened her new salon earlier in the week."

"Oh, well, you want to keep her. Your hair looks great." Donna smiled.

"Thanks. Now, did you need something?"

"No. I just came by to give you an encouraging fist bump." Donna reached across the desk and knocked her fist into Alexis's and then they both wiggled their fingers.

"Thanks, Donna. I'll see you tomorrow."

"You're not coming back by the office?"

"Nope. With any luck I'll get to leave at a decent hour this evening."

· · ·

Alexis's luck did hold. The surgery went well and when she got in her car to leave the hospital it was just before five o'clock. An idea found its way to the front of her brain and a smile followed. She pulled up her contacts and connected a call as she left the parking lot.

"Hey you!" CeCe Sloan's voice echoed around the car.

"Hey yourself. Are you working?" Alexis asked.

"I just finished my last client for the day. Whatcha need?"

"I need a drink. Are you interested?"

"I'm always interested if it has to do with you, Doc. I know just the place. Come by the salon."

Alexis smiled at CeCe's exuberance. "I'm on my way."

CeCe had been doing Alexis's hair for months now and every time she went to the salon they swapped stories of their lives. Alexis felt like she could tell CeCe anything. They didn't run in the same circles and it was nice to have someone to share the stress of her job with who wouldn't judge her.

In the same way, Alexis knew that CeCe confided things in her that she couldn't share with the other stylists or even her sisters. They were more than acquaintances, but they weren't friends who hung out together. Yes, they occasionally shared a glass of wine after Alexis's appointments, but they'd never been out to dinner or anything like that. Maybe it was time to change that.

Alexis walked into the salon and smiled at Ryan who was blowing out a client's hair.

"She's in the back," Ryan said, returning her smile.

"Thanks," Alexis replied and walked through the salon. She found CeCe sitting in her chair, scrolling through her phone.

"Hey," CeCe said warmly with a bright smile. She

CeCe Sloan is Swooning 23

hopped up and played with the ends of Alexis's hair. "Bad day?"

"No. It was a good day. I had a surgery that took most of the afternoon, but it went well."

"Of course it went well. You did it!"

Alexis smiled and shook her head as CeCe gave her another beaming smile.

"Cory has set up a little happy hour bar in the back of The Liquor Box. Come on, I'm buying."

Alexis grinned. "No you're not. I'm the one who invited you. Besides, I drank several glasses of champagne at the open house last week."

"We'll see," CeCe said, putting her arm around Alexis's shoulders, leading her to the front of the salon and through the adjoining entrance to Cory's store.

"How's this working out?" Alexis asked, pointing to the doorway as they passed through it.

"I haven't had many walk-ins from the liquor store or Cat's bookstore, but my clients have gone to both stores and shopped. I'm glad the salon is in the middle. It creates traffic for all of us."

They walked into the liquor store and Alexis noticed the counter to pay out across from them. There were refrigerated cases next to it that had beer, wine, and other cold drink offerings. Along the other wall were all kinds of liquor and spirits. There were several shelves stocked in the middle of the store as well. In the back there was a long bar with several stools.

"It's just open for happy hour," CeCe explained as they walked to the back of the store.

"And what is happy hour?"

"I think she serves from five until seven or so. It's just a place to stop off on your way home from work. The liquor store closes at nine and Cory didn't want people hanging around and drinking until then."

"It's kind of cute tucked in back here. You wouldn't know it's here," Alexis said, taking a seat on one of the stools.

"Yeah, I guess it's like Cat's little room in the back of her store," CeCe said quietly, taking a seat next to Alexis. "Speaking of that, how's the little toy you picked up last week?"

3

Alexis smiled but didn't say anything. Ignoring CeCe's question, she looked up to see what was offered at the bar. She could feel CeCe studying her profile and was sure she'd see a wide grin if she looked over at her.

"They only serve beer and wine for now, no fancy cocktails. Is that all right?"

"Sure," Alexis said. "You know I like wine."

CeCe held up two fingers to the bartender who was at the other end of the bar serving beer to two other customers. The bartender nodded and CeCe turned back to Alexis. "So your surgery went well today. I don't think you've ever told me what you specialize in."

"I'm a general surgeon. I decided not to specialize because I like to take what's wrong with the body and put it back together again. It could be any part of the body," Alexis explained.

"It's just incredible the things you do with your skillful hands. It's like magic," CeCe said as the bartender set their glasses of wine in front of them.

"It's not unlike what you do," Alexis commented, taking a sip from her wine glass. "You have such a talent to cut hair and make it do what we can't because we always look better when we leave the salon. My hair never looks as good when I do it at home, but at least it's better because of the way you cut it. You try to help me make it look good since you can't do it every day." Alexis chuckled. "Hey, I wonder if we could do something like that. I could come by the shop every morning and you could do my hair."

CeCe laughed. "Yeah, you're not the first to suggest that." But then she turned to Alexis with a serious look. "Doing hair is nothing like what you're doing. You save lives."

"I disagree. The things you do make people feel better. After you've done your magic," Alexis said, meeting CeCe's gaze and raising her eyebrows, "people can look in the mirror and feel more beautiful because you've done their hair, when inside they may not feel so beautiful. So, let's agree that we're both magical."

CeCe held up her glass. "I'll drink to that."

Alexis clinked her glass to CeCe's and took a sip. "We should do this more often. Now that you've moved the salon here we could."

"What do you mean?" CeCe asked, taking another sip of wine.

"You're right on my way home. I don't live far from here."

"Really? I knew we were on the edge of several swanky neighborhoods. Of course you live here," CeCe said.

Alexis smiled. "You'll have to come over sometime."

CeCe studied her for a moment. "I'd like that."

They both took sips from their glasses, but neither looked away. Alexis couldn't stop her mind from wandering to the back room in CeCe's salon. For a moment she could imagine them there, doing more than drinking a glass of wine.

"You didn't tell me about the toy you got last week," CeCe said, raising one eyebrow.

"You didn't tell me where you live," Alexis countered.

CeCe chuckled. "You didn't ask. I don't live far from here either. Do you know Marina Summit? She's a realtor."

"I don't know her, but I do know her business partner, Victoria Stratton. They have a design firm that matches renovated houses with buyers. They do good work."

"I couldn't agree more. Marina found the cutest little house not far from here that her company had remodeled. I bought it." CeCe shrugged. "Can you stay for another?"

Something was going on inside Alexis's mind. She knew the best thing to do would be to go home, but she didn't want to leave. She wanted to learn more about the vivacious CeCe Sloan and this was the perfect opportunity.

"Could we have another at the salon?" Alexis asked, fingering the necklace that fell at her chest.

CeCe raised her brows and stared into Alexis's eyes. "Sure," she replied with a seductive smile.

Alexis followed CeCe away from the bar and watched her snag a bottle of wine from a shelf as they walked by.

"Do we need to pay for that?" Alexis asked before they walked back into the salon.

"I've got it," CeCe replied.

Alexis could feel a push and pull between them. What could be characterized as playful flirting at times now seemed more serious. It was as if they were daring one another, seeing if either of them was bold enough to make the first move. Bold? Or foolish?

At this point Alexis didn't care. She was having too much fun watching CeCe swing her hips as they sauntered to the back room of the salon. Alexis had no doubt there was an extra sway or two just for her.

"You take this," CeCe said, handing Alexis the bottle. "I'll make sure everything is locked up."

Alexis took the bottle and started down the hall.

"Oh, Lex. There's a bottle opener in the top drawer next to the fridge. I'll be right there." CeCe grinned and walked back to the front of the salon.

"Damn," Alexis muttered as she walked into the back room. "Did someone turn up the heat in here?" She smiled to herself as she found the bottle opener and made quick work of uncorking the wine.

After finding wine glasses in a cabinet, she set two out. As she poured the wine she realized that CeCe had called her Lex. She didn't let anyone call her that, or Lexie or Alex. Why didn't she correct her on the spot?

"Hey," CeCe said, walking into the space. "You found the glasses, too." She smiled and added, "Ryan just finished his last client and is locking up."

Alexis handed CeCe a glass of wine then touched their glasses together. "You have to let me pay for this."

CeCe took a sip and raised her brows. "No I don't. Don't worry about it, Doc. I get a discount." She chuckled and moved to sit down on the couch.

Alexis followed her over and sat on the other end. She made a show of crossing her legs and watched CeCe take it all in. "Now I'll tell you about the toy."

CeCe's face brightened. "Finally! I thought you were going to keep ignoring me."

Alexis laughed and scooted a little closer. "That little toy is mighty powerful," she said with a sly smile.

CeCe moved in closer and her eyes widened. "Tell me."

CeCe Sloan is Swooning 29

Alexis sipped her wine but didn't take her eyes off CeCe's.

"Did you think of me when you used it?" CeCe asked softly.

Alexis took a deep breath, trying to calm her pounding heart. "CeCe Sloan, you are dangerous."

CeCe scoffed. "No I'm not. You're the dangerous one, Lex."

There was that name again. "You know, I don't let anyone call me that."

A sexy smile crossed CeCe's face. "You let me," she said, cocking one eyebrow.

Alexis leaned over and ran one finger along CeCe's cheek. She looked down at CeCe's lips and back into her eyes. She could feel CeCe leaning closer when there was a knock at the door.

"Hey, CeCe, are you still here?" Cat asked as she opened the door.

Alexis pulled back and watched as CeCe rubbed her lips together and sighed. "Yeah, I'm still here."

"Oh, hey. Hi Alexis," Cat said, walking over towards them. "I don't mean to be interrupting anything."

"We were just enjoying a glass of wine," CeCe said with a slight edge to her voice.

"Would you join us?" Alexis asked. She quickly glanced at CeCe and smiled.

"Nah, I'm headed home. I just wanted to remind CeCe about Cory's birthday," Cat said. "We're going out for drinks on Friday."

"You should come with us," CeCe said to Alexis. "It's just a few of us from work. Very low key."

"Yeah, it's Friday. We'd love for you to come," Cat added.

"Thanks, I'd like that," Alexis replied.

"I'll text you the address," CeCe said.

Alexis finished her wine knowing the moment between her and CeCe had passed. They were so close to kissing and Alexis was pretty sure she'd be using her new toy later tonight. "I'd better get going."

"Me too," CeCe said, draining her glass.

They all walked through the salon together.

"It was nice to see you again, Alexis. See you tomorrow, sis," Cat said, walking out the front door.

"I'm glad you stopped by tonight," CeCe said, turning off the lights.

Alexis walked out the front door and waited while CeCe locked it.

"I hope you'll be thinking of me when you get that cute little toy out tonight," CeCe said, turning to Alexis.

"Aren't you sure of yourself." Alexis smirked.

CeCe raised her eyebrows. "Am I wrong?"

Alexis grinned and ran her fingers along CeCe's cheek. "Dangerous," she murmured.

CeCe reached up and held Alexis's hand to her cheek for a moment. "See you Friday, Lex."

Alexis narrowed her gaze and chuckled.

On the short drive to her house Alexis couldn't keep from smiling. She meant it when she said CeCe was dangerous. There were times over the last few months when they'd exchanged a look or held each other's gaze in the mirror when CeCe was doing her hair. Nothing came of it, but now there was the possibility of seeing each other more often and not as stylist and client.

Alexis had to admit she was disappointed when Cat walked in this evening. She could almost feel CeCe's lips on hers and now she couldn't get the thought out of her head. This newfound flirting between them had lit a fire inside

CeCe Sloan is Swooning 31

Alexis. A fire that she thought had gone out long ago and honestly she hadn't had the time or inclination to try and relight it.

But when she'd stepped into the new salon that day and CeCe had given her such a grateful smile, something warmed in Alexis's heart. As they toured the shop and her sisters' stores, their playful banter became flirty and Alexis loved it.

Tonight it had started again and even though Alexis hadn't planned on ending up in CeCe's back room, there they were, about to kiss. Who knows what could have happened after that.

"And I get to see you again Friday, CeCe. Whatever will we get up to," Alexis said, smiling into the mirror as she removed her makeup and got ready for bed.

* * *

CeCe pulled into her garage, gathered her purse and appointment book, then walked into her house. She dropped everything on her table and went directly to the refrigerator. Peering inside, she grabbed a bottle of water and plopped down on her living room couch.

She turned the bottle up and took a long drink. "Whew," she sighed. "What are you doing?" she murmured.

There was a time when she'd been known as a wild party girl, but that was years ago. Back then, she was trying to figure out who she was and for whatever reason she thought she'd find the answer in a string of one-night stands. It didn't matter if they were male or female. She believed there was someone out there for her and she'd been determined to find them.

Thank goodness she'd figured out the error in her

thinking and hadn't suffered terrible consequences for her reckless ways. After a specific period of foolhardy behavior she'd vowed not to let sex make a decision for her ever again.

There had been a couple of relationships since her awakening that hadn't worked out. They were both amicable splits. Since then she'd gone on a few dates here and there, but no one interested her enough for a second date.

Her little crush on Alexis Reed began not long after she'd started styling her hair. This crush was nothing to worry about though because she knew Alexis could never reciprocate her feelings. At least that's what she'd thought until Alexis walked into the open house last week. Something was different that day. Their harmless flirting took on a new meaning and now CeCe knew that Alexis was interested.

But why? CeCe was just a hairstylist who loved to make people feel good about themselves and had a good time doing it. From Alexis's words tonight, CeCe felt like Alexis could see inside her soul. When Alexis looked into her eyes it felt like she wanted to see all of CeCe and she was determined to see the part of CeCe that she didn't let everyone see.

CeCe reached up and touched her cheek where not too long ago Alexis had laid her fingers. Her tender touch was a sweet caress and at the same time it felt like a sizzling flame spreading warmth through her body that culminated right between her legs.

CeCe inhaled deeply and slowly let her breath out. It had been so long since that kind of fire had burned inside her. But she had to be careful. She didn't want to lose Alexis as a client and that was one rule she abided by: CeCe did not date clients.

But those lips. They were so close to kissing when Cat walked in the back room tonight. And now CeCe couldn't get Alexis's lips out of her mind. She wanted to feel them pressed to hers and even more so she wanted to taste those sweet lips with her own.

She had until Friday to figure out what to do. Would it be so bad to kiss Alexis? Maybe that would end this crush and they could go back to their playful flirty ways.

CeCe rubbed her lips together and knew in her heart she couldn't stop this kiss. It was inevitable. But it was just a kiss. Alexis Reed was a respected, in-demand doctor. There wasn't a future there. This was just a little fun for both of them. And honestly, CeCe hadn't had any fun like this in a very long time.

She went to bed that night already looking forward to Friday.

4

Alexis was at her desk entering notes from her last appointment when she heard a knock on her opened door. She looked up to see Michael Pierce, one of her fellow doctors in the clinic and a friend, standing there smiling.

"Hey, Michael. What's up?"

"Do you have a minute?"

"Sure, let me finish this thought," Alexis said, making a few more keystrokes. She leaned back in her chair and smiled. "Come on in."

"I just wanted to invite you to our place Friday night. Lana wants to have a few of the doctors and their spouses over for drinks and snacks."

"Oh, well, I don't have a spouse," Alexis began.

"You know what I mean," Michael said, giving her a faux menacing look.

"I can't. I have plans Friday night."

Michael sat down in the chair across from Alexis's desk. "Oh, you do. Anyone I know?"

CeCe Sloan is Swooning   35

"No, but is it your business?" Alexis said, her tone playful.

"Yes," Michael replied. "I'm your friend and if you're seeing someone and Lana finds out, I'll be in big trouble for not telling her first. You know she's always looking to set you up."

"Oh, I know!" Alexis nodded animatedly. "But I think I made her understand that it's okay for me to be single."

Michael laughed. "That doesn't mean she likes it."

"She almost made me angry the last time and I think she finally realized she needed to ease up."

"Yeah, she just wants you to be happy and you know Lana. Her idea of happy and your idea of happy may be two different things. But she means well."

"I know that. That's why I said I *almost* got mad. If you must know, I'm meeting my hairstylist for happy hour. It's her sister's birthday."

Michael gave her a steely look. "You like her," he stated.

Alexis laughed. "Well, yeah. I do like her. She makes me look fabulous," she said, fluffing her hair.

"You do look fabulous, but CeCe can't take all the credit."

Alexis gave Michael a surprised look.

"What? Yes, I remember her name. You always talk about her for days after she's done your hair."

Alexis furrowed her brow. She had no idea she talked about CeCe to her friends and equally surprising was that Michael remembered her name. "Believe me, CeCe wouldn't take any of the credit, but she deserves most of it."

Michael smiled then hit his hands on his thighs as he got up. "Have a good time. I won't mention CeCe to Lana... yet." He winked at Alexis and walked to the door. "You will let me know if there's something to know, right?"

"It's just drinks with her sisters and the people who work at the salon."

Michael smiled. "You say that, but your eyes are sparkling and that grin tells another story. See ya."

Alexis smirked as Michael left her office.

Do I talk about CeCe at the clinic? She remembered recommending her to a colleague, but tried to think back to her last appointment. There was no way she could leave the salon without being in a good mood because CeCe was so full of life. It was like she infused her joy into her clients as she did their hair.

"Here are the files you asked for," Donna said, walking into Alexis's office with her hands full.

"Thanks, Donna. You can set them right here," Alexis said, clearing a space on the corner of her large desk.

As Donna set the files down Alexis leaned back in her chair. "Hey, Donna."

"Hey?"

"Do you know my hair stylist's name?"

Donna gave her a confused look. "Is this a test?"

Alexis chuckled. "No."

"Her name is CeCe. Why?"

"You know her name, too!" Alexis exclaimed.

"Yeah. Why is that a big deal?"

"Dr. Pierce just remarked that I talk about CeCe a lot after I've had my hair styled."

Donna seemed to think, then nodded. "Yeah, you do."

"Hmm, I didn't realize I did that."

"I always feel good after I've had my hair done, but..." Donna said, trailing off.

"But?"

"I don't know. You always come back with stories about

CeCe Sloan is Swooning 37

CeCe did this or CeCe did that. It's obvious you've had a good time and you like her. Aren't you friends?"

Alexis considered what Donna said and shrugged. "I guess we are. We don't see one another like friends do, but we do have fun when we are together."

"And who of your friends do you see and do friends things with?" Donna asked, giving her a pointed look.

"There's—" Alexis began. She put her elbow on her desk and raised a finger. "Uh, or—"

Donna raised her eyebrows and waited. After a moment she said, "Exactly. You don't do friends things."

Alexis bristled.

"It's okay, Doc. You are so busy during the week I don't know how you do anything on the weekends but catch up on sleep," Donna said. "Oh, wait. That's when you catch up by reading the latest news in your medical journals."

Alexis stared at Donna, knowing she was right. "That sounds dreadful."

Donna smiled. "It's not dreadful. But you don't have to save everyone in one week. You could spread your appointments out and actually have a little time to yourself. I've been trying to get you to let me do this for over a year. Why do you think I was so excited you wanted to leave early to go to your hairstylist's open house?"

Alexis smiled. "It was a lot of fun."

"I could tell. You were still smiling the next morning."

"Oh, I was not!"

"If that's what you want to believe," Donna said with a shrug.

Neither one of them said anything for a moment. Donna sat down in the chair opposite Alexis's desk which was something she rarely did. "Look, we have been working together a long time. You hide behind that self-assured, a bit cocky, surgeon's persona."

Alexis scoffed. "Don't you want your surgeon to be confident?"

"Sure I do and you're the best. But I also see you occasionally drop the mask and show off that beautiful smile of yours. It hasn't happened in a long time, but then I started to notice..."

"Notice?"

"When you get your hair done I see a flicker of that smile for several days."

"Do I look like a tired mean doctor the rest of the time?" Alexis asked, appalled.

"No! You are a professional and you do smile, but I'm talking about a genuine smile that comes from the heart. Not necessarily the one you give your patients when they are thanking you for making their lives better. I'm talking about the one that makes you feel all warm and fuzzy inside."

"Me? Warm and fuzzy?" Alexis exclaimed then laughed.

"You have a lightness to you when you talk about CeCe. I hope you're at least becoming friends."

"At least? What do you mean?"

Donna raised her eyebrows and dropped her chin. "It's been a while, wouldn't you say?"

Alexis sat back in her chair, shocked.

"I didn't mean that!" Donna exclaimed. "I meant it's been a while since you've gone out with anyone."

"Since you're so attuned to my schedule, when would I have time?" Alexis smirked.

Donna smiled. "Oh, I've seen you make time when you want to."

A slow smile crossed Alexis's face. Donna was right.

CeCe Sloan is Swooning   39

When Alexis was interested in someone she'd make time for them because on top of being a stoic surgeon, she could also be selfish. She was used to getting what she wanted, but with CeCe it felt different.

"Gotta go," Donna said, getting up and closing Alexis's door as she left.

The revelation from two of her co-workers about her behavior after seeing CeCe made her pause. What had begun as playful flirting was leading to much more and honestly, Alexis couldn't wait. She was up for a sexy little fling and from what she'd heard about CeCe she would be too. But was that all this was or was there more going on here than she thought?

Alexis furrowed her brow and tilted her head. "Nah, we're going to have a good time."

Satisfied with her conclusion she went back to her patients. Her friends were making too much of this. She couldn't help that, but she also couldn't wait for Friday.

* * *

"Look out, here comes trouble," CeCe said softly to the older woman sitting in her chair.

"Hi, Mrs. Eubanks," Cory said with a big smile. "How are you?"

"You're right, CeCe, that one's trouble."

Cory's mouth fell open in mock surprise. "I was about to tell you how lovely you look!"

"I know how pretty I look because your sister is just finishing up. Be sure and spray really well, CeCe."

"Yes ma'am," CeCe replied, reaching for the hair spray. She sprayed until a cloudy haze nearly choked them all.

"Good," Mrs. Eubanks said, patting her now stiff hair.

She looked into the mirror at both CeCe and Cory. "Your daddy would be proud of all three of you girls."

"Aww, thanks, Mrs. Eubanks. We sure do miss him," CeCe said with a nostalgic smile.

"Believe me, I do, too," Mrs. Eubanks replied. "Your momma and I are both widows now and we don't like it."

"I'm glad Mom has you though," Cory said. "Her friends mean the world to her."

Mrs. Eubanks smiled and handed CeCe several bills.

"Let me get your change," CeCe said, reaching for her money bag.

"No, you keep that. Go have a Coke later this afternoon on me."

"How about I have a beer or glass of wine this evening on you?" CeCe smiled.

Mrs. Eubanks giggled. "That'd be even better."

Cory and CeCe both held out a hand to help Mrs. Eubanks from the chair. CeCe handed her cane to her and Mrs. Eubanks smiled. "Thank you, dear."

"Thank you, Dottie. I'll see you next week," CeCe said.

"I'll be here. Bye, girls," she said as she toddled towards the front door.

"She always brightens my day," CeCe said.

"Your day isn't bright? We're going out for my birthday drinks this evening at Betty's, which just happens to be our favorite bar. How can you not be happy about that?" Cory asked, raising her arms to her side.

"My day is bright, but Dottie Eubanks always makes it that much better," CeCe explained.

"Oh, okay then." Cory narrowed her gaze. "Are you happy because it's my birthday or because Dr. Alexis Reed is joining us at Betty's?"

CeCe Sloan is Swooning 41

CeCe gave Cory a menacing look. "It's not your birthday yet. Please don't embarrass me again in front of Alexis."

"When did I embarrass you?" Cory said, then realization crossed her face. "Oh, you mean that comment about your crush."

CeCe put her hands on her hips and stared at Cory. "Yes! You can't say shit like that to someone like Alexis."

Cory's eyebrows shot up her forehead. "Someone like Alexis? I think your crush has morphed into something more, dear sister."

CeCe released a frustrated sigh. "No, it hasn't. Alexis is a respected doctor, Cory."

"I know that. She's also a very hot woman who thinks you are super sexy."

"What?" CeCe stared at her sister.

Cory shook her head. "CeCe, my sweet little sister. That doctor looks at you with lust in her eyes. Surely you've noticed."

"When have *you* noticed?"

"Oh gee, every time she's come in here since we opened," Cory commented.

"That would be once."

"What about the other night when you had drinks at the happy hour bar?"

"How do you know about that? You weren't even here," CeCe replied.

"Taylor told me you took a bottle of wine to go and she was pretty sure you two were headed to your back room," Cory explained.

"I'll pay for the wine," CeCe said sarcastically.

Cory smiled. "I don't care about the wine. So what happened?"

"Nothing. We did come back here and have a glass of wine. Cat came over as well."

Cory once again narrowed her gaze. "You mean Cat interrupted you and the hot doc."

"Hot doc, really! I'll have to say something to Taylor," CeCe said, trying to deflect Cory's intrusive gaze.

"I've seen the two of you together, CeCe, and felt the heat radiating from you both. I know you don't date your clients, but you may want to make an exception. How long has it been since you went on a date?"

"Oh, I don't know, Cory. How long has it been for you?" CeCe said defensively.

"Girls, girls, we're all friends here," Cat said, walking up. "And in this case, sisters, too." She chuckled.

"What do you want?" CeCe and Cory both said, turning to their little sister.

"Whoa!" Cat exclaimed, holding her hands in front of her.

"Sorry," CeCe mumbled.

"I was just telling our sister that maybe she should go out with Dr. Client. The sex oozes off of them," Cory explained to Cat.

"Uh, gross, Cory," Cat said, making an unpleasant face. "But she's not wrong."

"What! Not you, too!" CeCe exclaimed.

"All I'm saying is you and Alexis do have a certain chemistry. I felt like I was interrupting something the other night," Cat said.

CeCe looked from one sister to the other. "Look, I like Alexis. We have fun flirting and we both like wine, but that's it. Please don't invent something that's not there. She is so far out of my league—"

CeCe Sloan is Swooning 43

"No she's not," Cat said, cutting CeCe off. "She'd be lucky to be with you."

"Hell yes, she would," Cory added.

CeCe smiled at her sisters. They had always had each other's backs no matter what.

"Alexis wants you, CeCe. I could tell by the way she looked at you the other night," Cat said.

"I'm telling you both, it's playful flirting," CeCe declared. She couldn't help thinking back to the other night when they were about to kiss. There was nothing playful about that.

"I promise we will not embarrass you or the doc tonight," Cory stated, holding up her hands.

"Thanks. I appreciate that."

"Do you want to ride with me?" Cat asked CeCe.

"No, I'm going to run home and change. I have a perm this afternoon and I don't want to be all smelly."

"You mean perm smelly, not sweet CeCe smelly," Cat teased.

"Or is it sexy CeCe smelly," Cory added.

CeCe rolled her eyes. "Thank God, my next appointment just walked in. Y'all go back to your own stores. I'm sure someone needs you. Hi, Pam," CeCe said, greeting her client.

5

CeCe backed out of her driveway and looked at her reflection in the mirror. Her blue eyes were sparkling and her red hair fell in soft curls just below her shoulders. She smiled to herself and winked. "You've got this, Cecilia."

On the drive to the bar she couldn't help but think back to the conversation with her sisters. Did Alexis want her or were they just playing around? She could feel such a pull towards Alexis and she couldn't get the image of her lips out of her head since their near kiss. *What was she doing?* She was out of Alexis's league no matter what her sisters said. But maybe they could have a fun little fling that wouldn't do any harm. Couldn't they? There was that pesky little problem of Alexis being her client, though.

CeCe felt a flutter in her stomach as she walked up to the bar. Just thinking about Alexis made her smile. She was about to open the door when she heard her name.

"CeCe," Alexis called to her as she walked up. "What a sexy little smile. What were you thinking about?"

CeCe Sloan is Swooning   45

"Hmm, I reserve the right to reveal my thoughts later," CeCe said stealthily.

Alexis smiled. "I'm going to hold you to that."

CeCe laughed. "I'm sure you will." She turned to open the door. "I'm glad you could make it."

"I am, too," Alexis said, adding a little extra swing to her hips and wiggle of her eyebrows as she walked by.

Alexis had on a pair of jeans that looked like they were made just for her. *They probably were. Was there anything this woman didn't look sexy in*, CeCe wondered.

CeCe chuckled. "Dangerous," she mumbled to herself. "Hey," she said, reaching for Alexis's wrist and stopping her.

Alexis turned around and CeCe momentarily lost her breath. She felt like Alexis was looking right into her soul and reading every thought she'd ever had. "Uh," she stammered.

"Yes?" Alexis said, tilting her head.

"Uh, I..." CeCe shook her head and finally words began to tumble out of her mouth. "You look gorgeous, Doc, and it's obviously made me speechless."

Alexis smiled. "Thank you," she said softly. "You don't look so bad yourself," she added, leaning in a little closer.

Fuck, we're in trouble. "You can't believe anything my sisters tell you tonight. They will try to embarrass me."

"Don't worry, CeCe. You've already told me the stories about you are only half true, right?" Alexis grinned.

CeCe nodded. She realized she was still holding Alexis's wrist and she started to pull them both back out the door and to someplace where she could kiss this woman silly, but she thought better of it.

"They won't scare me away," Alexis added.

"Hey, CeCe! Over here," Amber called from a table near the bar.

She and Alexis walked over and CeCe made introductions. Amber, Ryan, and Heather were all there from the salon and sat at one end of the table. On the other end sat Cory, smiling from ear to ear.

"Hi, Alexis. So glad you could make it," Cory said.

"Happy birthday! And thanks for inviting me," Alexis replied.

"Hi, Alexis," Cat said from across the table. "This is Jessica; she works with me," Cat continued, "and this is Taylor. She works with Cory."

"Hi, Taylor," Alexis said. "We met the other night."

"That's right. You came in with CeCe. It's nice to see you again," Taylor said pleasantly.

"I think you've met everyone," CeCe said, looking around the table. "Oh, wait. This is Brandy. She grew up with us and for some reason she still likes hanging out with us."

"Ha ha," Brandy deadpanned. "It's nice to meet you, Alexis. The Sloan sisters have saved me a time or two."

Cory laughed. "Only because *you* got us all in trouble."

Brandy bumped her shoulder into Cat's. "But we had a good time, didn't we?"

Cat laughed. "As long as our parents didn't find out."

CeCe pulled out a chair for Alexis and sat down next to her. Just as they took their seats a waitress brought over a tray full of shots.

"Happy birthday to me!" Cory said, holding up her glass.

The entire table responded and downed their first shot.

As everyone took turns toasting Cory, Brandy and Cat entertained the group with stories from their youth to now.

"Hey," Alexis said, leaning over near CeCe's ear. "I'm the only client here. The rest of you work together."

CeCe smiled. "That doesn't matter. You know most of

CeCe Sloan is Swooning 47

the people here and they like you." CeCe furrowed her brow. "Are you uncomfortable?"

"Quite the opposite," Alexis replied. "I'm feeling kind of special."

"That's because you are, Doc," CeCe said, placing her hand on Alexis's arm.

"Come on, CeCe," Taylor said. "It's your turn for a story."

"I can't tell stories about my clients no matter how entertaining they might be." CeCe chuckled.

"Sure you can," Cat said. "You don't have to name names."

"What kind of stories has she told about me?" Alexis asked, raising her brows.

"Oh, I don't know if we should tell you everything she says after you leave the salon," Cory said.

CeCe gave her sister a desperate look, pleading with her eyes.

"She's never had one bad thing to say about you, Alexis. There are some clients that she looks forward to seeing and you would be one of them," Cory said earnestly.

"Besides, by the time she gets through with you, we all have to get a drink to cool down," Ryan said. "She has you looking so hot, you melt the salon." He reached over and touched Alexis's shoulder, pretending to get burned.

"Oh my God!" CeCe exclaimed.

Alexis threw her head back and laughed. "You are too much, Ryan. But," she said, catching her breath, "you're right. CeCe is magical."

CeCe met Alexis's gaze and watched as her eyes went from amused to something else as they darkened.

"All of you are magical," Cat said. "I don't know how you do it, but everyone feels better after they've been to Salon 411."

"I don't know about that," Amber said, chuckling. "Ask Misty Turner how she felt after I colored her hair."

"Nope," CeCe said firmly. "You tried to tell her it was going to be orange. She didn't believe you."

"Oh my," Alexis said, widening her eyes.

"It happens, but rarely," Amber commented.

"Yeah, most of the time the other stylists can make your client understand, but Misty just knew it would be the most beautiful shade of red." Ryan laughed. "Like CeCe's."

CeCe smiled. "Before anyone asks, this is the real deal." She swung her head from side to side as her hair flew around her shoulders.

"You've never colored it?" Alexis asked. "I thought you all had colored your hair at one time or another."

"Oh, I've colored it, but not in a long time," CeCe replied.

"Why would you?" Alexis said, reaching out and touching the ends of CeCe's hair. "It's beautiful."

CeCe caught Alexis's gaze and smiled. "Thank you," she said softly.

"However, there was that time when you colored all our hair green for St. Patrick's Day," Cory said. "Mom wanted to kill all of us, and CeCe twice."

Everyone laughed.

"We were trying to win a contest at a bar," Cat explained.

"Surprise, surprise," Heather deadpanned.

"We should've won, too!" Cory said.

CeCe shrugged. "That was pretty funny, until Mom got so mad."

"It was still funny," Cory said. "I heard her telling Dad about it and laughing."

"It sounds to me like the Sloan sisters have a lot of fun," Alexis stated.

CeCe Sloan is Swooning

49

"We do, most of the time," Cory said. "But this Sloan sister is done for the night."

"What? You're the birthday girl!" Brandy exclaimed.

"I know, but I'm opening in the morning," Cory said.

"Don't you make the schedule? Why would you open on a Saturday morning?" Heather asked.

"It's not that bad. Liquor stores don't open early. One of my workers that usually opens on Saturday needed off. As the boss, it's up to me," Cory explained.

"I'd have done it if you'd asked," Taylor said.

"You're already working tomorrow evening. You can't be there all day," Cory said.

"Why not? You are some days."

Cory scoffed. "But I own the place."

"Is that why you were swearing at the top of your lungs in the alley yesterday? Because you're the owner?" Cat asked.

Cory's face fell. "Sorry about that. I've got this sales rep for one of those big discount liquor stores who's making running my thriving new business more difficult than it should be."

"Have you turned on the Sloan sisters' charm?" Brandy asked.

"I don't think she's the kind of snake that can be charmed," Cory said.

"I don't believe that for a second. Cory Sloan, you are the sweetest Sloan sister and can get anything or anyone you want when you put your mind to it," Brandy said.

"I don't want this woman!" Cory exclaimed. "I just want her to stop undercutting my prices."

"You'll figure it out," Cat said, patting Cory on the back.

Everyone began to gather their things and Alexis turned to CeCe. "Do you have to work in the morning?"

CeCe shook her head. "No, but I do have to go back by the salon tonight. I left the money from today's sales and appointments there. I didn't want to carry it with me while I was out."

Alexis furrowed her brow. "Should you go back by yourself since it's dark out?"

CeCe grinned. "Aww, you want to come protect me."

"I'm happy to follow you."

CeCe chuckled and leaned in closer. "You're who I need protecting from."

Alexis gave her a faux shocked look then laughed. "Who's going to protect me from you?"

CeCe smiled, but didn't reply.

They all said their goodbyes and walked to the parking lot.

"Follow me around to the back of the building," CeCe said as she closed Alexis's car door.

Alexis gave her a smile and nodded.

CeCe kept an eye in her rearview mirror as she drove to the salon. She knew Alexis could get there on her own, but she had a hard time keeping her eyes off her all night. It felt as if the pull towards Alexis was even stronger tonight. There were times she could feel Alexis's leg rub against hers under the table and more than once they'd leaned in and rested shoulder to shoulder.

CeCe drove up to the back door of the salon and unlocked it. She waited for Alexis to get out of her car and held the back door open for her.

As they walked into the room CeCe said, "You know, ever since you asked me about this back room at the open house we seem to keep ending up here."

Alexis smirked. "You tried to tell me those stories weren't true."

CeCe laughed and opened a cabinet that held a small safe. After punching in the code, the door opened and she retrieved the money bag. When she turned around Alexis was standing right in front of her. CeCe could feel her heartbeat pick up.

"You never did tell me what that sexy little smile was all about at the bar," Alexis said with a sexy smile of her own.

CeCe raised her eyebrows and a slow smile crossed her face. "What if I said I was thinking of you?" She tossed the money bag onto the table and put her arms on Alexis's shoulders.

"You have been on my mind since I left this room the other night," Alexis said, putting her hands on CeCe's hips.

"Have you been thinking about what would've happened if my little sister hadn't walked in?"

Alexis pulled CeCe closer and leaned in. "I've been thinking about this." Alexis closed the distance between them and softly pressed their lips together.

What began as a slow sweet kiss heated up as CeCe wrapped her arms around Alexis's neck and pulled her even closer. CeCe moaned and melted into Alexis's arms. Their lips slightly parted and when their tongues touched for the first time, CeCe felt a rush of warmth and electricity flow through her body. Alexis moaned and CeCe knew she felt it too.

Their lips fit together perfectly and CeCe forgot that this was Dr. Alexis Reed, her client. These lips belonged to the sexiest, most interesting woman she had met in a very long time. She quickly discovered they were very good at this. Lips pressed together, moans from them both, and a tighter and tighter embrace made for several moments of sheer pleasure.

Taking a deep breath, CeCe pulled away and mumbled, "Even better."

"What?" Alexis asked, inhaling deeply.

"Your lips taste even better than I imagined," CeCe admitted.

Alexis smiled. "You've been thinking about my lips?"

"Pretty much nonstop since Cat walked in on us." CeCe leaned in and brought their lips together in another heated kiss.

Alexis backed CeCe up against the wall, never letting their lips part. As their tongues danced to the music of their moans, Alexis slid her hand up CeCe's side and cupped one of her breasts.

"Mmm," CeCe groaned. She pulled away, panting. Then she looked into Alexis's eyes and felt such warmth. Those usually soft brown eyes were dark molten chocolate waiting to wrap her in passion and she wanted to fall into them. When Alexis leaned in for another kiss, CeCe put her finger up and placed it on her lips.

"Wait," she panted, "I don't date my clients."

6

Alexis gave her a crooked little grin. "This isn't a date."

CeCe giggled. "Oh, what the hell," she muttered and crushed her lips to Alexis's. She devoured Alexis and was rewarded with a deep, sensual groan.

Alexis's hands were everywhere. She had CeCe pinned against the wall and cupped both her breasts, pinching her nipples through her shirt and bra. CeCe ran her fingers through Alexis's thick, dark hair, keeping their lips locked together in a long, soulful kiss.

CeCe could feel Alexis's hands move to the front of her pants and she quickly unbuttoned and unzipped them.

Alexis pulled away and looked into CeCe's eyes. CeCe ran her hands under Alexis's shirt so she could feel her skin next to her fingers. It reminded her of when Alexis ran her fingers along CeCe's cheek the other night. It was soft and laced with fire all at the same time.

CeCe gave Alexis a small smile and a slight nod then she claimed those lips once again. She felt Alexis run her hand down the front of her pants and into her panties. CeCe spread her legs a little further and couldn't believe she'd gone from wondering how Alexis's lips would taste to having her fingers stroking through the wetness she'd caused and circling her pulsating middle.

CeCe put her arms back on Alexis's shoulders and moaned. She leaned her head back against the wall and Alexis immediately began to kiss down her neck, finding her pulse point right below her ear.

"Fuck." CeCe moaned as the word escaped her mouth.

"I'm trying," Alexis whispered in her ear.

CeCe giggled then groaned as Alexis's finger slipped from divinely circling her clit to sliding inside her. She felt that heat and electricity pass through her body once again.

Her hips began to move and when she was almost over the edge, Alexis pushed firmly against her clit causing an explosion of sensations that made the earlier electricity feel like a hum. This charge flew up and through her body from Alexis's fingertip and back again and again.

CeCe had a death grip on Alexis's shoulders and held on until the last shudder left her body. She was glad Alexis had her pinned against the wall or she would have slinked right down to the floor.

Before she could say anything, Alexis's soft, luscious lips were on hers again, caressing and nibbling. *What did this woman just do to me?* CeCe couldn't think about that at the moment. All she could think about was that kiss as her body still tingled.

CeCe cupped Alexis's face as the kiss ended and gazed into her eyes. "You may have to get a new hairstylist."

Alexis furrowed her brow. "I don't want a new hairstylist."

"We'll see," CeCe murmured, softly kissing Alexis again.

She pulled back and gazed into her eyes once again and smiled.

"I knew it," Alexis said.

"What?"

"I knew this is what happened in the back room." Alexis reached down and buttoned CeCe's pants then zipped them up.

CeCe smoothed the tangles from Alexis's hair that her fingers had caused. She walked over to the refrigerator and pulled out two beers. She opened them, handed one to Alexis, and sat down on the couch.

After taking a long drink of beer, CeCe sighed. "I don't know what stories you've heard, but I have only done something like this two times since I started doing hair." CeCe held up two fingers and continued. "Both times were when I was in my twenties. One was with my boyfriend at the time and the other was with the girl I was dating. I'm now forty-two. I hope that shows you that I don't do this all the time like you heard."

Alexis's eyes had never left CeCe's as she told her story. "Then why did this happen tonight?"

CeCe took another sip and smiled. "You tell me?"

Alexis shrugged. "I haven't been able to get you off my mind since the open house. I look forward to coming to my appointments with you because I can leave everything outside the door once I step in here."

CeCe smiled. "I'm glad you can do that."

"I made an appointment with Nora next week for a pedicure," Alexis stated.

"It's not time for a haircut, so you scheduled a pedicure for a reason to come see me?" CeCe asked.

"Not exactly, but maybe."

CeCe giggled. "You don't have to make an appointment

to come see me. You came by after work the other day. Remember?"

Alexis smiled and took another sip of her beer. "How can I forget? That's when Cat walked in."

CeCe drank her beer and studied Alexis. *What am I doing?* Alexis might be finding reasons to come by but it wasn't serious. Now that they'd kissed and gotten that out of their systems, CeCe was sure things would calm down and go back the way they were. But how was that?

"You do have the most gorgeous red hair, CeCe. But I want to know what you're thinking. You are looking at me so seriously," Alexis said.

"I was just thinking about how things have changed since we opened the new salon," CeCe said.

"You mean between us?" Alexis asked.

CeCe nodded.

Alexis tilted her head. "Have they? What about your crush?"

"This may be the last birthday Cory sees."

Alexis laughed. "You didn't think I had a crush on you?"

"No! Why would you? I do your hair."

"So? Why would you have one on me?"

CeCe chuckled. "Do I have to spell it out for you? Okay then. Successful doctor, sexy as hell, gorgeous eyes," CeCe said, holding up fingers as she listed Alexis's attributes. "And a beautiful heart."

CeCe watched as Alexis's cheeks began to pinken. "Are you blushing?"

"No one has ever told me I have a beautiful heart," Alexis replied.

"Well, you do."

"How do you know?"

CeCe Sloan is Swooning 57

"Do you not remember the conversations we've had over the last year?" CeCe asked.

"Yes, I remember."

CeCe smiled. "Trust me, Doc. You're an incredible woman. Own it."

"My turn," Alexis said. "CeCe Sloan, you are the most vivacious person I've ever met. You bring joy to anyone who is lucky enough to spend time with you. I've already told you how beautiful your hair is, but it's your eyes that make my heart beat fast."

"What? I make your heart beat fast?"

"You couldn't feel it a few minutes ago?" Alexis exclaimed.

CeCe smiled. "I was too busy trying to grab a breath."

"Your crystal blue eyes make my heart smile when you look at me."

"How funny. Your soft brown eyes make me feel warm all over. Now that I know how your arms feel around me, it's like that," CeCe explained. "It's like you hug me with your entire body."

"Wow. It seems we do things to each other."

CeCe smiled and thought of lots of things she'd like to do to Alexis Reed.

They sipped their rest of their beers, simply gazing at one another and smiling.

Maybe it was a good thing to talk about what they'd been feeling. Now that it was in the open they could go back to stylist and client. Then why did CeCe want to lean over and kiss Alexis again?

"I'd better get going. That's probably enough honesty for one night," Alexis said, standing up and throwing her beer bottle away. "However, I don't believe Cory Sloan is the sweetest sister."

CeCe nodded. "She probably is. Behind that sometimes gruff exterior of hers is a total sweetheart," CeCe said as they walked to the back door. "Thanks for protecting me tonight."

"Anytime," Alexis replied. She reached out and took CeCe in her arms before she could open the back door.

Their lips met and this kiss was a sweet ending to the night, but there was a hint of more to come.

"I'll see you Tuesday," Alexis said as she opened the door.

CeCe smiled and nodded. She locked the door and walked Alexis to her car. "I was right," CeCe said.

"About what?" Alexis asked, rolling her window down.

"Everything. You're dangerous," CeCe said.

Alexis chuckled. "So are you!"

"And your lips." CeCe shook her head.

"Yours will keep me up at night." Alexis grinned, starting her car.

"Good thing I bought you that toy," CeCe said, stepping back from the car.

Alexis raised her eyebrows. "Maybe I want the real thing next time."

CeCe grinned. "Dangerous." Then she got in her car and they drove away.

* * *

Alexis drove home with a cocky smile on her face. That had to be the hottest sex she'd had in a long time. As she thought about it she shook her head. "Nope," she mumbled. "That was the hottest sex I've ever had."

How could that be? Was it because of all the flirting they'd been doing lately? Or was it that near kiss that had them

CeCe Sloan is Swooning 59

both wondering. Whatever it was, Alexis was not going to soon forget it. She could still feel the intensity pulsating through her body.

CeCe's body responded under her fingers like nothing she'd ever felt before. So did hers! When CeCe ran her hands up her back and lightly scratched across her skin with her nails, Alexis almost came undone right then and there. *With one touch?* This was confusing.

Alexis had been with her fair share of men and women, but she'd never felt quite like that with another person's touch. It was like their bodies had been waiting for this and once they were together, the intensity was fierce.

"You were in the back room of a beauty salon with your hair stylist backed up against a wall," Alexis said out loud. She'd imagined this exact scenario more than once, but the real deal was so much better. "Good God," she sighed.

She couldn't believe she felt this strongly about what had just happened when CeCe had yet to touch her. "It must be those kisses," she muttered.

When she pressed her lips to CeCe's that first time, something exploded inside her. She'd heard people describe when they were first with the love of their lives or soulmates or whatever the buzz word was now, that they felt like they were home. Alexis had thought that was rather ridiculous, but who was she to judge.

"Hmm." She had to admit there was some sort of feeling when their lips first met. It wasn't just lust, because she knew that was rushing through both of them. There was something about their lips, it was as if they'd been waiting for the other.

She'd experienced some bad kisses in her time and some good kisses. But the kisses she and CeCe had just created were on another level. That's kind of how she looked at it. Together they created a kiss, a touch, a sound, or even a feeling. There wasn't a familiarity necessarily, but it was like they knew what to do so they could feel the best of everything.

"Well, that sounds ludicrous. You're letting your analytical brain go too far. This isn't surgery. You were having great sex," Alexis chided herself as she pulled into her garage.

She sat in her car for a minute and stared straight ahead. *What does all this mean?*

Alexis took a deep breath and let it out. "All it means is that you hope to do this again when you see CeCe on Tuesday."

That made Alexis smile. Then she remembered what CeCe had said—she doesn't date clients.

Alexis raised her eyebrows. Did she want to date CeCe Sloan? Did that mean CeCe wanted to date her? Whatever it meant right now she couldn't wait to be in that back room with CeCe again.

7

CeCe's phone rang and for just a moment she hoped it was Alexis. They'd texted last night and again this morning briefly. When she picked up the phone she saw a picture of her big sister on the caller ID.

"Happy birthday to you, happy birthday to you, happy birthday, dear Cory, happy birthday to you," CeCe sang as she connected the call.

Cory's laughter bubbled out of the phone. "Thank you, sis, but I didn't call so you'd sing to me."

"Come on, you know you did. We don't celebrate you enough, big sister," CeCe said, laughing.

"Ha ha. I called to see if you'd go on a delivery with me," Cory said.

"You deliver?"

"Sometimes. Krista called looking for a specific bottle of wine and I happened to have it. I told her I'd bring it out to their place at the lake," Cory explained.

"I thought you were working," CeCe said.

62   JAMEY MOODY

"I was, but Taylor came in and insisted I take the day off since it's my birthday."

CeCe chuckled. "So the hard-ass owner is letting her employees boss her around."

"Krista happened to call when Taylor was there, so it all worked out. I hoped you and Cat would ride out to the lake with me. I'm sure Krista would love to see you."

"Come get me."

"Okay, see you soon."

A short time later the Sloan sisters were on their way to the lake resort.

"What do you have in the bag, Cat?" CeCe asked.

"I brought along a few toys from The Bottom Shelf to see if Krista might be interested," Cat replied.

CeCe giggled. "Krista will love it. Does she have a group there this weekend?"

"No," Cory replied.

"How does that work exactly?" Cat asked.

"It started as a secret hideaway for closeted gays in Hollywood. There are some women who are afraid that if the public knew of their sexual orientation, it could affect their careers," Cory explained.

"It's also a secluded place where couples can get away and not be bothered by nosy paparazzi," CeCe added. "I've been out here a few times and the women are so nice. Even the ones that have reputations of being divas are friendly."

Cory turned onto a small paved road off the main highway and after a couple of curves they pulled up to the main office and restaurant of Lovers Landing.

"I love the name of this place," CeCe said.

CeCe Sloan is Swooning 63

"It's almost as good as The Liquor Box," Cory replied with a grin.

CeCe and Cat shook their heads at their sister as they walked into the restaurant and found Krista sitting with her wife, Melanie, at a table next to a large window that looked out over the lake.

CeCe stopped and took in the view. The lake was calm and the water was a bright blue just like the Sloan sisters' eyes.

"Oh wow!" Krista exclaimed, standing up. "How did we get so lucky to have all three Sloan sisters here?"

"This is a treat," Melanie said. "Sit down and catch us up. How are things going with the shopping center?"

"So far, so good," Cory said, handing Krista the bottle of wine.

She looked at the label and smiled. "Tara is going to be so happy," Krista said. She looked over at Cory and added, "You said you'd have whatever I needed when you pitched your store to get our business."

"And we deliver," CeCe said with a grin. "It just happens to be our big sister's birthday."

"It is!" Krista exclaimed. "Let's have a drink." Krista went around to the bar. "Beer? Wine? Cocktail?"

"Beer is fine," Cory said with a big smile. She looked over at CeCe and shook her head. "You didn't have to say anything."

"Yes she did," Cat said, "and we brought a few products you may be interested in." She set the bag on the table.

Melanie looked up at Cat and raised an eyebrow. "Are those from The Bottom Shelf?" she asked, her voice low and sultry.

Cat smiled. "Well, they're not books."

Melanie laughed as Krista brought the beers over and

passed them around. "A toast to Cory since it's your birthday, but also we're so glad we've gotten to know all three of you."

They all clinked their bottles together and drank.

"Sit down and let's see what you've brought," Melanie said.

They gathered around the table and Cat took several boxes out of the bag.

"When is the next group coming in?" Cory asked. "Maybe Cat should leave a few of these for your guests."

Melanie chuckled. "Oh my God. Babe, can you imagine!"

Krista laughed. "Maybe one of these should be included in each cabin."

"We could try it with the group that's coming in on Wednesday," Melanie suggested.

"That's up to you and Julia, honey," Krista said.

"Are you not going to be here?" Cory asked.

"I am, but I'm having a little procedure done Wednesday, so I'm taking the week off," Krista explained.

"Oh? I hope it isn't serious," Cory commented.

"Not at all. I did not use sunscreen when I was a kid," Krista said.

"But you sure knew how to wear that tan," Melanie said, winking at Krista, who giggled.

CeCe watched this interaction and couldn't help feeling a bit of longing, wishing she had a partner. How wonderful it must feel to look at one another and share a knowing glance like Krista and Melanie just did. *Where did that come from!*

"Anyway, my doctor wants me to have a suspicious mole and the surrounding tissue removed and one of the best surgeons in the country happens to practice right here," Krista said.

Cory and Cat both looked at CeCe. "What?" Melanie asked.

"Is your surgeon Dr. Alexis Reed?" CeCe asked.

"It is! Do you know her?"

"Does she ever," Cory mumbled.

"She's one of my clients," CeCe replied, giving Cory a harsh look.

"What am I missing?" Krista asked.

"I smell a story here. Come on girls, spill it," Melanie said.

"Alexis is a brilliant surgeon who also has beautiful hair, thanks to my sister," Cat said.

CeCe sighed. "Alexis is my client, but we're also friends."

"There is a mutual crush happening and we have ringside seats," Cory said.

"Oh! CeCe, we love Alexis. She's been out here a couple of times. Why don't the two of you come out this weekend? Alexis can check on Krista and you can visit with me," Melanie said.

"There's a little problem. I don't date my clients," CeCe remarked. She thought back to last night when she told Alexis she may have to get a new stylist.

"It won't be a date. You're coming to see me while Alexis does a follow-up with a patient," Melanie said.

CeCe looked at Melanie and could see she was determined to make this happen. "I'll tell you what, Alexis will be in the salon Tuesday for a pedicure. I'll talk to her about it then."

"Good. We'll see her Wednesday morning," Krista said. "Now, Cat, show us what you brought."

CeCe sat back and watched Cat show the toys. She wondered if Alexis would agree to this non-date on Saturday. *What are you doing? You are not good enough for Alexis to date, much less come out here and party with these Hollywood people.*

But Melanie was insistent and she wasn't a celebrity like the others. And honestly, CeCe wouldn't know Krista was a celebrity if she hadn't seen all her movies.

CeCe smiled and listened to the laughter around the table. She'd been to parties out here before and hadn't felt out of place. So why did the thought of being here with Alexis make her so nervous, but also excited?

"What do you think, CeCe?" Cat asked.

CeCe shook the thoughts out of her head and joined the laughter and conversation.

* * *

Alexis walked into the salon and her eyes immediately found CeCe shampooing someone's hair in the back of the salon. She stopped and watched her for a moment. The smile on her face as she worked her fingers through her client's hair warmed Alexis's heart. CeCe really enjoyed what she was doing.

As if CeCe could sense her there she looked up and their eyes met. She wasn't prepared for the butterflies that fluttered in her stomach when CeCe smiled at her. Alexis hadn't felt anything like this in—she didn't know when. Had it been that long since she'd been excited about the possibility of something new?

She wasn't sure exactly what was happening to her and she didn't know if CeCe felt it too, but she intended to find out.

"Hi, Dr. Reed," Ryan said as Alexis started back to where Nora waited to do her pedicure.

CeCe Sloan is Swooning 67

"Hi, Ryan. It's nice to see you," Alexis replied, trying to calm her heart as it pounded in her chest.

"I've got everything ready," Nora said to Alexis as she reached the back area of the salon that contained Nora's nail station, the shampoo bowls on one side and CeCe's station on the other.

"Thanks," Alexis said with a smile.

As she rinsed her client's hair, CeCe looked up and winked at Alexis. "Hi, Lex. How's your day?"

Alexis smirked and put her hands on her hips. "It's been a good day, Cecilia. How about yours?"

"Oh, it's much better now," CeCe replied.

Alexis couldn't help but smile. CeCe Sloan was fun. With a look or a word she brightened any day.

"Right this way, Alexis." Nora led Alexis to her chair and slipped her shoes off then placed her feet gently in the water.

Alexis decided right then to do this more often. She had the perfect seat to watch CeCe. Today she was wearing a pair of jeans that hugged her curves in all the right places.

CeCe glanced at Alexis, as she put the cape around her client then began to cut her hair. Alexis could see in the mirror what CeCe was doing and also had a view of her back. She smiled as she watched CeCe deftly cut the woman's hair then she noticed CeCe had stopped. Their eyes met in the mirror and Alexis's heart began to thump wildly in her chest once again.

Alexis wasn't sure what was going on, oh, who was she trying to fool, she knew exactly what was happening. Alexis and CeCe were lusting after each other while pretending it was an ordinary day.

The idea made Alexis chuckle.

"Uh oh, are you ticklish?" Nora asked.

"No, it's okay," Alexis replied. She heard something hit the floor and looked up to see that CeCe had dropped her comb.

"Oops," CeCe commented and reached for another comb in a drawer.

Alexis continued to watch CeCe and was enjoying every second when once again something hit the floor. This time CeCe dropped her scissors.

"Sorry about that. I have butterfingers today," CeCe told her client.

"Alexis?"

"Hmm?"

"I asked if you've chosen a color you want me to paint your toenails," Nora said.

"Oh, sorry, Nora. Yes," Alexis said, handing Nora the bottle of nail polish.

"I like this one. It's a hot, hot, hot shade of red," Nora said.

When Alexis gave her a confused look Nora added, "The name of the color is 'Too hot to handle.' We just call it hot, hot, hot."

"Oh, okay. Wait just a second, Nora. Do you have a blue-green color?"

"Sure! That's a popular color this spring. I have a few," Nora said, getting up and going over to the display that held nail polish bottles with all the colors of the rainbow and everything in between.

"What about one of these?" Nora asked, showing Alexis three different shades of blue-green polish.

"Hey, CeCe," Alexis called. She waited for CeCe to turn around. "I don't mean to interrupt, but what do you think of this color?"

CeCe Sloan is Swooning 69

A slow grin crossed CeCe's face. "Are you trying to match a certain something?"

Alexis couldn't keep from chuckling. CeCe knew exactly what Alexis was doing. She was matching the color of the vibrator CeCe had given her on the night the shopping center opened. "Maybe. It does remind me of something."

"I like it. I think you should go with it."

"Thanks." Alexis gave CeCe her best smile.

As Nora worked on Alexis's feet and toes, Alexis couldn't keep her eyes off CeCe. They caught each other's gaze from time to time in the mirror and Alexis gave CeCe a sexy smile.

After CeCe dried the woman's hair, she removed the cape and smiled. Alexis couldn't hear what they were saying. She figured the woman was paying CeCe or making another appointment.

CeCe caught her staring when she turned to walk her client to the front. Alexis gave her another smile and CeCe smirked as she walked by.

Alexis turned her attention back to her pedicure and realized that Nora was almost finished. She looked around the salon and all the other stylists were gone. CeCe was locking the adjoining door to the bookstore then walked over to lock the door to the liquor store.

When CeCe walked back to her station she stood at Nora's back and stared at Alexis. She had her hands on her hips and a smirk on her face.

Alexis couldn't help but smile. CeCe was at her cutest when she was flustered and Alexis could see her cheeks were a frustrated color of red.

"Nora, could you lock the front door when you're finished with Dr. Reed?" CeCe asked.

"I'm almost done."

"Everything else is locked up. Dr. Reed, would you like to join me in the back when Nora's finished?"

"I'll be right there."

CeCe smiled at Alexis. "Good night, Nora. See you tomorrow."

"Bye, CeCe," Nora said.

As CeCe disappeared down the back hallway, Alexis couldn't wait to join her.

"Okay, that's it," Nora said. "I'd leave your shoes off a little longer."

"I brought these," Alexis said, holding up a pair of sandals she could slide her feet into.

"Perfect." Nora carefully slid them on Alexis's feet.

"Thanks, Nora." She handed her several bills. "Keep the change. These look great," Alexis said, wiggling her toes.

"You're welcome."

Alexis grabbed her shoes and stood up.

"Tell CeCe I'm leaving now. Thanks again."

"I'll tell her." Alexis started down the hallway and heard Nora lock the front door just as she turned the doorknob to the back room.

She felt a hand grab her wrist and she was suddenly pulled into the room.

8

CeCe shut the door and locked it as she held Alexis's wrist. She led them over to the couch, but stopped before sitting and whirled around, taking Alexis in her arms. They were nose to nose since Alexis wasn't wearing her heels.

"You come in here wearing that tight skirt and those heels and expect me to cut and style someone's hair while you watch?" CeCe said in a low, even tone, staring into Alexis's eyes.

Alexis gave her a sexy smile as her heart pounded in her chest. She'd never seen this take-charge side of CeCe and at the moment it was doing all kinds of things to her body. It was hard to breathe; she could hear her pulse throbbing in her ears and something else was throbbing even more under her tight skirt.

"You put on quite a show yourself, Cecilia, in those jeans that fit every curve and with those crystal blue eyes staring back at me in the mirror," Alexis said in a raspy voice.

CeCe raised one eyebrow and looked down at Alexis's lips and back into her eyes. Then she took Alexis's chin in her hand and crashed her lips to Alexis's in a passionate kiss.

Alexis felt her knees go weak as she held onto CeCe's shoulders with both hands and a groan escaped from deep in her chest. CeCe bit Alexis's bottom lip gently then sucked it into her mouth. *Good God, I'm going to come right here, right now.*

CeCe softened the kiss and caressed Alexis's lips with her own before she ran her tongue over Alexis's bottom lip. Their tongues met in a sensuous, sexy dance to the beat of their frantic breaths and melodic moans.

Here we go again, Alexis thought. *My God, this is fun!*

CeCe pushed Alexis down onto the couch and began another assault of hot kisses. She nibbled Alexis's earlobe and kissed down her neck then CeCe raised up and Alexis looked into her eyes as her chest heaved up and down.

What a beautiful woman, Alexis thought as she grabbed CeCe's face and pulled her down for another heated kiss. Alexis hadn't been this turned on...since she was last in this room with CeCe. She thought about raising up and turning CeCe over, but she liked the weight of CeCe pressing down on her body.

"Don't even think about it," CeCe whispered as she pulled her lips away and took a deep breath. "You're mine right now."

Fuck! Alexis couldn't form any words, but she looked at CeCe with such passion that she was sure CeCe knew what she was trying to say.

CeCe gave her a sexy smile. "You are so beautiful, Lex. Let me show you what you do to me," she whispered then began to softly kiss Alexis's neck once again. CeCe cupped Alexis's breast through her blouse. "I'll come back to this," she said softly.

Alexis watched as CeCe began to slide down her body. She pushed Alexis's skirt up her thighs then looped her fingers through either side of her panties and pulled them down her legs. CeCe stared at Alexis's wetness for a moment then looked back into her eyes.

The look coming from CeCe's dark blue eyes was more than lust. There was wonder and excitement and a sweet anticipation. Alexis had never felt wanted quite like this before. She'd have to think about that later because she really wanted CeCe to touch her.

"See something you like?" Alexis cooed.

CeCe smiled and quickly kissed Alexis's lips. "Watch me," she whispered.

Alexis did just that as CeCe blew air across her center. "Fuck." Alexis groaned and pushed her hips up. She saw CeCe grin then she ran her tongue from Alexis's entrance up and around her clit. Alexis didn't recognize the sound that passed her lips. It was somewhere between a satisfied 'ahhh' and a groan for more.

Alexis's fingers ran through CeCe's hair as she slid her tongue through and around her folds over and over. CeCe teased her entrance then licked up to her clit once again. Just when the pleasure began to build, CeCe would move her tongue to another spot and it would start all over again. Alexis's hips had a mind of their own as she opened her legs wider.

It felt like CeCe was everywhere and she wanted even more. The moans coming from CeCe's mouth along with her magical tongue made Alexis push her hips even higher. "So good," Alexis kept panting over and over.

"Mmm," CeCe moaned.

She reached up and took one of Alexis's hands and interlocked their fingers. Then she sucked Alexis's clit deeply into her mouth. Her hips bucked, and she fisted her fingers in CeCe's hair as a powerful orgasm began to shoot through her body.

She never wanted CeCe's mouth to move as wave after wave of luxurious bliss ran through her. Finally, Alexis fell back on the couch and eased her grip on CeCe's hair, but she didn't let go of her other hand.

"Fuck me!" Alexis exclaimed in a satisfied voice as her breathing began to slow.

CeCe giggled. "In a minute." She kissed the inside of Alexis's thigh then raised up and smiled down at her.

The look on CeCe's face made that throbbing between her legs start all over again. She'd just had one of the best orgasms she could remember! What was CeCe doing to her?

CeCe stared at Alexis and shook her head.

"What?" Alexis asked, suddenly confused.

"I thought we'd do this and that would be it, but it's not."

"Okay?"

"We keep ending up here. I can't stop thinking about you and from what just happened I think you're thinking about me too."

"I am," Alexis said softly.

"I can't be your stylist because we're not going to stop doing this. Are we?"

Alexis smiled and pulled CeCe down for another heated kiss. "Does that answer your question?"

CeCe ran her hand up the inside of Alexis's thigh and stared into her eyes. "Are you relaxed?"

Alexis's eyes widened. *What kind of question was that!* "No, I'm not relaxed. I'm about to come just thinking about where your hand is going next."

"I know you have surgery tomorrow and I wanted to take

all your stress away so you'd be relaxed when you enter the operating room."

Alexis's eyebrows crept up her forehead. "You know my schedule now?"

CeCe smiled. "No." She kept tickling the inside of Alexis's thigh until she bent her knee, raising her leg up. "I talked to Krista on Saturday and she told me you're her surgeon."

"Oh." Alexis nodded. "Are you going to relax me?"

CeCe grinned. "Oh Doc, I want to relax you over and over and over."

CeCe didn't wait for Alexis to answer. She pressed her lips to Alexis's and they both moaned. Her hand slid higher until her fingers found Alexis's center once again. She teased her opening with her finger and Alexis's hips raised to meet her.

"You are incredible, Lex," CeCe whispered as she pushed one finger inside.

There was that sound again coming from Alexis. When CeCe added a second finger, Alexis groaned even louder.

"Let's go," Alexis said, grabbing CeCe's face and kissing her hard.

CeCe began to move to the rhythm of Alexis's hips. They went faster and faster as the orgasm began to build.

"Are you close?" CeCe asked, pulling her lips away from Alexis's.

"Yes." Alexis forced the word out as she tried to breathe.

"Look at me, Lex. I want to see your eyes," CeCe demanded.

Alexis opened her eyes and locked her gaze on CeCe's bright blue eyes. She felt CeCe push inside her once again and curl her fingers. An explosion of sensation flowed through Alexis's body. She was filled with heat and her body stiffened as she squeezed CeCe's face between her hands and stared into those beautiful blue eyes.

CeCe smiled and the joy in her eyes made Alexis come again. "Kiss me," Alexis begged.

CeCe brought their lips together in a soft, sweet kiss. Alexis relaxed her hold on CeCe's face, but put her hand over CeCe's hand, holding it in place. There were still traces of the orgasm as Alexis closed her eyes and sank into the kiss.

"Cecilia," Alexis murmured when CeCe pulled away and rested her head on Alexis's shoulder. She wrapped her arms around CeCe and held her close for several moments.

CeCe finally sat up and looked at the floor. She picked up Alexis's undies and twirled them with one hand. "We've been invited out to Lovers Landing on Saturday."

Alexis chuckled and tried to snatch her panties from CeCe's hand, but just missed. "Are you going to let me have those back?"

"We'll see." CeCe grinned.

Alexis laughed. "Okay. Tell me about this invitation."

"Melanie invited us out. It's a non-date," CeCe explained.

Alexis raised her eyebrows. "A non-date? But if I'm getting a new stylist does that mean…"

"It means that the next time we have sex, it's not going to be against a wall or on a couch or—" CeCe looked around the room. "Or even in this room. We're going to have a bed and we're taking all our clothes off and—"

"And we're taking our time," Alexis said, finishing CeCe's sentence.

CeCe gave Alexis the most beautiful smile. It unexpectedly made Alexis's heart melt. "Uh, what about Saturday?" she said, wondering what CeCe was doing to her heart.

CeCe Sloan is Swooning 77

CeCe quickly told Alexis about going to Lovers Landing last Saturday with her sisters. She explained how she found out that Alexis was Krista's surgeon. "Melanie wanted us to come out Saturday so you could check on Krista and I could visit with her. She offered us a cabin for the night."

"Oh, she did? That's nice."

"Do you want to stay?" CeCe asked.

"Is it our first date?" Alexis asked with a grin.

CeCe gazed down at Alexis. "No." She narrowed her gaze. "Do you even *want* to go on a date with me?"

"I do now," Alexis said.

"What does that mean?" CeCe said, furrowing her brow.

"Can I sit up? You've kind of got me pinned down here," Alexis said, trying to move.

"You're just fine," CeCe said, looking down at her and waiting.

"Okay. I love flirting with you." Alexis reached for CeCe's hand and interlaced their fingers. "When you told me you don't date clients, I didn't know if you meant it or if you were trying to tell me something else. I can't stop thinking about you either and I would love to take you out on a proper date since you seem to want to go."

CeCe laughed. "You think I wouldn't want to go out with you!"

Alexis shrugged.

"Let's go on this non-date to Lovers Landing but then you have to promise to take me out on our first real date after that."

Alexis raised her hand. "I promise. But why can't you take me out?" she asked, raising one eyebrow.

"You're the one that started this," CeCe stated.

"Oh I did? How did I do that?"

"You came to the open house. That showed me I meant something to you."

Alexis's heart melted even more. "Let me up," she said earnestly.

CeCe moved so Alexis could sit up next to her.

Alexis gently cupped CeCe's face and gazed into her eyes. A soft smile covered her face and she said, "I want to know everything about you, Cecilia Sloan. I want to know why it doesn't bother me when you call me Lex, but if anyone else calls me that I cringe. I want to know what you taste like. I want to know why of all the people you could go out with, you want to go out with me. Your effervescent spirit washes over me every time you look at me or smile at me or I think of you. I'm not that kind of person, but with you, I am."

"What kind of person?"

"A happy, cheery person. I'm a fucking serious surgeon. I don't smile very often."

CeCe giggled. "You do with me."

"Exactly! I want to find out why. So you see, Cecilia, you very much matter to me."

"Well, when you put it like that... I'd love for you to find out all those things *with* me," CeCe said with a twinkle in her eye.

"What if I don't want to get a new stylist? I like the way you cut my hair and when you wash my hair it takes all my stress away," Alexis said.

"I have other ways to take your stress away, but if you want to go back to me washing your hair..." CeCe held up her hands.

9

"Nope. I'll talk to Ryan tomorrow." Alexis started to push CeCe down on the couch, but she stopped her.

"Did you not hear what I said? The next time we have sex—"

"Does that mean we have to start now?" Alexis said, nibbling CeCe's earlobe and kissing just below it. Alexis felt CeCe soften against her.

"We're jumping right in then," CeCe said, her voice serious.

Alexis pulled back with amusement on her face. "Is that fear I see in your eyes?"

"Maybe a little," CeCe said honestly.

"Why?" Alexis said, all humor gone from her voice.

"Because I really like you, Alexis." CeCe smiled.

Alexis trailed her fingers down the side of CeCe's face just as she'd done in the parking lot on open house night. "I really like you, too, CeCe. Why do you think I'm here?"

CeCe's eyebrows shot up her forehead. "I don't know, you tell me." She leaned in and kissed Alexis, smiles on both their faces, but the kiss quickly turned more passionate.

"Whatever are we going to do until Saturday?" Alexis asked, beginning to kiss down CeCe's neck.

"Mmm, I don't know," CeCe said breathlessly.

"We can go to my house. I was listening when you said no more sex in this room," Alexis said.

"I didn't mean never." CeCe looked into Alexis's eyes. "Is that all we are?" she asked softly.

"We *are* very good at it," Alexis replied.

CeCe giggled. "Yeah we are. But we're more than that, right?"

"That's what we're going to find out," Alexis said. "If you dare?"

A slow smile grew on CeCe's face. "That's what this felt like at first. I could feel you pulling me closer and closer, Lex. It's like you're daring me to push back."

"I like how you push back," Alexis said, pulling CeCe's lips to hers. "I kind of liked how you took charge when I came into the room."

"It's all your fault." CeCe grinned. "You drove me crazy."

"Do you feel better now?"

"I do," CeCe said with a satisfied smile.

"I know you wanted to relax me for Krista's surgery tomorrow," Alexis began as she slowly pushed CeCe down on the couch. "And technically, we're not dating yet."

"This is supposed to relax you?" CeCe asked as Alexis began to pull her pants down.

"Oh, yeah." Alexis nodded with a gleam in her eye.

"Well, I guess it would be my way of making sure Krista has a successful procedure tomorrow."

"There's that generous heart of yours coming through," Alexis said as she pulled CeCe's undies down her thighs.

CeCe Sloan is Swooning 81

"Are you sure a nice dinner wouldn't do the trick?" CeCe asked as Alexis leaned in to kiss her.

"Oh, no. This is just what the doctor ordered," Alexis said and pressed her lips to CeCe's.

* * *

As CeCe drove home later that evening she couldn't keep the smile from her face. She was going to spend a night at Lovers Landing with Dr. Alexis Reed. On top of that they were going on a real date next week. *This must be what heaven is like*, CeCe thought.

A part of her still couldn't believe someone like Alexis would be interested in her, but she had a feeling Alexis didn't let many people see the side of her she showed CeCe. And that made CeCe happy and feel special that Alexis could be herself with her.

She thought back to how crazy Alexis had driven her before she could get her hands on her. CeCe thought they might have sex again today, but when she saw Alexis walk into the salon she was sure of it. What CeCe thought would turn out to be another hot rendezvous became so much more. Alexis cared about her. She could see it in her eyes, feel it in her touch and hear it in her words.

CeCe was surprised when she admitted to Alexis that she was scared. But Alexis made it clear what may have started as hot sex was more than that to her. CeCe could still feel the relief wash over her when Alexis explained how CeCe made her feel. That was followed by the sweet anticipation of where they were going. CeCe was sure this would be one wild ride, but she was willing to give it a go.

"You'd be crazy not to," she said to herself as she walked into her house.

She couldn't wait for Saturday.

"Good morning," Alexis said cheerily as she pulled back the curtain and walked into the pre-surgery prep room cubicle. "How are you, Krista?"

"The question is: how are you, Dr. Reed?" Krista asked with a nervous smile. "Did you have a good evening? Plenty of sleep? Are you relaxed?"

Alexis smiled as flashes of last evening played through her head. CeCe's lips on hers, their hands entangled in each other's hair, and CeCe's smile. *That smile.* Alexis's heart warmed just thinking about CeCe.

"I think from the look on your face you had a fine evening," Melanie said from where she stood next to Krista's bed, holding her hand.

Alexis smiled again. "I did have a nice evening. I got a pedicure." She shrugged.

"That does sound nice. I need one," Krista replied. "You didn't happen to go to Salon 411, did you?"

"I did." Alexis grinned.

"Now I know why you're smiling." Melanie nodded her head. "CeCe Sloan didn't also happen to do your toes did she?"

Alexis gave Melanie and then Krista a measured look. "CeCe doesn't do nails. I recommend Nora."

"Oh, I see, but CeCe does your hair, right?" Melanie asked.

"Babe, can you leave Dr. Reed alone until after she does my surgery? You can talk about Salon 411 and CeCe all you want after that," Krista said.

CeCe Sloan is Swooning 83

"Everything is going to be fine, honey," Melanie said, giving Krista a reassuring look.

Alexis smiled. "I was thinking if everything goes the way I expect I may need to see you on Saturday," Alexis began. "I'd be happy to come out and do a follow-up."

"I knew you were amazing the first time I saw you. What doctor still makes house calls!" Krista exclaimed.

Alexis laughed.

"I'm guessing the ones that are invited on a non-date with an incredible hairstylist," Melanie said with a wink. "Her sister may have mentioned her rules. Or maybe she is no longer your hair stylist?"

Alexis felt her cheeks pinken.

"Yes, Doc, your name may have come up and that blush on your cheeks is adorable," Krista said. "Don't worry, we won't tell anyone."

"I do have a new hairstylist, but this is not a date on Saturday."

"Why not?" Melanie asked.

"We agreed our first official date will be next week," Alexis explained. She furrowed her brow and looked at Melanie and Krista. "Hey, y'all wouldn't have any ideas for a unique first date would you? Anyone can go out to dinner."

"Hmm, that will give me something to think about while you fix up my wife," Melanie said with a smile.

Alexis nodded. "This has not been the most professional pre-surgery visit. I apologize for that."

"No need, Alexis. We were thrilled to see the Sloan sisters last weekend, then when your name came up... Let me just say there was quite a sparkle in CeCe's eyes," Krista said.

Alexis couldn't keep from smiling.

"It kind of matched the sparkle in your eyes when I said CeCe's name," Melanie added.

"CeCe told me about her visit and your invitation," Alexis shared.

"We'd love to have you both stay the night. We're planning a night of karaoke and dancing," Krista said.

"However, we're not trying to push you too fast. There are two bedrooms in the cabin," Melanie said.

Alexis smiled. *Like we'll be sleeping in separate bedrooms.* Then she remembered what they'd both said about the next time they had sex: in a bed and they'd take their time.

"I'm sure the cabin will be perfect," Alexis said. "Now, we've got to get this procedure done. Let me put on my surgeon's face. I do not foresee any complications or problems. As soon as we're finished I'll come talk to you, Melanie."

"Okay. The nurse showed me the waiting area."

Alexis reached over and squeezed Krista's other hand. "I'll see you in a few minutes."

"Thank you, Alexis."

Alexis winked and left the cubicle.

"I see love on the horizon, babe. How about you?" Krista said, watching Alexis leave.

"They both have that look in their eyes, but may not realize it just yet. Hey, we need to concentrate on you." Melanie leaned down and kissed Krista tenderly on the lips. "I'll be right here when you wake up."

"I know," Krista said softly. "I love you."

Melanie smiled. "Oh, baby. I love you."

"Are you ready, Ms. Kyle?" a nurse said, walking into the cubicle. "We're here to take you to Dr. Reed. She's the best."

"Yes, she is," the other nurse said, unlocking the wheels on the bed.

CeCe Sloan is Swooning 85

"See you soon, love," Krista said to Melanie as they wheeled her away.

An hour later Alexis found Melanie in the waiting room. The anticipation and hope in a loved one's face always struck Alexis keenly. The look on Melanie's face was no different when she saw Alexis walking towards her.

Melanie hopped up and Alexis could see her trying to read her face. Alexis gave her a reassuring smile and reached for her hand. "Let's sit."

Once they were seated, Alexis looked into Melanie's eyes. "The procedure went well."

"Thank God," Melanie said, relief accenting her voice.

"There was a little more to it than I expected and I had to remove more tissue than we'd talked about, but it should heal beautifully."

Melanie suddenly put her arms around Alexis and hugged her tight.

Alexis knew this was a response to the stress of waiting and held her for a moment.

"Thank you," Melanie said with tears in her eyes. "You just never know."

Alexis nodded. "We're sending off the tissue, just to be sure, but I highly doubt it's cancerous."

Melanie responded with a nod. "When can I take her home? What do I have to do to take care of her?"

"There's a dressing on it now. All the instructions to care for the incision will be in her release papers."

"Okay, okay." Melanie nodded then she looked up at Alexis. "But hey, you'll be out Saturday to make sure she's doing all right."

Alexis smiled. "I will. If there's anything you need before

that don't hesitate to call me. Krista has my contact information. Call me directly on my cell phone."

Melanie finally leaned back in her chair and sighed. "Thank you, Alexis. I didn't realize how scared I was."

Alexis gave her hand a squeeze and smiled. "Will you do something for me?"

"Of course. Anything."

"Would you text CeCe and let her know everything went well? She's already texted me once this morning and I can't give her information about a patient."

"I'd be happy to. She's such a sweetheart," Melanie said, getting out her phone.

"Yeah, she is," Alexis agreed.

"I've got a group text to the family and I'll add CeCe to it," Melanie said as she pulled up the text.

"Thanks, I appreciate it." Alexis waited until Melanie had the message sent then said, "Would you like to see her?"

Melanie gasped. "Yes! I thought I'd have to wait."

"I have connections. I can get you in," Alexis said with a wink.

10

Alexis walked Melanie into the recovery room where Krista was beginning to stir.

Melanie grabbed her hand and bent down to kiss her forehead. "I'm right here, baby," she whispered.

A hint of a smile pulled up the corners of Krista's mouth as her eyes fluttered open.

Alexis was suddenly filled with such a sense of longing. To be able to elicit that reaction with a whisper. She could see the love between Krista and Melanie as if it was its own entity. *I want that!* She imagined the feeling inside her heart to love someone like that and to know they loved her back the same way.

Tears stung the back of Alexis's eyes. She blinked them away and cleared her throat, afraid her voice might expose the emotion she was feeling at the moment.

"Hey, Doc," Krista said dreamily.

Alexis grinned. "Hi, Krista."

"Everything went well, babe. You're going to be okay," Melanie said softly.

"No, I'm not. I need a kiss, baby. Your kisses will make me well," Krista said drunkenly.

Melanie chuckled and pressed her lips to Krista's. "I've got plenty of kisses for you."

"Oh, good," Krista said as she exhaled. "I love your kisses so much. I love you so much," she babbled, looking into Melanie's eyes.

"You'll be able to take her home in an hour or so," Alexis said, chuckling.

"Thanks, Alexis," Melanie said.

"Isn't she beautiful," Krista said, reaching up to touch Melanie's face.

"Thank you, honey. I think you're a little loopy." Melanie giggled.

"You're still beautiful. Can I have another kiss?" Krista asked. "Oh, oh, you've got someone to kiss, Alexis. You've got CeCe!" She pointed at Alexis.

Alexis couldn't help but smile. "I get it, Krista. CeCe's kisses are magical to me."

Krista laughed. "I knew it! They've been kissing, baby," she said, grinning at Melanie. "I'm so happy for them."

"I am, too," Melanie agreed.

"Krista, I think you're in good hands. I'll see you Saturday." Alexis turned to Melanie. "Call me if you need anything."

"Thank you," Melanie said.

As Alexis left the room her phone beeped in her pocket with an incoming text.

I knew you would be a rock star today. Thanks for letting me know in your own sweet way that Krista is okay.

Alexis smiled at CeCe's text, then replied.

Sweet? I'm not sure I've ever been called that. I'm a stoic surgeon. ;)

CeCe Sloan is Swooning 89

Alexis smiled as she waited for CeCe's reply. What was it about CeCe Sloan that could make her smile with a text? Yes, she was fun, but she had a way of making Alexis lower all her various masks. She could show CeCe her playful, not-so-serious side and not worry about being judged or hurt.

Alexis looked up from her phone as she realized how CeCe made her feel. A long time ago she decided not to give anyone her heart ever again. But CeCe Sloan made her feel safe.

Her phone pinged with another text and she looked down to read CeCe's message.

I see you, Lex.

"Hmm," Alexis mumbled. "You do, and I let you."

"Let what?" Melanie said, standing beside Alexis.

"Oh hey," Alexis said, putting her phone back into her pocket. "Everything okay?"

"Yes. I was just getting Krista some ice chips." Melanie studied Alexis. "Is everything okay with you, Alexis?"

"Uh, yeah." Alexis smiled. "Thanks for texting CeCe. She was just letting me know you reached out."

Melanie smiled and touched Alexis's arm. "I'm so glad I never have to date again, but there's excitement and a little trepidation while getting to know someone new. Enjoy the adventure."

With that, Melanie walked away, leaving Alexis to mumble,"CeCe is definitely an adventure and I can't wait for what comes next."

* * *

The next day Alexis was walking to her car after a difficult surgery. She was not pleased with the outcome and was worried about her patient. She got in her car and wondered if CeCe was still at the salon. One of her smiles would certainly make her feel better. If CeCe had already gone for the day or was busy, she'd go next door and buy a good bottle of wine. Or maybe she'd go to the bookstore and pick up a new book.

When Alexis walked into the salon she looked towards the back to CeCe's station but didn't see her there.

"Hey, gorgeous. Can I help you?" a sultry voice said from behind Alexis.

A smile immediately curled Alexis's lips and she turned to see a playful look on CeCe's face. "Yes, you can."

"Right this way," CeCe said, taking her hand and leading her to the back. "What's wrong?"

"Why do you think something is wrong?"

CeCe smiled. "I can tell."

"Are you finished for the day?"

"I have one more haircut and I'm done. What happened? Bad day?"

Alexis frowned. "Kind of."

"Heather, I'll be in the back," CeCe said to her coworker. "Come on." She once again took Alexis's hand and led them to the back room. Once inside she smiled at Alexis and held out her arms.

Alexis walked into her arms. This was the refuge she needed. CeCe held her for several moments.

"I'm sorry you're having a bad day. You just made mine very happy," CeCe said softly.

"I did?"

"Mmm, you did." CeCe ran her hands up and down Alexis's back. "It makes me happy to see you."

"I'm glad I could make you happy," Alexis mumbled.

CeCe pulled her head back so she could see into Alexis's

CeCe Sloan is Swooning 91

eyes. "This haircut will only take fifteen minutes and then I'm finished for the day. You can sit and watch me with a glass of wine," CeCe said with an enticing nod of her head.

"You won't drop your scissors or your comb?"

CeCe narrowed her gaze with a faux smirk. "I can't promise anything. You know what you do to me." Then she gave her a soft smile. "Please stay."

Alexis nodded. "I don't need wine. I'll wait until you can join me."

There was a knock at the door then Heather stuck her head in the room. "CeCe, Gabriel's here."

"Thanks, Heather."

CeCe leaned in and softly pressed her lips to Alexis's. "I'm glad you came by."

"Me, too," Alexis said hoarsely.

Alexis followed CeCe out of the room. "Nora's done for the day. You can sit over there or drag a chair over here by me," CeCe said as they walked back into the salon.

Alexis noticed a man sitting and spinning around in CeCe's chair.

"Hey, CeCe." The man smiled. "How's it going?"

"Hi, Gabriel." She turned to Alexis and smiled. "This is my friend Alexis Reed. She's going to hang out with us while I cut your hair."

"Hi," Gabriel said as he gave Alexis a long look.

"Hi," Alexis said, pulling a chair over, but staying out of CeCe's path.

"I'm sorry for staring, but you look familiar. Are you a doctor?" Gabriel asked.

"I am."

"Dr. Alexis Reed is a rock star," CeCe said, draping the cape around Gabriel.

"You operated on my father-in-law," Gabriel said with a

smile. "Actually, you gave him five more quality years. Thank you."

Alexis smiled. "I need you to remind me. What was your father-in-law's name?"

Gabriel chuckled. "Of course. I'm sure you can't remember all your patients and their families. His name was Javier Ramos. He was—"

"A wonderful man," Alexis said, her face brightening. "And quite a jokester."

"That was Pops," Gabriel said.

"As a matter of fact..." Alexis opened her purse and began to rummage around in it. Meanwhile, CeCe misted Gabriel's hair and glanced over at Alexis.

"Here it is." Alexis held up a coin and brought it over for Gabriel to see. "Mr. Ramos gave this to me. Before his surgery he told me that he needed my skill, but he also needed both of us to believe it was going to be a success," she explained.

"How about that," Gabriel said, looking at the coin.

"Let me see," CeCe said, taking the coin from Gabriel.

"It's a silver coin with the word 'believe' inscribed on it," Alexis said. "He told me that he believed in me and asked that I believe in him."

CeCe handed the coin back to Alexis and smiled. "That's so cool."

"I know. His chances were slim, but we believed." Alexis smiled. "I would say it was a miracle, but Mr. Ramos swore it was our belief that made it a success. I have carried this coin with me since then."

"What!" Gabriel exclaimed. "That was seven years ago."

"I know. Some patients stick with you. Javier Ramos is one of those patients."

CeCe Sloan is Swooning 93

"I can't wait to tell my wife. That will give her such comfort. Thanks, Dr. Reed," Gabriel said.

Alexis nodded and sat back down. It was such a good idea to stop by here, she thought.

"Hey, Lex. Gabriel works with Dru and Marina," CeCe said as she snipped his hair.

"Oh. Does that mean you work with Victoria Stratton, too? And Shelby?" Alexis asked.

Gabriel started to nod and CeCe placed her fingers firmly on his head. "Easy there, big fella."

He laughed. "Sorry. Yes, we all work together. I spend most of my time with Shelby. We've been working together since she started the staging business years ago. We've grown into quite the real estate establishment."

"I don't know Shelby well, but I do know Victoria. I was at their big bash after they got married. I still can't believe Victoria Stratton climbed a mountain and got married to Shelby when they came back down," Alexis said, shaking her head in amazement.

"Marina told me about that. It was so romantic." CeCe's face softened.

Alexis saw that sweet look on CeCe's face and was about to comment on it when Gabriel said, "That was some party."

"Yes, it was," Alexis agreed.

"I know there were a lot of people there, but I don't remember seeing you. Who were you with?"

CeCe stilled and gave Alexis a measured look. "Yeah, Lex. Who did you take to the party?"

Alexis couldn't keep the amusement from washing over her face. "I went alone."

"Hmm," CeCe muttered.

Alexis chuckled. "I left soon after their dads walked

them down the aisle to exchange rings, but I heard the dancing went on for hours."

"It did. We had the best time!" Gabriel exclaimed.

Alexis nodded and was mesmerized watching CeCe so skillfully style this man's hair, carry on a thoughtful conversation, make sure Alexis was okay, *and* make it all look easy. There was a little flutter in her stomach at the idea that this woman wanted to be with her.

"Okay, Gabe. Let's go over here," CeCe said. "I'll wash you up and have you looking pretty for your wife when you get home."

"Hey, do y'all like live music?" he asked as he sat down and leaned his head back.

CeCe looked over at Alexis and raised her brows. "I do."

Alexis nodded and filed that tidbit of information away for a future date night.

"One of the guys I work with sings on open mike nights at a club we frequent. I'll text you the next time and you can meet us. We have a great time," he said.

Alexis looked on as CeCe washed Gabriel's hair and felt so much better than she had twenty minutes earlier when she'd pulled into the parking lot hoping CeCe was there.

CeCe squeezed hair product into her hands and rubbed them together then she ran them through Gabriel's short hair, giving them a final scrunch.

"Oowww, wee!" Gabriel said. "CeCe's got me looking good!"

CeCe laughed as Gabriel pulled out his phone and sent CeCe payment for the haircut. Her phone chimed on the counter, indicating she'd received the funds.

"There you go," CeCe said.

"I'll see you in three weeks," Gabriel said with a grin

CeCe Sloan is Swooning 95

then he turned to Alexis. "It was so nice seeing you, Dr. Reed. Thank you, again."

"Be sure and text CeCe when your friend plans to sing." She looked over at CeCe and smiled. "We'd like to be there."

"Absolutely! Thanks, CeCe," he said and walked to the front of the salon.

CeCe turned to face Alexis. "Let me wash my hands and I'll be done." As CeCe dried her hands she smiled at Alexis. "Do you feel better, rock star?"

"I'm not a rock star."

"Yes, you are. Don't even try to argue with me." CeCe opened a cabinet underneath the mirror at her station. "Put your purse in here. You won't need it where we're going."

Alexis raised her brows, but did what CeCe said. She noticed CeCe put her keys in one back pocket of her jeans and her phone in the other.

"Do you trust me?" CeCe asked softly.

Alexis nodded. "How long have you been doing my hair? Yes, I trust you."

CeCe giggled. "Come on. You can tell me all about your day."

"Are we going next door to the happy hour bar?"

"Nope. You don't need alcohol. I've got something better."

Alexis wiggled her eyebrows and started to walk to the back room.

"Nope. Not that either," CeCe said, laughing.

11

After asking Heather to lock up the salon, CeCe took Alexis's hand and walked them out the front door of the salon.

"Are you sure there's nothing in the back room that can make me feel better?" Alexis said in a playful voice.

"Probably, but I've got a better idea," CeCe said as she walked them past The Liquor Box and over to a restaurant in the next shopping area. She dropped Alexis's hand and opened the door for her.

The restaurant was set up like a fifties-era diner with booths on the walls and a long counter set off from the entrance. There were also tables sprinkled through the expanse.

CeCe walked up to the counter and smiled at the waitress. "Hi, could I get two swirls in cones, please?"

"Coming right up," the waitress said as she turned to make the cones.

"Ice cream?" Alexis grinned.

CeCe nodded. "Soft serve. It's delicious. Trust me." CeCe could see Alexis's whole demeanor soften as she watched

CeCe Sloan is Swooning 97

the ice cream stream out of the machine into the waiting cone. The waitress did a little flair with her wrist, making a loop on the very top of the treat.

"Here you go," she said, holding the cone in front of her.

"You first." CeCe smiled.

Alexis reached for the cone and looked at CeCe.

"Don't wait on me. Have at it." CeCe grinned. She watched as Alexis ate the loop off the cone and closed her eyes, relishing what CeCe knew was the sweet taste along with the silky sensation.

"Mmm," Alexis moaned.

"I know," CeCe said, paying the waitress and taking her cone. "Let's sit outside."

There was a bench in front of the restaurant and they sat down, enjoying their treats.

"Better?" CeCe asked after they'd each had several licks.

Alexis nodded.

"Do you want to tell me about your day?"

"I had a surgery that didn't go as I'd hoped. When that happens I go back over everything and try to find what I missed," Alexis said, looking out and watching the cars whiz by on the roadway.

"As Mr. Ramos did, I believe in you, Lex. I'm sure your patient had the best surgeon and received the best treatment possible. All you can do is your best and I know that's what you did."

Alexis nodded. "I'm glad I came by here."

"I am, too. You've certainly brightened my day."

"What happened to you today?" Alexis asked, swirling her tongue around the ice cream.

"Oh," CeCe sighed. "I had a color that didn't turn out like I wanted, but the client was okay with it. Then I had a client who was late."

"And that makes the rest of your day late!" Alexis exclaimed.

"Exactly. Then I had one woman who simply didn't show up or call."

"What!"

"Yeah, it happens more than you think. Some of my clients don't value my time."

"That's terrible," Alexis said. She was about to go on when CeCe put her hand on Alexis's arm.

"This is not about my day. That's for another time. This is about you. Do you like the ice cream?" CeCe asked with a smile.

Alexis held up her cone to show CeCe that the ice cream was now level with the rim of the cone. "I'd say so."

CeCe chuckled. "Good."

"Hey, I want to know something," Alexis began.

"Okay." CeCe took a bite out of her cone.

"When Gabriel asked if we liked live music, how did you know I did?" Alexis asked.

"I've been cutting your hair for a while now. Don't you think we've gotten to know a few things about one another?" CeCe replied.

Alexis tilted her head. "I guess we do." She studied CeCe for a moment and grinned. "I know that you don't like onions."

"That's true. I don't."

"I remember once when you were cutting my hair, y'all were ordering food and you told them no onions. I started to ask you who you were kissing, and if that's why you didn't want onion breath."

CeCe laughed. "I would've loved that!" She took another little bite of her cone. "But I really don't like onions, kissing or not."

CeCe Sloan is Swooning 99

"How did you know I'd like chocolate and vanilla ice cream swirled together?" Alexis asked.

"I know you like vanilla because you've told me that before, but I also know you are dangerous and not afraid of anything," CeCe said, bumping Alexis's shoulder with her own. "I knew you'd try it and like it."

CeCe stuck her tongue down inside her cone, trying to get another bite of ice cream. She was aware that Alexis was watching her every move.

"This was a really good idea and it's giving me more ideas," Alexis said seductively.

CeCe leaned over and kissed a speck of ice cream from Alexis's lips. "It's almost Saturday," she said in a husky voice.

Alexis smiled. "Thank you for today."

CeCe smiled. "Anytime, Doc. You've made my day happy and hopefully there's something good about this one for you."

"I liked how you held my hand on the walk over here. That made me happy," Alexis said.

"Oh." CeCe nodded. "Does Dr. Reed have a little romantic side to her?"

"Can this be our first date?" Alexis asked earnestly.

CeCe swallowed the bite she'd just taken. "Why? Do you want to have sex?"

Alexis widened her eyes. "Not that I'm turning you down, but no." Her face softened. "I want to remember this as our first date because it's so perfect."

"Oh, Alexis Reed. Are you trying to make me swoon?" CeCe gazed into Alexis's eyes and felt her heart doing flips in her chest along with the butterflies in her stomach.

Alexis smiled as they finished their ice cream.

"Do you have a list of first dates or..." CeCe trailed off, handing Alexis a napkin.

Alexis wiped her fingers and smiled at CeCe. "I have a feeling we'll look back and remember this one day."

So many emotions were suddenly running through CeCe's head and heart. Alexis was saying all the right things and as much as CeCe wished they were in the back room tearing each other's clothes off, what she really wanted was to kiss this amazing woman.

"Definitely swooning," she whispered as she leaned in and softly kissed Alexis.

When they slowly pulled apart Alexis smiled. "Saturday can't come soon enough."

CeCe pulled into the circular drive in front of Alexis's house. It was a beautiful white brick home with black trim that gave it a sleek, clean look. It struck CeCe that it was a sizable home for only one person, but it also fit Alexis's persona. It was welcoming and the black accents gave it a modern, structured feel. To CeCe, it showed the Alexis she knew. There was the strict all-business surgeon, but also the exciting sexy woman she couldn't wait to spend the night with.

"You found me," Alexis said with a grin as she opened the front door.

"You did text me your address, Lex," CeCe teased her as she walked into the foyer. "What a beautiful home."

"Thanks," Alexis shrugged. "It's a place to sleep and it's a good investment."

CeCe looked around the living area and didn't see many personal touches. "Wait until you see mine. It has a more lived-in look."

Alexis smiled. "I imagine yours looks more like a home."

CeCe Sloan is Swooning 101

"This looks more like Dr. Reed than..." CeCe paused to find the right words.

Alexis raised her eyebrows waiting. "Than?"

"Than the Lex, who I'm dating."

"Are we dating?"

"How quickly you forget. Didn't we just have our first date two days ago?" CeCe teased.

Alexis took CeCe's hands in hers. "I'll never forget our first date." She leaned in and kissed CeCe softly. "Is this our first weekend away?"

CeCe shrugged. "We'll see." She pressed her lips to Alexis's and liked this little playful banter between them. "Ready to go?"

Alexis nodded, but didn't let go of CeCe's hands. She gazed into her eyes and CeCe felt those butterflies in her stomach again.

Alexis let her hands go and grabbed her bag that was sitting on the couch. "I'll give you a tour when you bring me home."

CeCe nodded. "Well then, let's go to Lovers Landing."

It was a thirty minute drive to the lake and Melanie had texted them earlier that she would meet them at the restaurant of the resort.

"You never did explain to me how you got us invited to Lovers Landing," Alexis asked.

"I'm not sure how it happened. We were talking about what a brilliant surgeon you are," CeCe said, reaching over for Alexis's hand. She laced her fingers through Alexis's and continued. "I mentioned that you were also my client."

"Not any longer."

CeCe laughed. "My big-mouthed sisters said something about our mutual crush and from there Melanie's imagination went into overdrive. She had it all planned before I knew what happened."

"But Melanie said it was a non-date," Alexis said.

"That's because I told her I didn't date my clients. She really wanted us to come out. It seems that we have both been out there at separate times and they like us."

"I like us, too." Alexis squeezed CeCe's hand.

CeCe glanced over at her and smiled. Alexis was showing her this soft side more often and CeCe loved it. She couldn't keep from wondering who else was lucky enough to see this side of Alexis. CeCe hoped this would be an opportunity to relax and get to know more about Alexis.

A short time later they pulled into the parking lot of Lovers Landing.

"I love it here," Alexis said, gazing down towards the lake.

"I didn't know you were the outdoorsy type," CeCe replied.

"I wouldn't say that." Alexis reached for CeCe's hand. "But I do like sitting by the water, perhaps enjoying a cocktail." She grinned at CeCe.

CeCe smiled back and took a moment to enjoy the fact that Alexis had taken her hand. She never had a problem with little public displays of affection: a touch here, maybe a quick kiss. But that wasn't always the case with other people she'd dated. CeCe thought back to the sweet kisses she and Alexis shared outside the diner and her stomach did another little flip flop. *What is wrong with me,* she thought. *We're just holding hands.*

Alexis tilted her head. "Are you all right?"

"Yeah." CeCe nodded. "I'm really glad we're here together."

"Me, too," Alexis said, then led them to the door and opened it for CeCe. "After you, beautiful."

"Watch it. You'll have me swooning again," CeCe teased.

Alexis grinned. "I thought that was a good thing."

"Oh, honey, it's a very good thing," CeCe said. She kissed Alexis on the cheek as she walked by.

12

They went in and Melanie was sitting at the same table by the window where CeCe had found her last Saturday. She looked up when she heard voices.

"Hey." She smiled and stood up. "Welcome."

CeCe and Alexis walked over and Melanie hugged each of them. "I'm so glad you're both here."

"Thanks for inviting us," CeCe said.

"It seems awfully quiet around here," Alexis said. "Is everyone getting ready for the evening party?"

"No," Melanie said. "Have a seat."

CeCe and Alexis sat down next to each other and across from Melanie.

"We were supposed to have a group this weekend, but I postponed them till next weekend. I was afraid Krista would try to do too much. Have you both met Julia, Krista's partner in the resort? She and her wife will be out later this evening."

"Yes," CeCe said. "I did her daughter's hair before she moved and Julia came to the salon with her occasionally."

CeCe Sloan is Swooning 105

"I met her and her wife, Heidi, when y'all needed a doctor that weekend," Alexis said.

"Oh my God! I'd forgotten about that, Alexis!" Melanie exclaimed. "We didn't need a doctor. A certain diva thought she did and you were gracious enough to come out."

"I didn't mind. You insisted I stay and treated me like one of your VIP's," Alexis added.

"Oh?" CeCe said, looking at Alexis then at Melanie.

"A nameless pain in our ass," Melanie began, "came for a week and had stitches from an earlier accident. She was sure they were infected and I couldn't convince her they were fine. I had been to see Alexis that week and called her for help. I wasn't about to take this woman to the emergency room in our little town's hospital. Can you imagine the spectacle!"

"I was happy to come out."

"Let me guess," CeCe said, grinning at Alexis. "You turned on that Dr. Reed charm, gave her one of your sexy smiles, and told her she had nothing to worry about."

Alexis smirked.

Melanie laughed and said, "That's exactly what happened! How'd you know?"

"I may have been on the other end of a few of those sexy smiles. Believe me, Melanie, you won't know what you're doing."

Alexis's mouth fell open and then she bit her bottom lip and shrugged. "I'm not the only one with a sexy smile. When you cock that one eyebrow, all coherent thoughts fly out of my brain."

"Really?" CeCe said, propping her elbow on the table and resting her chin in her hand.

Melanie chuckled. "I'd say things are going quite well

with you two. But I remember," Melanie said as she held up her hands, "this is not a date."

It was CeCe and Alexis's turn to laugh.

"I have a new hairstylist," Alexis said with a grin.

"Oh!" Melanie exclaimed.

"Is it so terrible that I have a rule against dating clients? It could cause all sorts of problems."

"I understand," Alexis said. "But I loved the way you styled my hair."

"You'll be fine," CeCe said with a wink.

Melanie laughed. "That sounds just like how you reassured the nameless diva that day, Alexis. I guess it's similar to you not operating on family."

"Oh no. I'm not comparing what I do with Alexis's skill," CeCe said earnestly.

"What you do is important, too, CeCe," Alexis said.

"I agree," Melanie added. "You boost mental health and that's just as important."

CeCe sat back in her chair and smiled at them both. "Thank you."

"So..." Melanie looked from CeCe to Alexis with a devilish smile. "It's a good thing you have another stylist because you'd be losing this one anyway. Lovers Landing will work its magic on you tonight. You'll see."

CeCe and Alexis stared at each other for a moment with soft smiles on both their faces.

"Then again, I don't think you'll need any magic," Melanie observed.

"Hey," CeCe said, pulling her eyes away from Alexis. "Where's Krista? She's doing all right, isn't she?"

"Yes. I wasn't sure what time you'd be arriving so I made her stay home and rest," Melanie explained. "Let's go check

CeCe Sloan is Swooning 107

on my love. It's a beautiful day for a fruity drink by the water."

"That's exactly what Alexis said when we got out of the car," CeCe said.

"Come on, we'll take the golf cart. I'll bring you back to get your car later." Melanie took them out the door that led from the restaurant to a deck that overlooked the lake. A golf cart was parked next to the stairs and they all got in.

"Krista and I live on the edge of the property in a cute little cabin that's perfect for us. We're putting you two in our favorite cabin," Melanie said as she drove them through a wooded area with views of the lake on their left.

"It's so beautiful. I wouldn't ever leave here if..." CeCe said quietly, gazing over at the water with a dreamy smile on her face.

"If what?" Melanie asked, looking back at CeCe.

"Oh—uh, you heard that," CeCe said, stumbling over her words.

Alexis turned around from the front seat and laid her hand on CeCe's knee. "Come on, you can't leave us wondering."

CeCe paused for a moment as Alexis squeezed her leg gently. "I'd never leave here if I had my...love here with me."

"Why would you? Now you know why Krista and I only go to town when we have to," Melanie said, keeping her eyes on the trail as they wound through the trees.

Alexis smiled at CeCe, but CeCe couldn't read the look in her eyes. Her face softened and her brown eyes were like decadent liquid chocolate shimmering at CeCe. *Does Alexis have any idea how much I love chocolate!* When Alexis turned back around, CeCe let out a shaky breath. Maybe Melanie was right; there must have been some kind of magic at that lake and in those woods.

Melanie pulled the golf cart around to the back of a cabin that sat near the water. It was nestled among a group of mature trees, but had a direct view of the lake where a small beach was visible.

"Oh my God, Melanie," Alexis said when she stopped the golf cart. "This is amazing."

"Thanks. We love it here."

"Hey!" Krista waved from a chaise lounge on the patio. "There's my doctor and new favorite friend."

"Favorite friend?" CeCe scoffed.

"Yes! I've been talking about you and your sisters all week. Haven't I, babe?" Krista said as they all walked over to her.

"She has. We love the Sloan sisters and don't see them often enough," Melanie said. "Let's go inside. While Alexis is examining Krista, CeCe and I will make drinks we can enjoy by the water."

"Oh, honey. That sounds perfect," Krista replied.

CeCe and Alexis followed them inside. The cabin was one large room with an area sectioned off for the kitchen that included an island with a table and chairs to one side. Two couches, chairs and a table were arranged to make a cozy living area. There were two opened doors that led to a bathroom and a bedroom.

"You wouldn't expect such a famous award-winning actress to live in such a small space, would you?" Melanie stated as she took glasses down from a cabinet.

"The only place I intend to live is with you," Krista said matter-of-factly. "This cabin happens to be perfect for us."

"It doesn't feel like a cabin," Alexis commented. "It's more like a lovely home."

"Why would you need a big house?" CeCe asked.

"We don't," Krista replied. "All we need is this right here.

CeCe Sloan is Swooning 109

When the kids and grandkids come to visit, we put them in a larger cabin close to the big beach and dock because they will be playing in the water anyway."

"I turned my investment business over to our daughters, so I'm retired," Melanie said.

"I'm retired, too, unless a role comes along I can't refuse, but I don't see that happening. There aren't many exceptional roles for fifty-something women, but occasionally one comes along."

"You do have this resort to run, so I wouldn't say either of you are retired," CeCe said.

"Doing this is fun. We get to decide the schedule and be as busy as we want," Krista said. "Can you examine me here?" she asked Alexis, pulling out one of the chairs at the table.

Alexis nodded and set her bag on the table. CeCe joined Melanie at the island and helped mix the drinks, giving Krista and Alexis privacy.

Alexis examined the incision she'd made on Krista's back near her shoulder blade. "This looks great," she said. "I brought along another bandage."

"Let me look," Melanie said. "We've kept it covered like you said to do, Alexis."

"You can look, too, CeCe," Krista said. "Come see how talented my surgeon is."

CeCe smiled, thinking she knew some of Alexis's talents already. "Oh, wow," she said, amazed. CeCe wasn't sure what she was expecting, but the small incision was sure to be barely noticeable when it healed. "You won't even know it's there, Krista. Does it hurt?"

"Not really. It was a little sore at first so I didn't sleep on my back. But I usually sleep on my side anyway."

"With my arms wrapped around you," Melanie said quietly, smiling down at Krista.

Alexis attached the bandage over the wound and smiled. "You're all set."

"Thanks for making a house call," Krista said with a grin.

"My pleasure."

"Everyone grab a drink and let's go soak up this gorgeous day," Melanie said.

CeCe and Alexis did as instructed and followed their hosts down to the water.

"Mmm, this is good," CeCe said, sipping her drink.

"I'm glad you like it," Melanie said. "I love a fruity drink with a splash of vodka to give it a little pep."

"Cory would be happy to show you a few more drink recipes. She's quite creative," CeCe said.

Once they were all seated and sipping their drinks, Krista looked over at CeCe and Alexis. "I got to thinking about this invitation and I hope we weren't too pushy. We didn't really ask either of you. It was more like we told you to come out today."

"Yeah, it's obvious you like each other, but we may have stuck our noses where they didn't belong. We don't want to push you into anything you might not be ready for, or even want," Melanie said.

CeCe looked at Alexis and furrowed her brow. "Did you feel forced to come spend time in this beautiful, romantic haven with—"

"A sexy dynamic woman who was once my stylist and now someone I can't stop thinking about?" Alexis finished CeCe's question with a sultry smile. "*Forced* isn't the word I'd use."

CeCe chuckled, looking Alexis up and down. "Me

CeCe Sloan is Swooning

either."

"I guess we didn't overstep after all, babe," Krista said with relief in her voice.

"This is new for us," Alexis continued. "But we're figuring it out. Wouldn't you say, CeCe?"

CeCe smiled and winked at Alexis. "So far, so good."

Krista and Melanie laughed. "Good. We're very happy you're here," Melanie said.

"We've had what I consider our first date, but I'm taking CeCe out for a real date next week," Alexis shared.

"Oh? Tell us." Krista dropped her chin and looked at them seriously. "You can see how invested we are in this."

"I'm beginning to get that idea."

"I was having a hard day and decided to go by the salon. Lucky for me, CeCe was just finishing up," Alexis explained.

"You knew CeCe would make you feel better. That's sweet," Melanie said.

"All I did was take her next door and buy her ice cream," CeCe said with a shrug.

"It was more than the ice cream and you know it," Alexis admonished her. "I knew CeCe would make me feel better, but she surprised me in the way she did it."

CeCe smiled. "It was an easy, laid-back moment."

"Ah, a safe place to be vulnerable. I'm guessing you may have thought you knew what you wanted, but received something even better," Melanie said.

"I did," Alexis agreed.

CeCe gazed over at Alexis and thought back to that day. Alexis might have had sex on her mind, but CeCe had known that's not what she'd needed. *How'd I know that?*

"I'm sure the daily stress that goes along with your job can weigh you down some days. It's good to have a place or a person," Krista said, looking at CeCe, "where you can let go and be yourself."

"That's what Lovers Landing is all about. We certainly understand that. I think we wanted to give y'all the time to connect, explore, and discover each other without the everyday pressures of life. This is a little escape for you," Melanie explained.

"I don't know what we did to deserve this, but I'm thankful you invited us," CeCe said.

"Think of it as our chance to get to know you better, too. We're still going to have a little party tonight. Julia and Heidi will be out later along with our friends Tara and Lauren."

"Tara Holloway!" CeCe exclaimed. "I'm such a big fan. I love her movies."

"She remembers you from the day you saved the photo shoot, CeCe," Krista said.

"Really?" CeCe smiled.

"Oh, no. Does that mean a big-time Hollywood movie star is going to steal you away from me?" Alexis teased.

Melanie laughed. "Tara was once one of the biggest players in Hollywood, but that all changed when she met her wife, Lauren, right here at Lovers Landing."

"They are both a lot of fun. We'll have plenty of dancing, singing, and fun tonight."

"I can't imagine anyone, even Tara Holloway, could steal someone away from you, Alexis," Krista said with a devilish smile.

"Especially when they only have eyes for you," Melanie added.

Alexis looked over at CeCe and raised her brows. CeCe reached out her hand and waited for Alexis to take it. "No one is taking me away from someone I want to be with," CeCe said.

13

Alexis felt CeCe's bright blue eyes stare into hers. When CeCe looked at her that way it made a warmth spread through her body. She took a sip of her drink, hoping it would mask what was happening inside her.

They had come here to have a good time and party. Alexis wanted to get to know CeCe better, but she also planned to get to know her body better as well. Those blue eyes kept staring straight into her heart and finding feelings Alexis had packed deep down a long time ago. She was actually surprised to find those types of emotions were still there.

"Hell yeah, CeCe!" Krista exclaimed. "No one is stealing you unless you want to be stolen."

"Maybe I'll do the stealing," CeCe said, raising one eyebrow. She dropped Alexis's hand and sipped her drink.

Alexis chuckled. "Oh, this is going to be fun."

"Speaking of fun, Alexis, I want to know if doctors and nurses are sneaking into the supply closets or empty rooms at hospitals and having sex. I swear when they were wheeling me back to my room I heard two nurses talking about meeting up somewhere," Krista said.

Alexis's eyes widened. "Are you sure you weren't dreaming? I don't think you were starting to wake up until Melanie and I walked into the recovery room."

"Oh, no you don't. It happens, doesn't it?" Krista pressed Alexis.

"Yeah, Krista. I want to know, too. I asked her that the other day and she changed the subject," CeCe teased.

"No, I didn't. I told you I don't kiss and tell," Alexis said to CeCe with a smirk.

"I knew it!" Krista exclaimed. She studied Alexis for a moment then asked. "So, Doc..."

"Yes?" Alexis replied slowly.

"You know my next question is going to be if you've ever hooked up at the hospital." Krista grinned.

"Babe, that's really none of our business," Melanie said.

"I know that, honey. But it's fun and a little scandalous." Krista giggled.

"It's okay, Melanie." Alexis said. "Have you hooked up on your movie sets, Krista? Don't you have your own little trailers? I can only imagine what happens in those."

Krista threw her head back and laughed. "It may have happened a time or two. How about you?"

Alexis gave Krista an amused look. "It may have happened once or twice for me as well."

"Oh really? Well, mine happened to be with my wife," Krista said.

"What!" CeCe exclaimed.

"I was visiting the set when she was shooting her last movie," Melanie explained.

"So?" Krista pinned Alexis with a look. "What about you?"

CeCe Sloan is Swooning 115

Alexis took a deep breath and slowly released it. She quickly looked over at CeCe and saw a curious look on her face as well. She looked back at Krista and said, "It happened to me twice and I later married him."

Alexis was afraid to look at CeCe, but she snuck a glance at her anyway. CeCe's eyebrows were raised, but when their eyes met she smiled at Alexis.

"Whoa! I didn't see that coming!" Krista exclaimed.

"That's what you get for being nosy!" Melanie chided her.

"It's okay," Alexis said. "It was a very long time ago. We were both doing our residencies and we were at the hospital all the time."

"Oh, I get it." Krista nodded. "Love in the operating room."

"Well, I did love him, but when I found out about the other women he was also loving, it was over for me."

"What an idiot," CeCe mumbled under her breath.

"I was married before I met Krista," Melanie shared. "That's where our girls came from."

"There were no kids involved here. When I made the decision to go into surgery I knew I couldn't be a good mother and follow the career path I wanted. So I decided not to have kids."

Melanie nodded. "What about you, CeCe? Do you want to have kids?"

"And you talk about me being nosy, babe," Krista said.

"It's okay. We're all getting to know each other, right?" She looked over at Alexis and smiled. "I had a pregnancy scare a long time ago. Believe me, no kid deserved this mess as a mother." She waved her hand in a circle in front of her. "It did make me take a hard look at myself and what I wanted."

"And?" Krista urged.

"Let's just say it put an end to hook-ups in the back rooms of beauty salons," CeCe said.

"Uh huh! What is it about sex in the workplace?" Krista asked.

"Is that what it is?" CeCe chuckled.

"Oh, I think there's a forbidden, secretive, let's-don't-get-caught aspect to it," Melanie offered.

"I guess," Alexis said with a smile. "But I think you're leaving something out."

"What's that?" Krista asked.

"It's fun!" Alexis exclaimed looking over at CeCe.

CeCe laughed. "Yeah, it is."

"Well, duh! Of course it's fun." Melanie laughed.

"That's enough questions for now," Krista said.

They both chuckled and sipped their near empty drinks.

* * *

Melanie took them back to CeCe's car and led them to their cabin. CeCe and Alexis dropped their bags inside as Melanie gave them a quick tour.

"You have your own private little beach over here," Melanie said, pointing to the sandy area that met the water not far from where they stood.

"Oh, wow," Alexis said. "That's so inviting."

Melanie turned towards them both and smiled warmly. "I hope our questions didn't offend either of you. We like you both and I think we see a little of ourselves in you. We weren't together when we were your age, but that doesn't mean we weren't in love with each other."

CeCe's eyebrows shot up her forehead. "You weren't together?"

CeCe Sloan is Swooning   117

"No." Melanie sighed. "It's a long story, but what's important is that we're together now and nothing will ever come between us." Melanie smiled and turned to leave. "We'll meet you at the restaurant around six."

"We'll see you then," Alexis replied.

As they walked back to the cabin, CeCe bumped her shoulder into Alexis's. "I can't imagine them ever being apart."

"Me either."

Once inside the cabin, CeCe walked over to the refrigerator and took out two beers. When she closed the door Alexis was standing in front of her. CeCe gave her the sweetest smile and draped her arms over Alexis's shoulders with a beer in each hand.

"Can I be honest?"

Alexis smiled and rested her hands on CeCe's hips. "Always."

"Part of me wants to take our clothes off, skip the party, and not leave this cabin until they make us," CeCe said with a devilish smile.

"I like that part of you," Alexis replied. "I feel like they wouldn't mind if we didn't show up for the party, but that could be something we do the next time we come to Lovers Landing."

"Oh?" CeCe nodded. "Are you going to bring me back here?"

"Or you could bring me."

CeCe shook her head. "You're the one that makes the big bucks, Doc. These are your kind of people. You'd have to bring us."

Alexis gave CeCe a confused look. "What do you mean? They wouldn't take our money, we're their friends."

CeCe leaned in and kissed Alexis softly. "Let's go check out the beach before we change our minds."

Alexis took the beer CeCe handed her. They made their way down to the water and CeCe spread out two towels side by side that she'd grabbed on their way out of the cabin.

"How's this?" she asked, plopping down on one of the towels.

"Just right," Alexis replied sitting next to her.

They sipped their beers and looked out over the water. CeCe leaned over just enough to where Alexis's shoulder nestled against hers. She closed her eyes and enjoyed the simplicity of the moment. It seemed like she and Alexis were always in some kind of tug-of-war. The looks they shared challenged one another with a sexy smile or swing of the hips, sometimes a sultry eyebrow raise, so when they were finally alone they couldn't wait to touch each other.

CeCe sighed and continued to look at the water. "So, you were married?"

"Mm hmm." Alexis nodded, taking a sip of her beer. "It was so long ago, I barely remember it."

"I'm sorry," CeCe said softly.

Alexis looked over at her. "You're sorry? Why are you sorry?"

CeCe met her gaze. "Because he hurt you. I'm sorry you were hurt."

Alexis tilted her head and smiled. "You think he was an idiot?"

Shock covered CeCe's face. "You heard me."

Alexis nodded. "I promised myself I would never give my heart to someone like that again."

"Oh, Lex," CeCe said softly.

"That's probably why I kept asking you about hook-ups

CeCe Sloan is Swooning

in the back room of beauty salons. Casual sex doesn't get your heart broken."

"Yeah, but look at the love Krista and Melanie share. Don't you want that?"

"My heart stopped feeling a long time ago." Alexis sighed and looked into CeCe's eyes. "It's my turn to be honest. I'm not sure what this is between us, but I do know it's more than just lust and sex. I can feel again."

CeCe reached up and touched Alexis's cheek. "It feels like more than that to me, too."

"It scares me, CeCe," Alexis stated.

CeCe nodded. "We can be scared together."

"Why are you scared?" Alexis asked softly.

CeCe scoffed. "Because, Lex, you may not have noticed but I'm just a hairstylist. You're a brilliant, sought-after surgeon. I'm not the kind of person you date. I'm more like the girl you have casual sex with. You know, in the supply room of a hospital or the back room of a beauty salon."

Alexis's mouth dropped open. "What? Why would you ever think that?"

CeCe shrugged and took a drink of her beer. "Because it's true."

"CeCe, that's the farthest thing from the truth," Alexis said with a concerned look on her face. "Have I ever made you feel like that?"

"No, no," CeCe said, turning to Alexis. "You make me feel wanted. Sometimes when you look at me I can't breathe."

"My God, CeCe. I do want you!" Alexis said nervously. "More than I want to admit. But I also think you're an amazing person. You have a way about you that brightens your clients' days. That's special. It's a gift."

"Just like you being a masterful surgeon is a gift? Do you see how they are not in the same league?" CeCe winced.

"Oh, honey. They are though. Actually, yours may be more important. Not everyone needs a surgeon, but they do need to feel valued and that's how you make people feel."

"Valued?" CeCe laughed sarcastically. "Do you know how my sisters and I were able to buy the shopping center? Someone had to die."

"What?"

"When we were kids, my dad's uncle died. He left Daddy a lot of money. Cory, Cat, and I were so excited. We weren't poor, but we thought we'd be able to buy better clothes and look like the rich kids in school. Do you know what my dad did?"

Alexis shook her head.

"He took us out for a nice dinner and told us to get any idea of spending that money out of our heads. He kept working and so did my mom. As the years passed we forgot all about the money. A few months ago Cory called Cat and me and had us meet her at the shopping center. It wasn't finished yet, but she had this idea for each of us to have our own business." CeCe looked over at Alexis and smiled. "It's been almost a year since my dad died."

"I remember," Alexis said quietly, putting her hand on CeCe's leg.

"That's right. You sent me flowers." CeCe smiled at Alexis. "It turns out that Dad invested the money. He left us a letter explaining that Mom would be taken care of, but he wanted the three of us to take the money and do something with it together. That way, he said, we would always be in one another's lives and take care of each other."

"Oh, my God, CeCe, that's beautiful," Alexis said, squeezing her leg.

CeCe Sloan is Swooning 121

CeCe wiped a tear away. "Yeah, it is, but there's no way I would've ever been able to run my own salon without someone dying and my dad taking care of the money. What I'm trying to say is that I'm not like you, Alexis. I don't come from money. I'm someone you have a good time with, not someone you make a life with." CeCe could see the horrified look on Alexis's face. "It's okay. I know my place."

14

Alexis couldn't believe her ears. Where was the confident, self-assured CeCe she knew? An anger was building inside her at all the people who had made CeCe feel less than in her life. She was the most generous and compassionate person and obviously didn't see it in herself.

"Your place? Listen to me, Cecilia Sloan. Your place is anywhere you fucking want to be! I would be privileged to be your date to anything. Your profession is making people look beautiful and you do it very well, but believe me, if you walked into a room on my arm, the heads would be turning to see you, not me."

CeCe shyly smiled. "Lex," she said softly.

"But that's not what pulls me towards you. It's what's inside," Alexis said, reaching to put her hand in the center of CeCe's chest. "When I'm not with you, I'm thinking about you. And that's a big deal for a surgeon. We're usually thinking about our next patient."

CeCe chuckled and the sound melted Alexis's heart like a favorite love song.

CeCe Sloan is Swooning 123

"I want to see your smile. I want to see that fire in your eyes when I give you a sexy look. You're waking up emotions in my heart that I thought were long dead, Cecilia Sloan. I'm the one that's not in your league. You somehow radiate your love for people. They can feel it with just a look. I may be a respected surgeon, but I can't make people feel like you do."

CeCe stared into Alexis's eyes. "You really mean that."

Alexis's face brightened. "It's true."

CeCe smiled and sighed. "Do you think there is hope for us, Doc?"

"I don't date, CeCe, and you haven't mentioned dating anyone in a very long time. But you asked me to change hairstylists so we could go out and I did. What do you want? Why would you go on a date with me? Is it just for fun?"

CeCe smiled. "I can't stop thinking about you, either. Yes, I want to have fun and we are very good at that part, wouldn't you say?"

Alexis smiled. "Yes, I would agree with you."

"I know you are a serious doctor and have to maintain your professionalism most of the time, but I get to see the playful, flirty, so fucking sexy, Lex. I want to be the doctor and make your heart feel good again."

Alexis could feel tears burn the back of her eyes. She couldn't remember the last time she'd felt cared for. "That sounds like someone to make a life with."

The smile that grew on CeCe's face was as bright as the evening sun. "We planned to come here and party then have hot sex all night, didn't we," CeCe said with a playful grin.

"We did."

"What do you say we go inside and get the party started."

"I swear, sometimes you read my mind."

CeCe chuckled then brought their lips together in a firm

kiss. "We've done enough talking for now." She stood up and offered her hand to Alexis.

Once on her feet, Alexis pulled CeCe close. "I want to hold you close, whisper in your ear, and dance real slow," she said, softly nibbling CeCe's bottom lip.

"Mmm," CeCe moaned, wrapping her arms around Alexis's shoulders. "You're not going to let a movie star steal me away?"

Alexis grinned. "Not a chance." She leaned in and brought their lips together in a tender kiss that quickly ignited and became passionate.

CeCe pulled away, gasping for breath. "You have nothing to worry about. I only have eyes for you, Lex."

"Oh, honey. I want more than just your eyes," Alexis mumbled, kissing CeCe again.

"My God, Lex," CeCe muttered, pulling her lips away. "We'd better get ready for this party before we both change our minds."

Alexis loosened her arms around CeCe's waist and reached for her hand. As they walked back to the cabin she looked over at CeCe. "You're not going to wear one of those cute little dresses you wear to the salon, are you?"

"I may have planned to wear a dress that's perfect for a mellow night at the lake. Why?"

"Oh, Lord, save me." Alexis sighed loudly. "I'll want to run my hand under your dress. That's why!"

CeCe giggled. "Isn't that the idea?"

Alexis stopped and stared at CeCe before they walked into the cabin. "Do you wear a dress on the days when I have an appointment to drive me out of my mind?"

CeCe grinned and shrugged. "I may have done that a time or two."

Alexis's eyes widened.

"Hold on! I only did it to see if you were looking."

"To see if I was looking! You couldn't tell! CeCe Sloan, you are a vixen!" Alexis exclaimed.

"Get in here," CeCe said, pulling Alexis inside the cabin. She closed the door and grabbed both of Alexis's hands.

Alexis's heart began to pound in her chest. She was reminded of the evening CeCe pulled her into the back room of the salon and she remembered what happened next.

"Are you trying to tell me," CeCe said, dropping Alexis's hands and walking around her, "you didn't plan on wearing that extra tight skirt the evening you got a pedicure?" CeCe's hand was tracing the curve down Alexis's shoulder, over her waist, until it rested on her ass. CeCe stopped in front of her, reached around with her other hand and firmly cupped both of her ass cheeks in her hands.

Alexis smiled and wrapped her arms around CeCe's shoulders.

"Are you trying to say you don't intentionally change into those form-fitting leggings before you come see me for a haircut?" CeCe asked, staring into Alexis's eyes, squeezing her ass cheeks. "You're dangerous, Doc, and you know it. Who's the vixen now?"

"I have one question," Alexis said, trying to maintain her focus which was becoming increasingly difficult with CeCe's hands squeezing and squeezing.

CeCe raised one eyebrow and waited.

"Oh, that look." Alexis sighed.

"Your question?" CeCe gave her an innocent smile.

"What took us so fucking long!" Alexis crashed her lips to CeCe's and kissed her with all the passion and heat she'd been holding back since CeCe picked her up earlier in the day. She held CeCe to her chest and could feel their breasts pressed together. Alexis couldn't wait until their clothes were gone and she could feel CeCe's bare skin next to hers.

They were both panting by the time Alexis tore her lips from CeCe's. She buried her fingers in CeCe's hair and pulled her in for another scorching kiss.

"Mmm," CeCe groaned. "Hold it, babe. Slow down."

Alexis pulled back and gulped breaths of air as she stared at CeCe. *How does she do this to me? She can turn me into a raging inferno with one touch!*

"I thought you wanted to slow dance with me and sneak your hand under my dress?" CeCe cooed softly. She ran her thumb under Alexis's lower lip.

"Do you see what you do to me?" Alexis asked shakily.

CeCe tilted her head and grinned. "Oh, no you don't. It's not me. It's that heart of yours coming out of the deep freeze."

A bark of laughter escaped Alexis's lips. "Oh, my God. I think you've made *me* swoon."

CeCe laughed with her. "Take me dancing, Lex. We've got the whole night ahead of us."

They changed for dinner and the party then walked the short distance back to the restaurant. There were two cars in the parking lot and Alexis thought she could just hear the sounds of music coming from inside.

Alexis remembered what CeCe had said earlier about the women at Lovers Landing being Alexis's people. At the time she hadn't understood what CeCe meant, but now she knew that CeCe didn't see herself on the same level as Krista and her friends. Alexis smiled and couldn't wait to show CeCe that she not only fit in, but these were her people as well.

CeCe Sloan is Swooning 127

* * *

"What's that sweet little smile about?" CeCe asked as Alexis held the restaurant door open for her.

"I'm about to walk into a room full of incredible women, but the most amazing woman of all is walking in with me." Alexis beamed.

CeCe smiled and stopped in front of Alexis. "And this amazing woman is also leaving with you." She sealed her statement with a quick kiss on Alexis's lips and wiped a smudge of lipstick away with her thumb. "Do you have any idea how beautiful you are, Alexis?" she said, staring into Alexis's eyes. Her stomach did a little flip as she watched Alexis smile at her. "I can't wait to get you back to that cabin."

Alexis gave her a wink and CeCe walked through the door. "Fuck me," she said on an exhaled breath. She could hear Alexis chuckle behind her.

"Hey! There they are!" Melanie exclaimed as CeCe and Alexis walked into the restaurant.

"Over here!" Krista called to them from the bar. "You have to get a drink first."

CeCe felt Alexis slide her hand into hers and was surprised at the feeling that washed over her. She'd held Alexis's hand before, but the sweetness of the moment and the feeling of togetherness eased the nervous butterflies in her stomach. Yes, she was a little nervous even though she'd met and been to a party with everyone there before, except for Alexis.

While CeCe was getting dressed she'd thought about what Alexis had shared earlier about being married. It really hurt her to know someone had broken Alexis's heart like that, so much so that she hadn't taken a chance on love since. Maybe CeCe could at least show her what an amazing woman she is. Love? Time would tell, but definitely a lot of like.

"I brought an excellent bottle of wine," Tara said, walking up to the bar next to CeCe and Alexis. "It's so nice to see you both again." Tara glanced down at their joined hands and smiled. "Alexis, I hope you realize how talented this beautiful woman is."

CeCe watched as Alexis gave Tara a measured smile. "Believe me, I do know what an amazing woman CeCe is." She turned to CeCe and continued. "And I can't believe I'm lucky enough to spend time with her."

Tara nodded. "I don't know you very well yet," she said to Alexis, "but I do believe you."

"Ladies, ladies. What is all this fuss over little ol' me?" CeCe said with a sly smile, secretly loving every second of this.

Tara laughed. "Hold onto this one, Alexis."

"Oh, Tara. No one holds onto CeCe Sloan unless she allows it. Right, babe?" Alexis said, with a grin.

CeCe chuckled. "You know the right things to say," she said to Alexis with a wink.

"Okay, if y'all are through with all this good-natured flirting, how about a drink?" Krista asked again.

"I'd love a glass of Tara's wine," CeCe said. "I know she has good taste because my sister supplies her spirits."

"I'll have the same," Alexis said.

"Tara, I appreciate your compliments, but don't forget what Alexis's skillful hands did for Krista this week," CeCe said.

"Oh, I'm sure Alexis's hands are quite skillful," Tara said with a roguish look.

CeCe Sloan is Swooning 129

"Let's all agree this room is full of exceptional women," Melanie said from the table where she, Lauren, Julia, and Heidi sat. "Now come over here and join us."

15

"Let's go, ladies. My wife has spoken," Krista said, coming around the bar.

Everyone found a seat and welcomed CeCe and Alexis.

"CeCe, how are things at the new shopping center?" Julia asked.

"It's going great. You should come by and see Cory and Cat," CeCe replied.

"Look at this hair!" Julia exclaimed. "I need to come see you!"

"I once had an exceptional hairstylist," Alexis lamented, looking up at the ceiling.

"Oh, we heard about CeCe's rules," Heidi said. "Good for you. There's a fine line when working with friends."

"What are you talking about?" Julia said. "You're a lawyer and you work for our friends all the time."

"I do, but you have to be careful," Heidi stated.

"I know what you mean," Lauren said. "Friends will ask you to sell their houses for them and they expect you to get

CeCe Sloan is Swooning 131

them a better price as their realtor. Unfortunately, it doesn't work that way."

"I disagree," Tara said, putting her arm around Lauren. "You knew exactly what you were doing when you showed me the house that would eventually become our home."

Lauren laughed. "Yeah, I came with the house." She leaned over and kissed Tara on the cheek.

"Best deal I ever made," Tara said with a grin.

"I've heard about your lovely home," CeCe said.

"You and Alexis are welcome anytime. I'd love for you to come out some Saturday. We can take a boat ride and enjoy the lake," Tara said.

"Oh, wow." CeCe looked over at Alexis and smiled. They had just been invited as a couple to Tara and Lauren's home.

Alexis raised her eyebrows and nodded. "We'd love to."

"Okay," Lauren said. "We'll plan it for a Saturday soon."

"I want to know about the private room in the back of your sister's bookstore," Julia said suggestively.

"You'd have to ask Cat or"—she looked over at Alexis with a twinkle in her eye—"Alexis might be able to enlighten us."

"Oh really?" Krista said, taking a sip of her drink.

"At the open house I was given a private tour that came with a gift," Alexis replied with a devilish look at CeCe.

"I don't remember a private tour or a gift when we stopped by," Melanie teased.

Alexis shrugged and winked at CeCe.

"But Cat did bring you a few samples last week," CeCe said, eyeing Melanie. "Did you not share with your friends?"

A rumble of laughter came from Krista as she looked over at her wife. "She may not have shared with her friends, but—"

"I thought we were going to be dancing tonight!" Melanie said, getting up from the table.

"I'll turn up the music." Krista laughed.

CeCe laughed along with her, stood up, and extended her hand to Alexis. "Will you dance with me?"

Alexis took her hand. "I'm not a very good dancer."

CeCe took her into her arms and whispered into her ear, "I've been waiting to dance with you since Melanie invited us. Can you hold me?"

Alexis nodded.

"Play us a slow song, Krista," CeCe yelled over her shoulder.

"This is one of the first songs I ever sang to Melanie," Krista said as the first notes of Madonna's "Crazy For You" began to play.

CeCe looked into Alexis's eyes and smiled. "I think I know how Krista feels. I'm kind of crazy for you, Lex." She pulled Alexis even closer and nuzzled her neck as they slowly moved to the music.

"There's no 'kind of' to it for me. I am crazy for you," Alexis whispered.

CeCe closed her eyes and let the music take her away. She'd remember this as one of the most romantic moments of her life. Here she was, dancing with an incredible woman, surrounded by more amazing women who treated her as a friend. Times like this didn't happen to her. She happily sighed.

As if reading her mind, Alexis whispered, "You're not Cinderella, Cecilia. You belong here, with me."

CeCe raised her head and looked at Alexis. Those soft brown eyes made her feel like she was surrounded by a velvet hug. Maybe she did belong here, but more importantly, maybe there was a chance for her and Alexis after all.

CeCe Sloan is Swooning 133

CeCe leaned in and softly kissed Alexis. "I'm all yours," she said with a smile.

Alexis's eyes brightened with desire and a sexy smile crossed her face.

The song ended and the sound of Whitney Houston's "I'm Your Baby Tonight" began to fill the air.

CeCe and Alexis laughed and danced around the room with the others. The group took a break to have dinner and laughter filled the air. Just as Alexis said, CeCe did feel like she belonged there, but it was also a bit magical. What had started as a little sexy flirting had become an intense attraction between them, but tonight it felt like much more than just a fling.

CeCe rested her chin in her hand as she watched Alexis talking with Krista and Tara at the bar.

"You two fit together," Lauren said, sitting next to CeCe.

"Excuse me?"

Lauren giggled. "You fit together," she repeated. "Like Krista and Melanie, or Julia and Heidi."

"Or you and Tara," Julia added.

"Sometimes two people look like they belong together. That's how you and Alexis look," Lauren explained.

"Plus, the way you gaze at each other says a lot," Julia said.

CeCe smiled. "Like we want to rip each other's clothes off," CeCe admitted. "We do have quite a pull towards one another, but it's still very new."

Lauren studied CeCe for a moment. "You know, when Tara and I first got together I didn't think there was any way I could fit into her world."

"Really?" CeCe asked.

"Yep, but I was wrong," Lauren replied, smiling at CeCe. "Don't get me wrong, there are some of her friends..."

"Who think their shit doesn't stink," Julia stated.

"Exactly, but those aren't the people Tara wants to hang out with," Lauren said. "She wants to hang out with people like us, like you and Alexis."

"Who are nice," Julia said.

"I wonder about Alexis's doctor friends. I mean, come on, I do hair," CeCe said.

"I'm a realtor and my wife is a fucking movie star," Lauren said, her eyes widening.

"I was a stay-at-home mom when I talked Krista into buying this place," Julia said.

"My wife is a fucking movie star, too. I was just a businesswoman," Melanie said, joining the conversation.

CeCe looked at each of these remarkable women and realized what they were trying to tell her. "Is it written all over my face or something?"

"Not at all," Lauren said. "The way you look at her tells me you want more than just a weekend at a romantic place with lovely people." Lauren raised her arms and gestured to the others at the table. "I recognize the look, CeCe, because that's the way I looked at Tara. I wanted more than just a fling."

CeCe gazed over at Alexis and smiled. She wanted more than a fling, too, but it wasn't entirely up to her, was it?

"Don't worry, honey," Melanie said, patting CeCe on the shoulder. "Alexis wants more than that, too."

CeCe smiled.

"Those doctors and their spouses are going to love you. It's Alexis who should worry. She's got to convince the Sloan sisters she's good enough for you." Melanie grinned.

CeCe laughed. "She's already working on them."

"What am I working on?" Alexis asked, walking up to the table.

CeCe Sloan is Swooning 135

"Your dance moves," CeCe said, grabbing her hand and spinning them onto the dance floor.

"What were y'all talking about?" Alexis asked as the music slowed and she could hold CeCe close. "You looked kind of serious."

CeCe gazed into Alexis's eyes and sighed. "Lauren was telling me how she didn't think she'd fit into Tara's world when they first got together."

"I can imagine. Tara is quite a force," Alexis replied.

"Kind of like someone else I know," CeCe said, amused.

Alexis gave her a confused look.

"You are quite a force as well, Dr. Reed," CeCe said.

Alexis scoffed then tilted her head. "Are you concerned about the doctors I work with?"

CeCe shrugged.

"You have nothing to worry about, honey. You'll see when you meet them."

CeCe narrowed her gaze. "Am I going to meet them?"

"I guess. I don't really socialize." A smile grew on Alexis's face. "Lately I've been going to my new favorite place."

"Oh? And where is that?" CeCe asked.

"It's a beauty salon."

CeCe chuckled. "A woman as gorgeous as you? Why would you be going to a salon so often?" CeCe asked, playing along.

Alexis laughed. "Do you realize I was ready to make hair and nail appointments every week just for a reason to come see you?"

"What? No you weren't. You came by that afternoon when you were having a bad day. You didn't have an appointment then."

"Do you remember my pedicure?" Alexis asked.

CeCe nodded. She remembered yanking Alexis into the back room and kissing her like her life depended on it.

"After that," Alexis said, dropping her head and staring into CeCe's eyes, "I was looking for any reason to come by and see you."

CeCe giggled. To think she could have that effect on someone like Alexis made her heart soar. "Hey, I noticed earlier that you aren't drinking much. If you don't like the wine, I'm sure Krista will get you something else."

Alexis leaned in and softly said, "There is no way I'm getting drunk tonight. I have you in a cabin, with not one but two beds, and no one to interrupt us. We get to take our time and I can hardly wait."

CeCe could feel the heat rush to her cheeks. "Good God, Lex. You're making me very hot right at this moment. I may have to take you to the restroom."

"Oh no," Alexis said. "You made the rules. In a bed, not in the back room *or* a bathroom, and we get to go slow."

CeCe gave her a dreamy look.

"Are you swooning, CeCe Sloan?" Alexis said with a sexy smile.

"I fucking am." She nodded.

Alexis laughed then leaned in and gave her a romantic kiss. When she pulled away, CeCe grabbed the front of her shirt and brought her back in for another long, soulful kiss.

"Do you think they'd care if we go back to the cabin now?" CeCe asked, taking a deep breath.

"Nope."

A short time later they said their goodbyes and walked back to the cabin.

"Could you feel all the love in that room?" CeCe asked, holding Alexis's hand.

"Yes. I felt like we were being whisked up into some kind of magical romantic haze," Alexis replied.

"I feel like I'm still there." CeCe stopped and turned to Alexis before they stepped into the cabin.

"I feel a heightened sense of possibility with us, CeCe," Alexis said softly.

Was this the beginning of what CeCe had been waiting on? She was through with flings and one-night stands, but she still had doubts she could be the one for Alexis. There was only one way to find out.

* * *

They'd come into the bedroom, hand in hand, and stopped at the edge of the bed. Alexis was surprised at how much she'd been looking forward to this moment and now that it was here, she was nervous. There was always a certain thrill of how her heart pounded when she was about to have sex. Sometimes it was a look or touch with someone else that led to a quick bout of passion and climax.

Wasn't it simply a physical need? That's how she'd looked at most of her past dalliances. There were a couple of women she'd seen for a short time, but they certainly weren't relationships. Those had happened quite some time ago and neither had come close to breaking the ice that encased her heart.

But CeCe Sloan was different. Alexis knew this the first time CeCe did her hair. She'd envisioned a friend, maybe a confidant, because she knew CeCe liked to have fun just as Alexis did away from the staunch confines of the hospital.

All of that changed when Alexis walked into Salon 411 and CeCe met her with a glass of champagne. The look

CeCe gave her along with the accompanying smile began to crack the ice around Alexis's heart.

Right now, CeCe was giving her the same look as Alexis slowly pulled CeCe's dress over her head. CeCe's eyes were like some kind of x-ray vision warming Alexis's heart until she thought it might explode.

CeCe put her hand in the middle of Alexis's chest. "Breathe, baby, just breathe."

Alexis smiled then inhaled and slowly let it out. "You are so beautiful, Cecilia. Sometimes you make it hard to breathe."

"I know," CeCe whispered. She lifted Alexis's shirt over her head and dropped it on top of her dress. "As much as I like you in these tight black jeans, let's get you out of them."

Alexis shimmied out of her jeans and smiled at CeCe. "You first," she whispered.

CeCe gave her a daring look and slowly lowered the straps of her bra and reached around to unhook it, letting it fall to the floor.

Alexis was taken by CeCe's beauty. Her gaze started at CeCe's long thick red hair as it flowed over her shoulders and stopped to drink in her ample perfect breasts.

"Your turn," CeCe said softly.

16

Alexis brought her eyes back to CeCe's then unhooked her bra and let it slowly slide down her arms revealing her forty-five year old breasts that were beginning to dip slightly. But the way CeCe looked at her made her feel like the most beautiful woman in the world.

"I've waited to touch, kiss, nibble, and feel every part of you. Don't think I want you any less than I did the last time we were together, but I love looking at you, Lex. You are exquisite."

This must be what it feels like to swoon, Alexis thought. She had never been self-conscious about her body, but she wanted CeCe to find her desirable, so she slowly lowered her undies and stepped out of them. Alexis reached for CeCe's undies and slid them down her legs.

On her knees now, Alexis wrapped her arms around CeCe's middle and pressed her cheek to CeCe's skin. She could feel CeCe's fingers comb through her hair.

Alexis began to kiss up CeCe's body until her hands cupped both of CeCe's breasts. An appreciative moan grumbled low in Alexis's throat. She pressed her lips to CeCe's as she rubbed her hardened nipples between her thumbs and forefingers.

CeCe gasped. "Fuck, Lex, that feels so good."

Alexis deepened the kiss and could feel CeCe hold their lips together as she fisted Alexis's hair. Without their lips parting, Alexis eased them onto the bed. They made their way up to the pillows and Alexis pulled away.

She saw the most beautiful sight. CeCe's hair looked like flames spread across the pillow and her clear intense blue eyes were laser focused on Alexis asking her for more.

"Oh, CeCe, I'm trying to go slow, but you are so beautiful, so sensual..." Alexis said, shaking her head.

CeCe gave her a sexy little smile. "I'm all yours."

Alexis felt her heart stop, butterflies ravaging her stomach, and then she kissed CeCe with all the emotion that was in her heart. CeCe had put it there and it was for her, so she received it all.

Their moans, groans, grunts, and breaths began to echo around the room.

Alexis kissed and nibbled down CeCe's neck, over her breasts, and lavished each one with a swirl of her tongue. She pinched and caressed one breast while feasting on the other.

Alexis ran her hand down CeCe's leg then up the inside of her thigh. She knew how CeCe felt in her hand, but she'd longed to taste CeCe from the moment they'd first kissed. She could feel CeCe's fingers gently stroking through her hair. Their passion crackled like electricity. This was no longer a spark, it was full on high voltage.

Alexis needed one more kiss before she reached her ultimate destination. She claimed CeCe's lips in a kiss that promised of what was to come. Her fingers began to slip

CeCe Sloan is Swooning 141

through CeCe's folds and she felt the wetness she couldn't wait to taste.

CeCe moaned with every touch of Alexis's tongue and each touch of her fingers. She once again kissed down CeCe's body and could hear her moans of anticipation followed by words gasped through her teeth. "Fuck, Lex. You are amazing!"

Alexis started at CeCe's belly button and traced her tongue around then down. She could smell CeCe's heavenly scent and felt drunk on the essence of this incredible woman. Alexis couldn't wait any longer and ran her tongue from CeCe's opening up over and around her clit.

CeCe raised off the bed with her fingers now embedded in Alexis's rich brown hair. "Good God, Lex."

As Alexis continued to lick through CeCe's folds, "Yes, yes, yes," echoed around the room on CeCe's heavy breaths.

Alexis gently sucked CeCe's clit in her mouth as she slowly slid one finger inside then another, filling her.

The most glorious sound bellowed from somewhere deep in CeCe's chest. This only urged Alexis on—as if she needed any encouragement. She slowly began to move her fingers in and out as her tongue swirled around CeCe's clit.

"Oh, Lex," CeCe gasped.

Alexis could feel CeCe's fingers pull her hair as CeCe came closer and closer to the edge. She pulled her fingers out then pushed them back in once again and curled them up until she felt CeCe tighten around them. Then Alexis sucked CeCe into her mouth until she could feel the explosion of sensations shoot through CeCe's body.

Alexis held them like this, not daring to move until CeCe felt every last wave of this fierce orgasm.

CeCe fell back onto the bed, her chest heaving and her

eyes closed. She eased her hold on Alexis's hair as she tried to breathe.

"Alexis Reed, I may need a doctor," CeCe cooed.

Alexis smiled and gently kissed CeCe's stomach then raised up and pressed her lips softly against CeCe's.

When she pulled away, CeCe reached up and put her hand behind Alexis's head. "Come back here. I need another one of those."

Alexis leaned in and kissed her again tenderly.

* * *

"Mmm," CeCe moaned as Alexis pulled away. She raised up and pushed Alexis onto her back. CeCe stared into her eyes and reached for both her hands, pinning them on either side of Alexis's head.

"Are you going to let me show you how you made me feel?" CeCe asked softly.

Alexis smiled but didn't say anything.

"Will you let go and simply feel, Alexis?" CeCe continued to search Alexis's brown eyes. "I'm not asking you to fall in love or give me your heart." CeCe smiled. "Can you turn that very smart brain of yours off, just for the night, and feel me against your body?" She placed her thigh between Alexis's legs and began to slide her body over Alexis's.

"I want you to feel every touch, every breath, every whisper that passes over your skin. Don't think, just feel me, Lex," CeCe whispered against her lips.

CeCe watched as Alexis closed her eyes, took a deep breath, and bit her bottom lip. She saw Alexis let the sensations wash over her as CeCe continued to gently move against her.

CeCe Sloan is Swooning 143

"I'm ready to feel you," Alexis said softly as she opened her eyes.

"Here we go," CeCe murmured and softly pressed her lips to Alexis's. She squeezed Alexis's hands and ran her tongue over her bottom lip. She sucked Alexis's lip into her mouth and bit down gently.

"Feel me?" she teased.

"More," Alexis mumbled.

CeCe deepened the kiss and lost herself for a moment when Alexis moaned. She loved Alexis's lips and tonight she planned to kiss them as much as she wanted.

She let Alexis's hands go and they immediately grasped at CeCe's back, holding them chest to chest.

"Please keep kissing me," Alexis gasped. "I love the feel of your lips on mine."

CeCe smiled and did what Alexis asked. Again, she felt like sometimes Alexis could read her mind.

After Alexis's pedicure that day, CeCe had been so caught up in the moment she'd neglected to give Alexis's breasts the attention they deserved. She planned to rectify that misstep right now. Even though their lips were melded together in a passionate dance, CeCe worked her hand in between their chests.

Alexis eased her hold on CeCe enough so that her fingers could skate down Alexis's chest and cup her breast. CeCe noted how it fit perfectly in her hand and moaned as she ran her thumb over Alexis's pebbled nipple.

CeCe pulled her lips away from Alexis's and stared into her eyes. "My lips have to kiss you all over."

"I feel you," Alexis whispered.

CeCe smiled and nuzzled Alexis's neck. She kissed just below Alexis's ear because she knew it would drive her wild. CeCe was rewarded with a deep, pleased groan. She could feel Alexis's hands rub up and down her back as her kisses marked a path down and around the nipple she'd been rolling between her finger and thumb.

CeCe sucked the hardened nipple into her mouth gently at first and then firmly. She felt Alexis shudder and began to flick her tongue across the tip as she held it with her teeth.

Alexis arched her back and buried her fingers in CeCe's hair. CeCe held on and continued to lavish Alexis's breast with her tongue.

"Oh, oh, oh," Alexis panted. "God!"

Encouraged, CeCe let her hand skim across Alexis's stomach through her curly hairs until her fingers found the wetness she sought. She kissed her way across Alexis's chest to her other breast and began to pamper it with the same lavish strokes of her tongue and lips.

Alexis's gasps and moans were followed by her body writhing under CeCe's hand.

Suddenly CeCe felt Alexis place her hand over hers. She smiled against Alexis's breast as Alexis pushed CeCe's hand so her fingers found her opening.

CeCe raised up and found Alexis staring. Her brown eyes were pleading with CeCe to touch her.

"I've got you, babe," CeCe whispered. She pushed two fingers inside and held them there as Alexis's hand fell away.

Alexis grabbed CeCe's face. "Take me, baby!"

CeCe crashed her lips to Alexis's and started a rhythm that began slow and gained speed and intensity. Alexis spread her legs wider and CeCe could feel her getting closer and closer.

With one more deep thrust, CeCe curled her fingers just as Alexis had done earlier and pushed her thumb against Alexis' clit.

CeCe Sloan is Swooning 145

Once again CeCe felt Alexis wrap her arms around her back and squeeze. The most glorious shout came from deep inside Alexis as CeCe pulled her lips away.

"Look at me, Lex. Look at me! I want to see you feel!"

Alexis's eyes flew open widely and CeCe swore she could see the bright colors of this intense orgasm play across her now very dark brown eyes.

Alexis never took her eyes from CeCe's as her breathing began to calm. The most beautiful smile grew on her face as she cupped CeCe's cheek.

"I felt everything. I felt it all," she said softly.

CeCe saw tears pool in Alexis's eyes and she gently kissed the corners before one drop could fall. A quick flash of anger ran through CeCe at the thought of the man who caused Alexis's heartbreak. Alexis had shielded herself from feeling that kind of pain again, but at the same time it prevented her from experiencing all this pleasure.

"Thank you for trusting me, Lex," CeCe said softly.

"I felt it all," Alexis said again. "And it was glorious!"

CeCe released a relieved breath. She knew she'd made Alexis feel good, but she wanted more than good. She wanted that orgasm to course through Alexis just the way it had for her earlier.

CeCe sighed and smiled. "We are very good at this."

Alexis laughed and pulled CeCe to her chest. "Wanna do it again?"

CeCe raised up in disbelief, but when she saw Alexis's playful grin she chuckled. "I'm ready when you are," CeCe teased.

"Let me say now and going forward," Alexis began, "I'm always ready for you."

"Then kiss me," CeCe challenged her.

Alexis reached up and gently pulled CeCe's lips to hers.

CeCe could feel that same love swirling around them that they'd felt earlier at the restaurant with the others. There was some kind of magic at work in this place.

But what if it wasn't the place? What if it was CeCe's heart grabbing onto Alexis's? Either way, CeCe wasn't letting go.

17

"Hey, Mom," CeCe said, looking up from her phone. She got out of her chair where she'd been waiting for her next appointment. "What brings you by?"

"Your sister has a book for me and I wanted to hear about your weekend," Christine Sloan said, sitting down in CeCe's salon chair.

"My weekend?" CeCe replied innocently.

"Yes. I'm guessing by the smile that's on your face, whomever you were just texting is probably the same person you spent the weekend with at the lake."

CeCe's phone made a noise and she quickly glanced at it before putting it into her back pocket.

"There's that smile again," Christine said, raising her brows. "Tell your mama what's going on, Cecilia Sloan."

CeCe chuckled. "And why do you think something is going on? Hey, wait—" CeCe narrowed her gaze at her mother. "How do you know I was at the lake this weekend?"

It was Christine's turn to chuckle. She spun around in the chair. "I'm your mother. I know things." She stopped when she was in front of CeCe. "And if you think your sisters can keep a secret from me..." Christine dropped her chin and smirked.

"It wasn't a secret. I was invited to Lovers Landing," CeCe said.

"And who went with you?"

CeCe stared at her mom and put her hands on the arms of the chair, trying to decide how to reply. "I went with the same person whom I have a date with tonight." CeCe gave her mom another spin in the chair.

"Stop! You'll make me dizzy!"

CeCe laughed and brought the chair to a stop. "Her name is Alexis. I've been doing her hair for a while now and we've become friends."

Christine raised her brows. "What have you told me about mixing business and pleasure?"

CeCe smiled. "Ryan does her hair now."

Christine nodded. "I can tell that you like this woman."

"I like a lot of women, Mom."

"Don't get smart with me. What are you holding back?"

CeCe sighed. "I do really like her, but she's a doctor."

"So?"

"I wonder if—"

"CeCe Sloan, don't you dare tell me you're not good enough for this woman or anyone else," Christine said firmly.

CeCe smiled. "It's not that, Mom. We come from different worlds."

"CeCe, my sweet girl. Look at what you have done here," Christine said, standing up and spreading her arms wide. "You own your own business, but even if you didn't, are your worlds that different? Doesn't she go to work every day just as you do?"

CeCe Sloan is Swooning 149

"Yeah, but she saves lives! She operates on people!"

"So do you! You provide a service just as she does."

CeCe scoffed.

"It takes all kinds of people to make our world go around, honey. Why would you want to be with someone just like you?"

"I don't."

"Exactly, so what makes you think your doctor wants to be with someone like herself?"

CeCe smiled. She'd never thought about it like that. "Her name is Alexis. Would you like to see a picture?"

Christine smiled and nodded. CeCe took out her phone and pulled up a picture she had taken of the two of them with the lake in the background. They were both smiling and Alexis had turned to look at CeCe just as she'd snapped the photo.

Christine admired the picture and turned to CeCe. "It looks like you put the same kind of smile on her face that she puts on yours. That's a good thing, honey."

CeCe looked at the picture and smiled. She'd found herself looking at it several times since they returned from the lake.

"Walk me to the bookstore before your next client gets here," Christine said, putting her arm in CeCe's. "Maybe some weekend you'd like to cook hamburgers for me and your sisters. We could eat on your patio; you have such a lovely backyard. Perhaps Alexis would like to join us."

"I'm not trying to scare her away, Mom."

Christine laughed as they walked through the entrance to Your Next Great Read.

"Maybe you should be asking my little sister the same questions," CeCe said.

Cat was in the reading nook at the side of the store

having a conversation with a woman. Neither of them saw CeCe and Christine watching.

"I haven't seen her smile like that at another woman since—"

"Don't say her name. She's finally left Cat alone and we do not need that heart-breaking ex-girlfriend of hers anywhere near this bookstore," Christine said sternly.

CeCe waved at Cat and she quickly excused herself and joined them.

"Hi Mom, I have your book at the register," Cat said, her cheeks showing a healthy shade of pink.

"I see Elena is here again. I think she may like the owner as much as she likes books," CeCe teased her little sister.

"Do you think Alexis likes her new hairstylist?" Cat asked, giving CeCe a warning look.

"Okay, Mom. I've got to go," CeCe said, quickly leaving the bookstore. She chuckled to herself at her sister's quick reaction. Cat was quiet, but that didn't mean she was shy.

* * *

"What is with you?" Michael said, standing in Alexis's office doorway.

She looked up from her phone and knit her brows together. "What are you talking about?"

"You're smiling. You've been doing that a lot lately," he said.

Alexis looked back down at her phone and quickly responded to a text from CeCe then put it on her desk. "You're almost as funny as Donna," Alexis deadpanned.

"We're not the only ones that have observed a pleasant change in our most esteemed colleague," Michael teased in a snooty voice.

CeCe Sloan is Swooning   151

Alexis shook her head and rolled her eyes. "Is there something you need or are you just stopping by to harass me?"

Michael smirked and plopped down in the chair across from her desk. "We had to cancel the little party last Friday because Lana got sick."

"Oh, that's too bad. I hope it's nothing serious."

"Nah, she ate something at lunch that day that didn't agree with her. Anyway, the party is back on for this Friday. So, please, please, please, come," he pleaded, holding his hands clasped together in front of him.

"What's with the begging? I thought it was just a small drinks and snacks kind of thing."

"It is, but it's always so much more fun if you're there," he said earnestly.

Alexis sighed. Michael was one of her oldest friends and she did love his wife, Lana. An idea popped into her head. "Can I bring someone with me?"

Michael gasped and clutched his chest. "No shit!"

Alexis rolled her eyes again. "Never mind. If you're going to act like that..."

"No, no! I'm just kidding. Someone *did* put that smile on your face." He leaned over and whispered loudly, "Tell me!"

Alexis couldn't stop the grin that grew on her face. "I've..." She narrowed her eyes. What was it she and CeCe were doing? Were they dating? "I'm...uh, going on a date tonight with someone I really like."

"Okay, how about you invite—"

"Her," Alexis interjected.

"Her." Michael nodded with a huge grin. "To the party Friday. Lana is going to die!"

Alexis sat back in her chair. She wanted CeCe to meet

Michael and Lana at some point, but was it too soon? Was this the right setting?

"Come on, it will be fine. What are you worried about?"

"I don't want y'all to scare her away!"

Michael smiled. "Lana will take her under her wing and protect her from the assholes we sometimes invite to these little get-togethers. And she'll have you." He shrugged.

"Okay. I'll ask her and let you know tomorrow."

"Now, tell me all about her. If you don't, Lana will keep calling you until you answer and she'll mess up your date tonight," Michael rambled.

Alexis laughed. "Are you sure it's Lana who wants to know?"

"Alexis, this is the first time in years I've seen you have more than a passing interest in another person. Of course I want to know!"

"Her name is CeCe Sloan," Alexis began.

"I knew it!" Donna exclaimed from the doorway. She walked in, set several files on Alexis's desk, and sat down in the chair next to Michael. "That's her hair dresser. Every time she has an appointment she comes back smiling and is happy for a week," she explained to him.

Wide-eyed, Alexis looked at Donna. "What the…"

"It's true." Donna shrugged.

"Well?" Michael said, staring at Alexis.

"She *was* my hairstylist, but now she's my friend and—"

"They're going on a date tonight!" Michael said excitedly to Donna.

Alexis couldn't quite believe her ears or eyes. She wasn't an unhappy person, but to hear Michael and Donna talk, she didn't smile very often. It wouldn't be a stretch to say she was very focused at work, but she did have peoples' lives in her hands.

CeCe Sloan is Swooning 153

She leaned back in her chair and thought about the past few days. Her attention was still on her patients, but when she had a spare moment her thoughts drifted to CeCe. Alexis couldn't not smile when CeCe crossed her mind, so she certainly was smiling more often.

"Where are you taking her?" Donna asked.

"Like I would tell either one of you!" Alexis exclaimed. "That's enough about my love life. I have patients to see, so if you two will excuse me." Alexis got up, shooed them out of her office and closed the door. Then she leaned against it and smiled.

* * *

"Is this date going to be as good as the one at Lovers Landing?" CeCe asked coyly as Alexis drove them towards downtown.

"I didn't think that was a date," Alexis replied with a grin, glancing over at CeCe. "You know, you're putting a lot of pressure on me for this date to be spectacular."

"Hmm, you don't think I'm the kind of woman who should be wooed on a spectacular date?"

Alexis sighed contentedly as she thought back to their weekend at Lovers Landing. It had only been a few days, but she couldn't wait to see CeCe again. Donna had seen a change in Alexis and had bombarded her with questions all week, wanting to know how she'd spent her weekend and what caused the change in her usually stoic doctor.

"You're thinking about last weekend, aren't you?" CeCe asked, reaching for Alexis's hand. "I'll admit it may have crossed my mind a time or two in the last few days."

Alexis chuckled at CeCe's attempt at nonchalance. Last

weekend was special for both of them and Alexis hoped that same vibe would continue tonight.

"You don't have surgery tomorrow?" CeCe asked, pulling Alexis's hand into her lap.

"Nope, but that doesn't mean you can't relax me the way you did before Krista's surgery." Alexis wiggled her eyebrows suggestively.

CeCe chuckled. "We'll see about that."

That little chuckle had become one of Alexis's favorite sounds along with the little moans that their kisses seemed to elicit from both of them.

Alexis could feel CeCe gently tracing her fingertip into her palm as she took the exit that would take them to the streets that criss-crossed through the jungle of tall buildings and skyscrapers.

"You really are taking me downtown," CeCe said, looking up at the tall buildings as Alexis navigated the one-way street.

"I am," Alexis replied, glancing at the street names displayed next to the stoplights they proceeded under. Alexis turned into an opening in the middle of the block that led them into a parking garage. She drove them up and up until she steered into a parking space near the elevator that led to the apartment building adjacent to the garage.

Alexis looked over at CeCe and smiled. "Ready for a little urban adventure?"

CeCe grinned. "I'm always ready for an adventure with you."

They got out of the car and, hand in hand, walked the short distance to the elevator. Once inside Alexis punched the button for the top floor. The doors closed and Alexis took CeCe into her arms. She smiled then kissed her softly.

CeCe Sloan is Swooning 155

When she pulled away the bell dinged in the elevator indicating they'd reached the top floor.

Alexis took CeCe's hand and stepped out of the elevator. They walked down the hall to a stairway that led to the roof.

CeCe's eyes widened. "We're going to the roof?"

Alexis nodded and pulled a key card from her pocket and waved it across the lock on the door. After they made the short climb up the stairs, she opened a door. "After you," she said to CeCe.

18

Alexis watched as CeCe walked further onto the roof and spun around taking in the three hundred and sixty degree view.

"Oh, Lex, this is incredible," she exclaimed, settling her gaze on Alexis.

"It's not the tallest building, but there's something I want you to see a little later. For now, let me show you around."

Alexis guided CeCe to each side of the roof and pointed out the different buildings that surrounded them and explained what the lights were in the distance. Then she led them to a small table with two chairs. On the table sat a cooler.

"I didn't even see this," CeCe said with a huge smile.

"You had a lot of other things to notice first," Alexis said, opening the cooler.

She brought out a bottle of wine and two glasses. There were also several containers filled with crackers, olives, cheese, and other finger foods.

After she poured the wine she looked up at CeCe and handed her a glass. "I hope this is okay," she said tentatively.

CeCe Sloan is Swooning

"Okay?" Laughter bubbled out of CeCe's throat. "Oh, Lex. This is more than okay."

"There's nothing fancy here, but as I said, in a little while you'll see why I brought you here. In the meantime a toast... To swooning," Alexis said, holding up her glass.

CeCe laughed. "Swooning?"

"Yes. You've said more than once that I've made you swoon. I wasn't exactly sure what that felt like, but I do now."

"You do?" CeCe asked, holding her glass next to Alexis's.

Alexis nodded. "When we took our clothes off that night at Lovers Landing, you said you like to look at me."

"I did." CeCe smiled. "I do."

"The feeling I had when you looked at me must be what it feels like to swoon." Alexis hurriedly swallowed the lump that had suddenly formed in her throat.

"To swooning," CeCe said, clinking their glasses together.

Alexis took a sip of her wine and the gaze she shared with CeCe was both intense and enlightening at the same time.

In the past, Alexis may have taken a woman to dinner before having sex, but it was just meant as nourishment, nothing more. She hadn't done something for someone because she cared about them in ages. But right now, she felt an overwhelming sense of joy at the look she'd put on CeCe's face.

Alexis had planned this night because she wanted to do something special for CeCe. She wanted to give her a little happiness. Yes, she wanted to spend time with CeCe but they could have done that anywhere. This was an adventure for them, a surprise for CeCe. They were making a memory.

The poignancy of that thought caused the lump in Alexis's throat to return.

"Are you okay?"

"Yes," she gushed. "I just realized we're making a memory tonight. I haven't done that, nor wanted to, with anyone in years."

CeCe set her wine glass down and cupped Alexis's face. "We're taking some of the seriousness away, Lex, and letting the joy come through."

CeCe pressed her lips to Alexis's in a soft sweet kiss. Then she reached for her glass.

Alexis smiled and clinked her glass to CeCe's. "To joy."

"To memories," CeCe replied with a grin.

They sat down and sampled the food and drank more wine. CeCe shared a few stories from the shenanigans at the salon over the last few days. Their laughter echoed into the air as the lights of the city twinkled around them.

As it grew darker Alexis looked around then set down her glass. "Let me show you why we're here."

"You didn't tell me how we got here. Who do you know?" CeCe asked, taking Alexis's offered hand.

"One of the doctors in my clinic has an apartment in this building. I inquired about the roof access and she was happy to help out."

"I see. Did you tell her why you wanted to come here?"

"I did. After she picked her jaw up from the floor, she was more than happy to help me. It seems a few people, namely my office manager and a couple of colleagues, have noticed a change in my demeanor since the weekend."

"Is that right?" CeCe said with an exaggerated southern drawl.

Alexis took CeCe's shoulders and turned her around.

"Oh my God, Alexis," she exclaimed. "This is amazing."

CeCe Sloan is Swooning 159

"So are you," Alexis replied softly.

Between two of the tall buildings there was a view of the night sky. It wasn't completely dark yet, so the sky looked dark blue. The buildings provided a shield to block out the lights of the city and a beautiful crescent moon appeared in the cobalt sky. There were two stars just below the crescent shape and it looked like the moon had tipped over and the stars had spilled from it.

"Those bright stars below the moon are actually Venus and Jupiter," Alexis explained. "The larger and brighter one is Venus and the other is Jupiter."

"It's incredible," CeCe said with awe in her voice.

"Do you remember the other night when I was late leaving the hospital?"

"Yes," CeCe replied.

"I noticed the moon and the planets on my drive home. I meant for us to look for it at the lake, but I forgot."

CeCe chuckled and put her arm around Alexis's shoulders. "I can't imagine why you'd forget," she teased.

"Me neither. Surely it didn't have anything to do with you."

"This is beautiful, Lex."

"I wanted to do something special. Anyone can go out to dinner for a first date. I wasn't sure we'd be able to see the moon, but I knew the view from up here would be gorgeous, just like you."

CeCe put her finger on Alexis's chin and turned her face towards her for a quick kiss. "I know we won't be able to see this celestial show for long, but it's so romantic I had to kiss you."

"I am not known for being romantic, but I swear, CeCe, you have done something to me."

"I hope it's a good thing."

Alexis nuzzled CeCe's neck and kissed below her ear. "It's a very good thing."

As they gazed at the moon, planets, and stars, Alexis topped off CeCe's wine. "Are we officially dating now?"

CeCe smiled and sipped her wine. "I remember you telling me that you don't date."

"I didn't, but now I do. Well, I want to date you," Alexis said with hope in her voice.

CeCe laughed. "Are you asking me to go steady?" she teased. "Who are we kidding? We've been dating since we both can't seem to keep our hands off each other."

Alexis reached out and took CeCe's hand in hers. "How true. I was wondering..."

"Yes?"

"Would you go with me to a small get-together at my friend's house?"

Surprise covered CeCe's face. "Really?"

"Yes, really. One of the doctors at the clinic also happens to be a friend. His wife loves to throw informal parties with drinks and snacks." Alexis gave CeCe a shaky smile. What was wrong with her? She knew CeCe in the most intimate of ways, yet she was nervous to ask her to meet her friends.

"Are these your friends as well as colleagues?" CeCe asked.

"Most of them are." Alexis nodded.

"So it would be like meeting the family for the first time," CeCe said.

"I guess you could look at it that way, but we don't have to go if you don't want to," Alexis said.

"Oh so now you're taking back the invitation?"

"No!" Alexis said with a frustrated sigh. "I want you to go with me. I want you to meet them. They know I've been seeing someone and they want to meet you."

CeCe Sloan is Swooning

CeCe furrowed her brow. "You're nervous about this. Why, babe?" CeCe's face fell. "Oh, no! Are you afraid I'll embarrass you?"

"What? No! You won't embarrass me. If anything I'll embarrass you."

"Are you sure?"

Alexis tilted her head. "Yes, I'm sure. They're going to love you and wonder how I managed to charm you into coming with me."

CeCe raised one brow. "Oh, you do have charms, Lex."

"Mmm, so do you," Alexis said as she felt a familiar warmth spread through her body. CeCe could make her melt with that look. "Will you go with me?"

"You want to take me to meet your friends and colleagues, huh. That makes me think your heart may be coming around."

Alexis stared into CeCe's eyes. *If only CeCe knew what's happening in my heart.* "Is that a yes?"

CeCe nodded. "Yes, Lex. I'd love to go with you."

Alexis let out a relieved breath then leaned over and kissed CeCe tenderly.

"Mmm, if you keep kissing me like that you might get lucky tonight."

"I'm already lucky," Alexis whispered and brought their lips together again.

CeCe looked back at the moon with her arm still around Alexis.

"Oh wait, I almost forgot," Alexis said, walking back over to the table. She grabbed her phone and in a couple of moments music began to play.

"Dancing, too?" CeCe smiled.

"I didn't realize how much I like to dance," Alexis said,

taking CeCe in her arms. "Well, how much I like dancing with you."

CeCe tightened her arms around Alexis's shoulders. "Maybe the next time you come by the salon we'll add dancing to our back room fun."

Alexis stared into CeCe's eyes. "Would you come home with me tonight?"

CeCe raised her brows. "Why the serious look?"

Alexis smiled but didn't say anything.

"We could've simply ended up at your house and you wouldn't have to ask," CeCe said.

"I want you to know that I want you there. I'm not assuming anything," Alexis said.

"Oh. Did other women assume they'd spend the night?" CeCe asked.

"No." Alexis shook her head. "I haven't invited anyone to stay the night with me."

"What?" CeCe asked, surprised.

Alexis sighed. "I told you that I don't date."

"I know, but no one has spent the night? You know, after a little fun?"

Alexis smiled. "Nope."

"But you're asking me?" CeCe narrowed her gaze.

"I am."

"You don't date, but now you're dating me," CeCe said.

Alexis nodded.

"You don't have women spend the night at your home, but you're asking me?"

"That's correct."

"You made this night special for us because it was supposed to be our first date," CeCe said.

"I hope it's special."

CeCe Sloan is Swooning 163

"Oh, Lex, it's special. I'm not sure what to make of all this."

"We're not a fling. We don't just meet in your back room or hide out at Lovers Landing," Alexis stated. "You're an incredible woman who I hope is my girlfriend. And I want you to spend the night with me." Alexis sighed nervously. "I sound like an idiot."

"No you don't!" CeCe exclaimed. "A lot is happening all at once."

"It is?"

CeCe tilted her head. "Yes! You've whisked us to a rooftop for an incredibly romantic evening, you've asked me to go to a party with your colleagues, and you want me to spend the night."

"CeCe, what about this is surprising? You knew we were going out tonight and it had to be special. Of course I want you to stay the night. I can't get last weekend out of my head. I roll over in the night and think of you. Oh wait—" An alarmed look grew on Alexis's face. "You don't feel the same way." Alexis dropped her hands and stepped back.

"No, no, no!" CeCe said, reaching for Alexis. "I do feel the same. I want to stay with you tonight."

Alexis sighed in relief. "My God, you scared me to death."

CeCe began to laugh and Alexis joined her.

"Okay, here's the deal," CeCe said. "This"—she held out her arms—"is the most romantic date I've ever been on. I tend to mask my nervousness with senseless teasing or flirting. I was fine until you asked me to go to the party with you."

"We don't have to go!" Alexis exclaimed.

"It's not that, baby. I want to go. I'm just nervous because these are your people."

"CeCe," Alexis exhaled in frustration. "You are my people! You are the person I want to be with."

CeCe smiled. "Okay, okay. You may have to remind me of that from time to time, but I believe you."

A big smile grew on Alexis's face. "I asked you to spend the night because it's a big deal for me, CeCe."

"Okay?"

"I may have had sex from time to time with people, but that was a long time ago and I never let anyone stay at my home. I didn't want you to think I was an asshole and expected you to spend the night with me because of the weekend or—"

"The back room at the salon?" CeCe asked.

"Yes. I want you, it's true. But I also want to fall asleep with you in my arms and wake up in yours. That's new for me."

CeCe smiled and put her hand on Alexis's cheek. "I want that too. I was kind of teasing about your heart earlier, but it makes me angry that someone hurt you so much that you closed it off. I want your heart to feel good emotions again because you make my heart happy, Alexis."

Alexis smiled. "The moon is about to disappear behind the buildings. Let's take one more look then can we go home?"

CeCe nodded and brought their lips together in a sweet kiss. Alexis deepened the kiss for just a moment and hoped CeCe could feel the happiness she put in Alexis's heart.

19

"Thank you for dinner, the wine, and the show," CeCe said as Alexis drove them out of the parking garage.

"The show?"

"Yes, it was amazing how the moon and planets lined up perfectly between the buildings." CeCe reached for Alexis's hand and took it into both of hers. "You are so talented, Dr. Reed, I wouldn't have been surprised if you orchestrated the entire thing."

Alexis laughed. "I have no control over the moon and stars."

"I don't know about that," CeCe said softly. She believed Alexis Reed could do anything she set her mind to. "You've become quite adept at making my heart swoon and that can be difficult to do."

"Can it?"

CeCe chuckled. "Yes, it can, but not for you."

Alexis smiled and quickly glanced at CeCe. "Hmm, I wonder what's going on then. We seem to make each other happy."

CeCe squeezed her hand and grinned. This was new for them both, but right now CeCe didn't want to think about that; she wanted to enjoy it.

"Hey, speaking of happiness, do you go to the hospital every day?"

"Yes, that's where the operating room is," Alexis replied.

"Don't be a smartass. You don't perform surgery every day."

"You're right, I don't, but I do go to the hospital every day to check on my patients or for other things."

"I'm going to be at your hospital in a couple of weeks," CeCe stated.

"You are?" CeCe could feel Alexis's concerned eyes glance her way. "Is something wrong?"

"No, babe, I'm fine. I do a makeover event for the women in the oncology department. Patients, nurses, and staff are included. I'd love for you to come by and see me when I'm there."

"Of course I'll come by. Tell me about it," Alexis said.

"I get a group of stylists together to do facials, manicures, and pedicures. We also do hair for some patients and the nurses and staff. Not all patients lose their hair."

"I'd heard about this program, but didn't know you did it! That's incredible, baby!"

CeCe smiled "Never in a million years did I ever dream that Dr. Alexis Reed would be calling me 'baby.'"

"It just slipped out! Is there something else you'd rather I call you?"

"No, *baby*!" CeCe teased. "I love it," she added softly.

"Tell me more about the makeovers?"

"The salon I left to open Salon 411 is owned by a good friend. We came up with the idea when one of our clients had cancer. It gives the women such happiness to be

CeCe Sloan is Swooning   **167**

pampered for a little while. And the nurses give such incredible care that we wanted to include them as well. It's a fun day for everyone."

"You are amazing, Cecilia!" Alexis exclaimed. "I'm not surprised, though. You always take such care with your clients. I should know, I used to be one."

CeCe chuckled. "I'll still do your hair. If you haven't noticed, I rather like running my fingers through it." CeCe leaned over and tucked a strand of Alexis's hair behind her ear and kissed her on the cheek.

"Are you trying to make me wreck the car?"

"Just giving you a little incentive to get us to your place."

"We're almost there," Alexis said, turning onto her street.

Sure enough a few minutes later CeCe followed Alexis into the kitchen from the garage.

"I have a hard time believing you haven't had sex in this house," CeCe said.

"I didn't say that," Alexis said, setting the cooler on the table.

CeCe stared at her for a moment then her face brightened. "Oh, that's right. I did give you that cute little toy."

Alexis giggled. "You did." She rested her hands on CeCe's hips and smiled. "More dancing?"

"Do you want to dance?"

"Not really." Alexis leaned in and kissed CeCe softly.

"Mmm, let's play," CeCe said, deepening the kiss. It had been such a romantic night and now that they were back at Alexis's house she wanted to feel Alexis's skin next to hers. The vibrator might make an appearance at some point, but she wanted Alexis all to herself.

"Do you want something else to drink?" Alexis offered as she caught her breath.

CeCe shook her head. "All I want is you."

Alexis gave CeCe such a heated look that CeCe felt a jolt between her legs. She hoped this was the beginning of many nights they spent together.

"I had such a good time tonight," Alexis said as she led them into the bedroom.

"It's not over yet." CeCe crooned.

"I know, but one of the first things you asked me was, were we more than just sex. Remember?"

CeCe nodded. "I know that I mean more to you than just a roll in the hay. I also know we may not have the words yet for just what this is and that's okay."

"Can we keep trying to figure it out?" Alexis leaned in closer.

"Will you try to open your heart?" CeCe asked, raising one brow and putting her arms around Alexis's neck. She knew it would be hard for Alexis to be vulnerable again, but if they were to have a chance, Alexis had to try.

"I trust you to be gentle with my heart."

CeCe smiled. "And will you do the same for mine?" CeCe searched Alexis's eyes. She also knew there was no way Alexis would hurt her intentionally, but sometimes the heat was so intense between them that CeCe was afraid their feelings might not be the same. It would be very easy for CeCe to fall head over heels for Alexis Reed, but it would be hard for Alexis to do the same.

"I can't imagine a heart as good as yours could feel anything for mine."

"What?" CeCe said. "You have a wonderful heart, Alexis, you're just afraid to use it."

"Do you think we really have any control over our hearts?" Alexis asked.

CeCe smiled. "Maybe we don't."

CeCe Sloan is Swooning   169

"You've made me feel things that I haven't felt in such a long time that at first I didn't know what was happening."

"Oh, Lex," CeCe cooed, cupping Alexis's face.

"And I don't want it to stop. So, yes CeCe, my heart is open to you. When you turned around and saw the moon tonight then turned back and looked at me, I knew I had put that smile on your face. The joy your smile put in my heart in that moment almost brought me to tears."

CeCe could feel tears sting her eyes.

"Oh no." Alexis ran her thumb under CeCe's eye and caught a single tear.

"It's okay, baby. You're speaking with your heart."

Alexis smiled. "I don't seem to have any control over it and that's way out of my comfort zone."

CeCe laughed. "I know you're used to being in control, but it's okay. I won't tell anyone."

Alexis chuckled. "How did that turn so serious?"

"Because we had such a special night and you created it for us."

"We created it," Alexis said, leaning in and kissing CeCe gently.

"I think we've done enough talking," CeCe murmured, kissing Alexis's neck.

* * *

CeCe's eyelids fluttered open and for a moment she didn't know where she was. She'd been having a dream and it seemed so real. Her eyes closed again and she inhaled. A smile played at the corners of her mouth as she breathed in Alexis's scent. Her head was resting on Alexis's shoulder and CeCe could feel her arms around her. A wisp of Alexis's chocolate brown hair tickled her nose.

She gently swiped the hair away and opened her eyes. It was dark in Alexis's bedroom, but she could make out the outline of the furniture and see there was still darkness behind the window. Her hand rested on Alexis's chest where not too long ago her lips had been exploring and kissing.

CeCe took a deep breath and tried to recall the dream she'd been having. Maybe if she thought about it, she'd fall back to sleep and the dream would continue. In the dream, CeCe was at the salon finishing a client's hair when Alexis walked in. She smiled at CeCe as she walked to the back of the salon and kissed her on the cheek. When CeCe finished, she'd known they would leave together and go home or be off for a date-night. Is that the way a happy relationship looked?

CeCe remembered having that thought right before she woke up. Is that where she and Alexis were headed? Was this the beginning of their happy relationship? They had such a good time last night and Alexis was so cute, asking CeCe to spend the night.

She could feel the shift inside Alexis. What had started as playful challenges between them were now heated kisses and touches fueled with emotions other than lust. CeCe could see the difference in how Alexis looked at her and felt it in her touch.

CeCe knew she was in trouble the first time Alexis kissed her. As much as she wanted to keep it as playful flirting, that kiss went straight to her heart. She'd been trying to contain her emotions since. It would take time for Alexis to trust her heart, but she could see it happening.

Alexis stirred and CeCe raised her head, slightly sitting up.

"Mmm, is everything all right?" Alexis mumbled.

CeCe put her arm around Alexis and eased her head

onto her chest. "It's perfect," CeCe whispered. "I want to hold you."

"Mmm," Alexis moaned and snuggled in closer as she drifted back to sleep.

"Swooning may become my middle name," CeCe muttered. Alexis did something to her, whether it was a simple look or something bigger like asking her to stay the night. She knew she should tamp down these feelings so Alexis could catch up or she might get hurt. CeCe smiled. "It won't hurt to fall into these feelings for one night," she said softly, kissing Alexis's forehead and pulling her arms a little tighter.

"Mmm, I'm so glad you're here," Alexis whispered as she snuggled a little deeper into CeCe's arms.

* * *

"You didn't have to make breakfast," Alexis said, walking into the kitchen with a cup of coffee.

"It's just oatmeal," CeCe said, putting two bowls and spoons on the table. "You need a good breakfast to go out and save lives." She turned around to pour them more coffee and stopped in her tracks. "Damn, Dr. Reed. You are rocking that suit!"

Alexis smiled and sipped her coffee. "Thank you."

CeCe pulled out the chair for Alexis and waited for her to sit.

"You looked particularly beautiful in the shower this morning, Ms. Sloan," Alexis said in a low, seductive voice. "I could get used to this." She kissed CeCe on the lips and sat down.

CeCe giggled "Careful, Doc. Your heartstrings are showing."

Alexis knew what CeCe was doing to her heart, but she wasn't ready to make any declarations. The fact that she asked CeCe to spend the night was quite a step for Alexis, but this morning they'd awakened in one another's arms and Alexis was shocked. She couldn't believe how natural and easy it felt. For a moment she'd imagined this scenario on a weekend morning where they lazed in each other's arms, slowly made love until they were both spent, and leisurely planned the day.

Alexis took a bite of her oatmeal and raised a brow. "This is delicious. Thank you for making breakfast."

CeCe smiled. "My mom makes it with brown sugar, so that's how I make it. Speaking of my mom, she wants to meet you."

Alexis's spoon clamored against her bowl.

"Are you okay?"

"Uh, your mom wants to meet me? Now I know why you're nervous to meet my doctor friends."

CeCe chuckled. "My sisters told her I was with you at Lovers Landing last weekend."

"Oh fuck! She knows we spent the weekend together!" Alexis could feel her heart speed up.

"Honey." CeCe reached for Alexis's hand. "My mom also knows we are both adults and can spend the weekend or nights with whomever we please."

"But I pleased her daughter, not *whomever*." Alexis winced.

"That you did," she said in a low, throaty voice. "My mom is a sweetheart. She'll love you."

"You think so?"

"A better question is: why do you care what my mother thinks?" CeCe said, eyeing Alexis.

20

Alexis took another bite of oatmeal and a sip of coffee. "You know how you have your rules about not dating clients?"

"Uh huh." CeCe nodded.

"I have a rule or two also. One of those rules is that I don't have women spend the night with me."

"Is that right?" CeCe replied, batting her eyelashes.

"It is. You may have noticed I broke that rule with Christine Sloan's daughter when you spent last night with me."

"I've always been a rule breaker," CeCe stated.

Alexis laughed. "Should I be surprised?"

"Does that mean you've done away with that rule?" CeCe asked, amused.

"Not at all. That rule is still in effect, but you're not just any woman, Cecilia," Alexis said, her face softening.

CeCe smiled. "I intend to be the only woman who spends the night with you."

Alexis liked the sound of that. "And that is why it's so important to me that your mom likes me. I want you to spend more nights with me and maybe I'll get to spend a night or two with you."

"You want to spend the night in my little house?" CeCe's forehead creased.

"Why does that surprise you?"

CeCe shrugged. "I don't know. My house isn't like this," she said, gesturing with her hand.

"Your house feels like a home," Alexis said earnestly. "Maybe if you were here more often my house would feel like that, too."

Alexis watched as shock covered CeCe's face. She was the one usually surprised by CeCe's antics, but she meant what she said. Waking up in CeCe's arms that morning gave Alexis the feeling of home. She'd never had that in this house. It was where she lived, but it never felt like a home. It was a place, but it felt like more than that this morning.

"You're not saying anything." Alexis looked at CeCe and felt her stomach drop. Had she said something wrong?

"Every time I think I know you, Lex, you do something that surprises me," CeCe confessed.

"Surprise in a good way?"

CeCe chuckled. "Yes, in a good way!"

"Well, it still surprises the hell out of me every time you call me Lex and I like it." Alexis grinned.

CeCe leaned over and cupped Alexis's cheek. "I call you that because no one else does. It's *my* name for you."

"I know." Alexis leaned into CeCe's touch.

"I realize that I am the rule breaker, not you. I don't want you to be late for work," CeCe said, standing up and taking their bowls to the sink.

Alex grabbed their coffee cups and followed CeCe. She reached around and set the cups in the sink, trapping CeCe

CeCe Sloan is Swooning 175

against it. She pulled CeCe's hair back and kissed her neck. CeCe leaned back, giving her better access.

"Thank you for breakfast," Alexis whispered as she kissed just below CeCe's ear.

"Mmm, maybe we can do it again sometime," CeCe mumbled, stroking the side of Alexis's face.

Alexis turned CeCe around and their lips crashed together in a passionate kiss. Their tongues touched, immediately followed by moans. Their arms tightened around each other as the kiss continued to flame.

"We have to stop," CeCe said breathlessly, pulling her lips from Alexis's "You can't be late the first time I stay over."

Alexis smiled. "Oh, baby. I won't be late."

"I know you won't." CeCe wiggled out of Alexis's arms and got her things together.

Alexis laughed. "You do realize I'm the boss, right?"

CeCe stopped and stared at her. "What do you mean?"

"I have plenty of time to take you home and make it to the hospital for rounds before my first appointment," Alexis explained.

"Please tell me you are not one of those doctors who make their patients wait forever."

"I am not. There will always be a good reason if one of my patients has to wait," Alexis said.

"Good to know," CeCe said, walking toward the door to the garage.

"Wait!" Alexis exclaimed and hurriedly put her computer in her bag. She walked over to CeCe and kissed her softly on the lips. "I want a goodbye kiss."

CeCe leaned in and kissed her again. "One for the road." She winked and walked out the door to the car.

* * *

Alexis closed the patient files she'd been working on and checked her schedule for tomorrow.

"That was your last patient," Donna said, walking into Alexis's office. "Here are the files you'll want in the morning."

"Thanks, Donna."

"Now, how did the date go last night?" she asked, tapping her foot nervously.

Alexis blinked several times and sighed. "When did my love life become of such interest around here?"

"Do I really need to explain that to you? Okay," Donna said, sitting in her familiar spot across from Alexis's desk. "About fifteen years ago you waltzed into this clinic, fresh out of residency. You were a young, shiny surgeon ready to show the world your talent and skill. You were confident, almost arrogant, and only focused on your job." Donna paused for a moment.

"Almost arrogant?"

"Almost. Some people thought you were a little cocky, but you backed it up with your work. Very impressive," Donna said. "But in those fifteen years I've rarely seen you go out with a woman or man more than a couple of times. Michael, Lana, and a couple of the other doctors have tried to set you up or introduce you to other people only to fail. But now, out of nowhere, Dr. Alexis Reed suddenly smiles more. You are almost chipper!" Donna exclaimed. "I would never call you chipper!"

Alexis gasped in faux amazement. "I should hope not!"

"We now know the change in you is because of a woman! A woman who you have seen several times! That, my friend, is why your love life is so interesting."

Alexis sat up and leaned towards Donna. "I'm bringing

CeCe Sloan is Swooning **177**

CeCe to Lana and Michael's party. I do want her to meet you all, but I also hope—"

Donna raised her hand. "We won't embarrass you."

"I know you're going to embarrass me." Alexis smiled. "What I hope is that I still have a girlfriend at the end of the party."

"Girlfriend, huh?" Donna said with a wide smile.

Alexis nodded. "Since I'm finished for the day, I think I might go see my girlfriend on my way home."

"I'm happy for you, Alexis. And I look forward to meeting your *girlfriend*," Donna said.

Alexis smiled and liked the way that sounded. *My girlfriend.*

When Alexis got in her car she noticed a pair of earrings in her console. She picked one up and smiled. CeCe left them there last night after they'd come down from the roof. "I should return these." Alexis chuckled and smiled at herself in the rearview mirror then headed to the shopping center.

She walked into the salon and could see CeCe at her station in the back. There was a woman in the chair, but suddenly CeCe looked over and saw Alexis walking towards her. The smile on CeCe's face made Alexis's heart skip a beat.

She smiled at the woman in the chair as CeCe took a step towards her. "Hey," Alexis said, kissing CeCe on the lips. "I thought you might be missing these." She held up the earrings and grinned.

"Where'd you get those?" CeCe asked. "Oh, I remember. I took them off last night."

"CeCe, are you going to introduce me to your friend?" the woman in the chair asked.

178   JAMEY MOODY

"Oh, I'm sorry," Alexis said. "I didn't mean to interrupt. I'll wait over here." She started towards the empty chair at Nora's station when CeCe grabbed her arm.

"Oh no you don't." CeCe gave her a devilish smile.

Alexis's eyes widened. "What?"

CeCe took her hand and led Alexis around in front of the woman. "Alexis, I'd like you to meet my mom, Christine Sloan."

Alexis felt the color drain from her face. She'd walked in here, kissed CeCe, and dangled her earrings in front of her suggesting they'd spent the night together. *Oh my God!*

CeCe chuckled. "It's okay, babe. Mom, this is Dr. Alexis Reed."

Christine laughed and Alexis was struck by how much she sounded like CeCe. "I am so happy to finally meet you, Alexis. It is okay to call you Alexis, isn't it?"

"Yes ma'am," Alexis said, finding her voice. She took Christine's offered hand. "It's so nice to meet you." She hadn't noticed it at first, but Alexis could see the resemblance now, especially in those striking blue eyes.

Christine held Alexis's hand for a moment and smiled. "CeCe's sisters tell me you are a brilliant surgeon and also a very nice person. It's a shame CeCe hasn't introduced us before now."

"Oh stop, Mom." CeCe took Alexis's hand and smiled at her. "Did you not just see this gorgeous woman walk in here and kiss me? I want her to keep doing that." CeCe turned to her mother and continued. "All you'll do is ask her question after question until she's so happy to get out of here she'll never come back!"

Alexis couldn't keep from laughing at the comedy of it all. "Christine—is it okay if I call you that?"

"Absolutely."

CeCe Sloan is Swooning

179

"In CeCe's defense, I could claim to be busy with work, but honestly, we've been having such fun together—"

"We didn't want anyone else around," CeCe added with a grin.

Alexis felt warmth spread through her body, but quickly looked back at CeCe's mother. "I'm happy to answer any and all of your questions. When you're finished here, would you like to go next door to Cory's bar?"

"I'd love to," Christine replied with a beaming smile.

"We're almost done," CeCe said, leading Alexis a few steps away. "Are you sure you want to do this?" she said softly to Alexis.

"Yes." Alexis nodded with a sweet smile. She leaned in and whispered in CeCe's ear, "I want to keep coming in here and kissing you."

A throaty chuckle slipped from CeCe and it was Alexis's turn to melt a little.

"What if I have another appointment after Mom?" CeCe asked.

"That's okay. We'll visit until you can join us." Alexis shrugged. "I'm sure Christine and I can find plenty to talk about, right?"

"That's right," Christine said, watching them in the mirror.

CeCe finished by spraying a little hair spray on Christine's hair. "That'll be $19.95," CeCe teased.

Christine scoffed. "As if you'd let me pay you."

"You did, Mom, by paying for beauty school. Remember?" CeCe held Christine's hand as she stepped out of the chair.

"Thank you, sweetie. It looks lovely, as usual," Christine said, looking into the mirror.

Alexis looked on and couldn't keep from smiling. She

immediately liked Christine Sloan and hoped Christine would like her as well.

"I can join you in a few minutes."

"We'll be fine, honey," Christine said, patting CeCe on the back. "Let's go, Alexis."

Alexis grinned at CeCe and held up her hand with her fingers crossed as they walked past her.

21

"You know, CeCe is right. I do like to ask questions," Christine said as they left the salon and walked into The Liquor Box.

"My dad used to say that you can't learn anything if you don't ask questions," Alexis said as she followed Christine to the bar at the back of the store.

"Well, well," Cory said from behind the bar as Christine and Alexis climbed onto stools. "Did CeCe finally introduce you two?"

"Don't be a smart ass, Cory," Christine chastised her daughter.

"Yes ma'am," Cory replied. "I have opened a very nice bottle of wine that I think you'll like, Mom."

"Wonderful," Christine replied.

"How about you, Alexis?" Cory asked as she poured her mom a glass.

"I'll have what Christine's having," Alexis said with a smile.

Cory poured her a glass as well. "Where's CeCe?"

"She'll be here shortly. Is there something else you could

be doing, hon?" Christine asked, giving her daughter a pointed look. "Don't you need to be working on your strategy to outsmart that discount liquor store?"

"Uh, okay. It's nice seeing you again, Alexis," Cory said, walking to the end of the bar.

"I am well aware CeCe did not intentionally keep me from meeting you, Alexis," Christine began. "I knew she would introduce us when the time was right for her."

"I may have interfered with that. She didn't know I was coming by this afternoon," Alexis explained.

"She hoped you would," Christine said.

"Oh?"

"She told me about your date last night and how beautiful the night sky was from that rooftop." Christine took a sip of her wine. "She promised me that if you didn't come by today that we would meet soon."

Alexis took a sip of wine, letting Christine's words sink in. She knew CeCe had had a good time last night, but knowing she'd shared it with her mother meant more to Alexis than she'd thought it would. "I'm very glad I came by today."

Alexis could feel Christine's eyes look her up and down, measuring her next words. "From the way you look at my daughter, I can tell you like her very much."

"I do," Alexis agreed.

"For CeCe to even mention you, much less tell me about your date, means you two have spent time together."

Alexis wasn't sure exactly what Christine was implying, but she hoped this was an opportunity for CeCe's mom to help her.

"We have been spending time together and you may be able to enlighten me about something," Alexis began.

"What's that?" Christine replied, taking another sip of

wine.

"CeCe is going with me to a small get-together with a few friends from my clinic and the hospital. I know she's a little nervous about it, just as I am about meeting her mother," Alexis said, looking into Christine's familiar blue eyes. "CeCe has made the comment to me a few times about being out of her league or not fitting in. I know that CeCe has no idea how truly amazing she is. She is one of the most interesting, generous, thoughtful people I've ever met. I can't seem to make her understand, if anything, that she's so much better than the people she'll be meeting."

Christine nodded. "I've been telling her for years that there is no one who is better than she is unless she lets them be. But for my sensitive sweet girl, sometimes that's hard."

"I want her to know how amazing she is," Alexis said.

Christine smiled. "When CeCe was in elementary school there was a girl who loved to make it known that her family had money. They were members of the country club and we weren't. In the summer, my girls went to the public swimming pool, but this little girl bragged about the pool at the country club. She would invite other little girls to go with her as her guest, but she never invited CeCe."

"I can't tell you what that makes me want to do to that little girl," Alexis said, surprised at the emotion filling her heart.

Christine reached over and patted Alexis's arm. "I know. When CeCe was in high school she went to the country club with another friend and her parents for dinner. She came back home and the first thing she told me was that the swimming pool at the country club was small and they didn't even have a slide," Christine said. "I think that's when she realized the grass wasn't always greener, but it still bothered her that she wasn't included. That little girl made her feel less than. I tried to instill in her that anyone who would make someone else feel that way wasn't worth another thought. I think that's why she makes such an effort for every one of her clients to feel special."

"That's just it, Christine. CeCe is the one who is special."

Christine looked into Alexis's eyes and smiled. "You make her feel special. Keep doing that and she'll believe you."

"Oh, I hope so."

"Hope what?" CeCe said, throwing her arm over Alexis's shoulder.

"We hope you'll buy the next round," Christine said.

"You do have to drive home, Mom."

Christine scoffed. "I have three daughters that own this place. Surely one of you can drive me home."

"CeCe and I will drive you home. Hey, Cory. We need another glass," Alexis said, looking towards the end of the bar.

Cory brought another glass and emptied the bottle of wine.

"We'll take my mother home?" CeCe said softly into Alexis's ear.

"Yes, we." Alexis grinned. She turned to Christine. "Now, tell me more about when CeCe was a kid."

"Please," CeCe said, standing between Alexis and her mother. "There is nothing you need to know about awkward, shy CeCe."

"Shy!" Cory exclaimed. "You've never been shy a day in your life!"

"Oh, dear sister. I cover it well."

"No way. You may have been awkward, but you weren't shy," Cory said. "Was she, Mom?"

"I don't think you were shy or awkward. You didn't

realize the other girls wanted to be like you," Christine said.

"Like me?" CeCe scoffed. "Who wanted this mass of unruly, flaming red hair, along with the freckles and legs that could barely walk without stumbling?"

"Are you kidding me! Your hair is gorgeous, your freckles are adorable, and as for your legs, well, we can talk about them when your mom isn't around."

Christine laughed and sipped her wine. "I know all of my girls are beautiful in their own ways."

Alexis noticed CeCe and Cory exchange a look.

"Thanks, Mom," CeCe said.

"Yeah, thanks," Cory echoed her sister.

"I want to know what you're going to do to top this rooftop date last night," Christine asked Alexis.

"It's CeCe's turn," Alexis said, turning her stool to face her.

"If you'll remember, I got us invited to Lovers Landing for the weekend," CeCe said.

"But you're the one who said last night was our first date," Alexis countered. "Um, should we be having this discussion right now?"

CeCe chuckled. "You said our first date was the day we had ice cream next door."

"Isn't this cute, Mom?" Cory said, taking a drink from her beer.

"It tells me these two don't know what dating is," Christine said.

"Oh, and you're the expert," CeCe said. "You and Daddy were high school sweethearts and were married for nearly fifty years."

"And we dated until the day he died," Christine said matter-of-factly.

"Oh, wow!" Alexis said, amazed. She couldn't imagine

knowing someone for fifty years, much less being married to them for that long. She looked over at CeCe and suddenly saw an image of them in their old age together. Alexis shook her head and took a much needed sip of her wine. When she set her glass down she looked up to see Christine staring at her and smiling.

"It was wonderful," Christine said.

"You say that now, but I remember some not so wonderful times when you grounded us for various lame reasons," Cory said, sounding like a petulant teenager.

Christine laughed. "Those were great times! Your dad and I were on the same page, but we suffered more than you girls did because you were moping around the house."

"I don't know about Cory's childhood, but mine was the best and I knew it."

"Okay, girls. It's time for me to go home. I can drive," Christine said.

"Oh, no, Mom. I'll drive you home," CeCe said. "Alexis can follow me."

Alexis started to get money out of her purse to pay for their drinks, but Cory stopped her. "I've got this, Alexis. I hope you'll come by more often."

"Thanks, Cory. I appreciate it."

As they got up to leave Christine handed her keys to Alexis. "Why don't you drive me home and CeCe can follow us."

"Okay." Alexis smiled, taking her keys.

They walked back into the salon then to the front door.

"My car is in the back. I'll meet you at Mom's," CeCe said to Alexis. "Are you sure about this?"

Alexis gave CeCe a big smile. "You do trust me with your mom, don't you?"

"Of course I do."

CeCe Sloan is Swooning 187

"Let's go, Alexis," Christine said, walking out the front door.

Alexis shrugged and followed her to her car. Once they were on their way, Alexis looked in the rearview mirror and could see CeCe a few cars back.

"CeCe is right. I do like to ask questions," Christine said. "I wanted you to drive me so I could ask you one more thing."

"I'm happy to answer any questions. Shoot!"

"This may sound old-fashioned, but I was wondering why a woman like you chooses to be alone. You are obviously successful and beautiful, so as they used to say, women or men are probably lined up to be with you."

"Uh, thank you for the compliment." Alexis sighed. She could tell that Christine Sloan wasn't necessarily trying to be nosy. She was probably just looking out for her daughter.

"Many years ago I got my heart broken. Since then I haven't been willing to go through that again, so I've remained single."

"No one has come along who you thought might be worth a chance?" Christine paused. "Let me say this. If you can't tell CeCe is worth that risk then I hope you'll stop seeing her now. I don't want either one of you to get hurt and from what I've observed, both of your hearts are already tangled."

Alexis knew Christine was right.

"Turn here," Christine said. "I'm the second house on the right."

Alexis turned into Christine's driveway and saw CeCe right behind them.

"The last thing I'd ever want to do is hurt CeCe," Alexis said, turning to look at Christine.

"That should tell you something, honey."

22

CeCe pulled in behind her mother's car. She watched as Christine got out of the passenger side, but Alexis sat there for a moment. CeCe walked to the driver's side door and opened it. Alexis had a thoughtful look on her face as if she was considering something then she looked up at CeCe and smiled.

"Is everything okay?" CeCe asked.

Alexis's smile widened. "Sure."

"CeCe, thank you again for doing my hair. I'll see you next week," Christine said.

"I'm sure I'll see you before then."

"Thank you for driving me home, Alexis. I enjoyed our visit."

"It was so nice to meet you, Christine," Alexis said, handing Christine her car keys.

"Maybe we'll see one another again. You girls have a nice evening," Christine said, walking into the house.

"Okay then," CeCe said as she watched her mother close the front door. "That was a little weird." She turned to Alexis

CeCe Sloan is Swooning

and took her hand. "She didn't say anything to offend you, did she?"

"Not at all. You're right. Your mom is a sweetheart."

"Do you have plans tonight?"

Alexis smiled and CeCe could feel the butterflies come alive in her stomach. *How does she do that?*

"I hope so. With you," Alexis said, walking towards CeCe's car.

"I just happen to have an opening this evening," CeCe quipped. "I can take you back to your car and we can grab dinner."

"Could you take me to my car and I'll follow you home?"

CeCe smiled. "And order dinner in?"

"What a great idea." Alexis leaned in and kissed CeCe on the lips before walking to the passenger side of CeCe's car.

"So you want to come home with me," CeCe said as she backed out of her mother's driveway.

"Is that all right?"

CeCe glanced over at Alexis and grinned. "I guess that means my mom didn't scare you off."

"Nope, but your mother is direct."

"Uh oh, what did she do?" CeCe asked warily.

Alexis chuckled. "She asked why I was single."

"Oh gosh, Lex. I'm sorry."

"No, babe, it's okay."

CeCe smiled.

"You like it when I call you babe," Alexis said.

"I do."

"Your mom is easy to talk to."

"More like demanding." CeCe glanced over at Alexis. "You don't talk about your family much. Is your mom hard to talk to?"

"I wouldn't say that."

CeCe pulled into her garage and looked over at Alexis. "You don't have to talk about them if you don't want to."

"I don't mind. Let's order dinner and I'll tell you about them."

They went inside and decided to order a pizza.

"Would you like a glass of wine or a beer?" CeCe asked.

"No thanks. Water is fine."

"Here you go." CeCe handed Alexis a glass of water and led them to the living room couch.

Alexis looked around the room and smiled. "I like your house. It feels like a home."

"You've mentioned that before."

Alexis shrugged. "I don't think I've lived anywhere that felt like a home. I've lived in houses."

"Even growing up?"

"Oh yeah, I was going to tell you about my family." Alexis took a drink of her water and set it on the table. She leaned back on the couch and pulled one leg under her. "My dad is a banker and my mom is a doctor. They are both retired. I have an older brother who is married with two daughters."

"You're an aunt." CeCe smiled.

Alexis nodded. "I don't see them very often, but we keep in touch with the magic of technology and FaceTime."

"Did your mom inspire you to be a doctor?"

"I suppose. She was a pathologist. She didn't see patients, but was into research. From a very young age I saw cadavers and body parts in her lab. I wanted to help people who were alive, though. She did teach me how to stitch and I practiced when I'd go to the lab with her."

"Wow! So you had a head start on your colleagues when

CeCe Sloan is Swooning

it came to that part. No wonder Krista's incision will disappear as it heals."

Alexis chuckled. "I hope it will. My brother went into finance and worked in banking with my dad. We are not close like you and your sisters. I mean, we get along okay, but not like you, Cory, and Cat."

"It might be different if you saw him every day like we do."

Alexis shrugged. "Maybe." She reached for her water and took a sip.

CeCe saw the wistful look on Alexis's face and rubbed her hand on her thigh.

Alexis smiled. "I grew up knowing we had money, but my parents made sure we worked and weren't spoiled. I can't help thinking about that little girl that wouldn't take you to the country club swimming pool."

"What?"

"Oh." Alexis looked up at CeCe. "Your mom told me about that little girl and how it hurt you."

"Bethany Hinson," CeCe spat. "I still can't stand her. It wasn't that she wouldn't invite me to go with her, it was the way she acted. She paraded around like she was better than everyone else."

"I came from money and I have money, but CeCe, my parents would not tolerate that kind of behavior. I don't ever remember wanting to behave that way, you know?"

CeCe reached for Alexis's hand. "That's because you are kind, Lex. You don't have a mean bone in your body. I don't know what made Bethany Hinson be such a little bitch, but she didn't grow out of it."

"Does she still live around here?"

"No, after she graduated from college, she got married and doesn't live here."

"What would you do if she walked into your salon?" Alexis asked with a devilish grin.

"Well, let's see, I could offer to give her a dazzling spa experience and then botch her hair." CeCe laughed.

Alexis laughed with her. "You wouldn't do that." Alexis scooted a little closer and put her arm on the back of the couch. "You would give that mean woman your best treatment, just like you do me or any of your clients, because you, CeCe Sloan, are a wonderful human being."

CeCe smiled and leaned a little closer to Alexis. "Is that right? Why don't you show me just how wonderful I am?"

Alexis gave her a slow, sexy smile and leaned in just as the doorbell rang.

CeCe giggled and rested her forehead on Alexis's. "To be continued." She started to get up, but stopped. "Will you stay the night?"

"I thought you'd never ask!"

CeCe laughed as the doorbell rang again. She quickly got up and answered the door.

They shared the pizza and took turns telling stories from their childhood.

Alexis's phone rang and she smiled at the caller ID. "This is my friend Lana. She's having the party tomorrow night and has already called me several times."

"You work with her husband, right?"

Alexis nodded. "Do you mind if I get it?"

"Of course not." CeCe got up and began to clear the table as Alexis answered the phone.

"Hi, Lana," Alexis said.

CeCe could feel Alexis's eyes on her as she moved about the kitchen.

"Yes, I was with patients when you called earlier. I'm

CeCe Sloan is Swooning

excited for her to meet y'all. I think," Alexis said into the phone.

CeCe smiled and put their dishes in the dishwasher.

"Yes, she's beautiful, but you'll have to find out the rest tomorrow when we see you," Alexis said.

CeCe imagined Lana was asking all sorts of questions about her. She knew if the tables were turned her friends would be doing the same thing. She turned around and Alexis was staring at her while she listened to Lana on the phone.

CeCe hadn't hidden the fact that she was nervous about meeting Alexis's friends. But when she met Alexis's gaze, those brown eyes gave her such a feeling of belonging. It didn't matter that she was a hairstylist surrounded by medical professionals because she was with Alexis. They belonged together no matter where they were. She hoped to remember this feeling when they went to the party.

"Okay, see you tomorrow," Alexis said, ending the call.

Alexis got up, walked over to where CeCe leaned against the kitchen counter, and put her hands on CeCe's hips. "What is that look?"

CeCe lazily rested her arms on Alexis's shoulders and gave her a smoldering look. "I'm yours," she said softly, pressing her lips to Alexis's. She should be afraid that Alexis might not feel the same, but CeCe had decided last night while she held Alexis in her arms that she wanted the chance to love Alexis's heart like it should've been loved all along.

Alexis deepened the kiss and CeCe was glad she was leaning against the counter otherwise she'd melt right to the floor.

"Mmm, I'm having you for dessert," Alexis moaned into CeCe's ear.

CeCe took a steadying breath and led them to the bedroom. "When I left this morning I didn't know I wouldn't be alone when I came back."

"Plan on it from now on," Alexis said.

CeCe turned just as Alexis claimed her mouth with the most sensuous, luscious lips. She felt like Alexis was kissing them into some kind of lavender haze just like the Taylor Swift song.

The next thing CeCe knew, they were lying on her bed, face to face, no longer wearing clothes. Alexis was stroking the side of her face with her fingers and staring intensely into her eyes.

"You make me feel things I've never felt before. When I'm not concentrating on a patient, my mind drifts to you. Let me show you what you make me feel."

CeCe smiled. Her heart soared with Alexis's words. Maybe she did feel it, too. "Let's do this together," she whispered.

Alexis's brows rose then CeCe could see her take a deep breath.

They started with a kiss and began to create the most intimate dance that only their hearts knew. CeCe understood what Alexis meant earlier. They had both been in love at one time or another, but it hadn't felt like this. CeCe knew Alexis might still be afraid to call it love, but what she felt for Alexis was better than any love she'd felt before and she intended to show her.

"I've never wanted you as much as I do right this moment," CeCe said softly as she pulled her lips from Alexis's and stared into her eyes. She slid her hand from where it had been splayed on Alexis's back down her side and over her hip.

CeCe Sloan is Swooning

"I want you just as much." Alexis gasped as she mirrored CeCe's movements.

"I want to feel you inside me as I'm inside you," CeCe whispered. She wanted to give herself to Alexis, but she also wanted to show Alexis she could let go and trust CeCe with her heart.

Alexis nodded. "Show me."

CeCe lifted her top leg and bent it, resting her foot on the bed. She waited for Alexis to follow her lead. When Alexis raised her leg, CeCe reached for Alexis's hand and placed it on her sex. Her eyelids fluttered closed as she felt Alexis's fingers explore her wetness. CeCe opened her eyes and found a smile playing at the corners of Alexis's mouth.

"You feel so good," CeCe said, exhaling. She ran her fingers through Alexis's folds and saw her eyes shut as well.

"Mmm," Alexis groaned. "You're right, this feels so good."

CeCe leaned in and kissed Alexis softly on the lips. "Be careful, you'll make me come with those magic fingers of yours before we even get going."

Alexis pressed their lips together again. "Then let's go."

CeCe replied with a throaty chuckle. She pushed two fingers inside Alexis and they both groaned as Alexis did the same with her fingers.

CeCe knew this would be an amazing feeling but she wasn't prepared to lose her breath as she felt filled with Alexis and at the same time her fingers were surrounded by Alexis's velvety warmth.

"Oh, God," Alexis moaned.

CeCe brought her eyes back to stare into Alexis's bliss-filled face. "Mmm, you like this," CeCe cooed.

"Very much," Alexis replied on a shaky breath.

Their gazes were locked on each other and together they began a slow rhythm.

"Oh, yeah," CeCe hummed.

Their breaths came quicker now and Alexis gasped. "I really like this, but I'm close."

CeCe nodded. "Keep looking at me, babe." CeCe pushed her fingers in deeper and curled them up.

Once again, Alexis mirrored her movements and they held one another in place long enough for the orgasm to explode through them both.

"Can you feel that!" CeCe exclaimed.

"Yes!" Alexis shouted. "Don't move, baby."

CeCe wasn't about to move. She wanted this feeling to go on and on and on. Wave after wave of pleasure ran through her body, filling her everywhere. She hoped Alexis was feeling the same thing.

As her pulse began to slow, CeCe was certain her heart had never been this full. She'd tried to give Alexis all her love, so was Alexis's love now filling her heart? *God she hoped so!*

Although she wanted to profess her love to Alexis, she didn't think either one of them were ready for that.

"My God, CeCe, that was amazing," Alexis said softly, pressing her lips to CeCe's.

"Yeah it was," CeCe agreed.

Alexis rolled over on her back and exhaled. "I've never done that before."

CeCe raised up on her elbow and rested her head on her hand. With her other hand she traced her fingers over Alexis's stomach. "You are such a beautiful woman, Lex," she said. "But you have done that before, with me!"

Alexis grabbed CeCe's hand and laughed. "I meant like

that." She looked at CeCe and smiled. "You know, both of us at the same time."

"Stay with me, honey, and there's no telling what we can discover together," CeCe said, wiggling her eyebrows.

Alexis rolled over on top of CeCe. "I'm discovering that I really like you, CeCe Sloan."

"I really like you too, Alexis," CeCe said earnestly.

Alexis softly pressed her lips to CeCe's and once again CeCe lost her breath. What was Alexis doing to her? If she wasn't sure before that Alexis felt what she was feeling this kiss made her believe. She could feel the love.

23

Alexis lazily drew circles on CeCe's back with her finger.

"Mmm, your hands cannot be still, can they, Doc?"

"Not when I'm with you," Alexis said, pleasantly sighing.

"I had fun last night. How about you?" CeCe said, raising her head.

"I'm still having fun," Alexis leaned in and kissed CeCe softly.

A big yawn escaped CeCe's mouth as she pulled away. "Sorry." She quickly turned her head.

Alexis chuckled. "My little sleepyhead."

"Someone kept me up past my bedtime," CeCe said with a grin.

"You started it!"

CeCe laughed. "Oh, we're both equally responsible and I wouldn't change a thing."

Their lips met again in a soft kiss. This time when CeCe pulled away she sweetly said, "Good morning, honey."

CeCe Sloan is Swooning

"Good morning." Alexis smiled. "I'll pick you up for the party tonight. Do you want to stay at my place or yours?"

CeCe's face lit up with surprise. "You're confident I'm not going to embarrass you?"

"How could you embarrass me?" Alexis shrugged.

"I could tell everyone that the amazingly gifted Dr. Reed has a weakness," CeCe said.

"Oh?"

"Yeah, when I kiss her right here," CeCe said and softly kissed just below Alexis's ear. "She'll do anything I say."

Alexis moaned. "You are not wrong."

"Or I could tell them behind this serious, usually stoic surgeon," CeCe said in a severe tone, "is the most generous, beautiful heart."

"You think I have a generous heart?"

"I know you do." CeCe grinned.

Alexis felt that funny little flutter in her heart. Add that to the list of things CeCe Sloan did to her. "Why don't we spend the weekend together?" Alexis said.

CeCe looked at Alexis and wondered what she was thinking.

"Is that too much? I would love to spend all day with you. We don't have to do anything, just a normal day, hanging out..." Alexis rambled.

"And discovering things like last night?"

"Among other things."

"What things do you usually do on weekends?" CeCe asked with a twinkle in her eye.

"I catch up on any medical reading I didn't have time for during the week. What do you do?"

"I clean my house, but I'm pretty sure you have someone who does that for you."

"I do."

"I don't blame you!" CeCe exclaimed, sitting up in the bed. "I usually go to the grocery store and go by the shop to check on things. I try not to schedule any Saturday appointments."

"Do you watch TV?" Alexis asked.

CeCe nodded. "I love cooking competition shows."

"Oh, that sounds like fun. Maybe we could cook something together."

"I didn't say I could cook," CeCe pointed out.

Alexis laughed. "Maybe I can cook."

CeCe studied her face and grinned. "I wouldn't be surprised. I'm pretty sure you can do anything, Lex."

"You can too, Cecilia."

"Do you also read for pleasure? Because I do love to read," CeCe said.

Alexis wiggled her eyebrows. "Anything I do with you brings me pleasure."

CeCe smacked her on the arm. "Please!"

Alexis chuckled. "I can't help it! I have fun with you."

"I like to read romance novels, especially sapphic romance." CeCe grinned.

"You might be surprised to know that I, too, read sapphic romance."

"No way!" CeCe said, smacking her on the arm again.

"Easy there, I have to use that arm to perform surgery next week," Alexis teased.

"I'll spend the weekend with you if you'll do something with me," CeCe said.

"Name it!"

"I want to laze around in bed with you in the morning," CeCe said. "Don't tell me you're one of those people who get up early even on the weekend."

A smile grew on Alexis's face. "That sounds like a

wonderful morning to me. You have a deal." Alexis held out her hand for CeCe to shake it.

"I don't want your hand." CeCe slapped it away and grabbed Alexis's face. "I want this." She leaned down and sealed their agreement with a kiss.

Alexis looked up at CeCe with the happiest lopsided grin. "Do you want to stay here or at my place?"

CeCe shrugged.

"I like it here. We're close to things to do. We can go to Cory's and have a drink or maybe find a book at Cat's," Alexis suggested. "Or go to the diner and have ice cream!"

CeCe chuckled. "You sound like you're going away for the weekend."

Alexis' face softened. "Maybe it could be every weekend with us?"

"Careful, Lex."

Alexis smiled. She knew what that meant. "You're about to swoon?"

CeCe nodded. "It's time to get up."

"Wait!"

CeCe stopped and turned back to Alexis.

"Just one more kiss."

CeCe smiled and shook her head. "You know I can't resist your kisses."

* * *

CeCe put her supplies away and walked towards the front of the salon.

"Okay, Ryan, I'm through for the day. Heather is supposed to be back. Will you make sure one of you locks everything up?"

"I'll make sure," Ryan replied. "Have fun at the party."

CeCe smiled. "Yeah, I'm not sure how wild a bunch of doctors can be."

Ryan chuckled. "You never know."

CeCe laughed and walked over to The Liquor Box. She found Cory at the bar talking to Cat. "Well, well, are you having a meeting without me?" she teased.

Cory laughed. "We were just talking about your big party. Are you nervous?"

"I was, but now I feel like anywhere that Alexis and I are together, we belong. I don't know how to explain it but she makes me feel like I'm supposed to be there. It doesn't matter what I do or how much money I have."

"Finally!" Cat exclaimed.

"I say that now, but who knows how fast my heart will be beating when we get there."

"I get it," Cory said. "What you do for work and how much money you make shouldn't matter. It does to some people, but those aren't our people."

"Exactly," Cat agreed. "And besides, you own your own business. We all do!"

"That's how Lex makes me feel." CeCe smiled.

"Lex? I don't see her as a 'Lex,'" Cory said.

CeCe chuckled. "She's not, but she is to me and I call her that."

"Someone is falling in love," Cat said, her voice rising playfully.

CeCe released a breath. "I'd love to tell you you're wrong, but I can't. I'm falling for her. Hard!"

"Oh, CeCe." Cory sighed. "It's too late to tell you to be careful. I just don't want you to get your heart broken."

"Alexis isn't going to break her heart," Cat said confidently.

CeCe Sloan is Swooning 203

"Everything has happened so fast," CeCe said. "But I think she's falling for me, too."

"How could she not!" Cat grinned. "But it hasn't been fast. Y'all have been getting to know one another for a year."

"Still! Don't say anything!" CeCe warned her sisters. "I've got to give Alexis time."

"Okay, okay."

"We'll see how the party goes, but we're spending the weekend at my place. We'll probably see you both tomorrow."

"Oh wow, first it was a weekend at Lovers Landing and now at your place," Cat said. "I'm happy for you, CeCe, but that won't ever be me. Never again."

"Don't say that, Cat. Someone could walk in your book store and right into your heart." CeCe smiled at her little sister.

Cat gave her a skeptical look and shook her head.

"I have volleyball practice tomorrow afternoon, but I'll be here after that. Come by and I'll buy y'all a drink," Cory offered.

"Thanks. I'll tell Alexis. It's time for me to get out of here and get ready for this party. Wish me luck."

"You don't need luck. You'll dazzle them with the Sloan sisters' magic," Cory grinned.

"Have fun," Cat added, giving her a hug.

* * *

Alexis tapped on her steering wheel to the music playing through the speakers as she waited at the stoplight. She smiled as her eyes were on the car in front of her, but she was thinking about CeCe. Her eyes roamed until she looked into the rearview mirror. She'd taken a little extra time with her hair and soft curls fell just to her shoulders.

A smile curled the corners of her mouth. "When was the last time I fussed with my hair to impress a woman?" She chuckled, knowing it had been a long time.

As the light changed and she headed towards CeCe's house, her thoughts drifted to last night. Something changed between them when they got to CeCe's last night. Well, changed wasn't really the right word, perhaps strengthened or deepened was more accurate.

After Alexis's talk with Christine, she had no intention of backing away from CeCe. She could feel CeCe give herself to Alexis last night and in return Alexis's heart had split wide open. There was no fear, which had been her earlier reaction. She was falling for CeCe and couldn't wait to see where that took them.

It didn't matter how things went at the party tonight. She was sure her friends would love CeCe, but if they didn't, oh well. After last night, Alexis knew where she and CeCe belonged. Together.

She may not be afraid, but it was still overwhelming. Her heart had been closed off for so long, she needed to ease into this idea of love.

They were in no hurry. All Alexis wanted to do was be with CeCe because when they were together they were both happy. Who wouldn't want to be happy?

She pulled into CeCe's driveway and stopped the car. One more check in the mirror then she grabbed her bag from the front seat and went to pick up her date.

"Hey!" CeCe said, opening the front door.

"Cecilia," Alexis said with wonder in her voice. "You look amazing."

"Thank you." CeCe stepped out of the way so Alexis

CeCe Sloan is Swooning 205

could come inside. "I need you to be on your best behavior tonight. Just because I'm wearing a dress does not mean you're supposed to slide your hands under it."

Alexis chuckled. "I will control myself until we get home."

"This dress isn't too much is it?" CeCe suddenly asked, sounding hesitant.

Alexis scoffed. "I'll say it again. You look amazing. Are you ready to go?"

"Hold it, Lex!" CeCe exclaimed. "Give me a moment to appreciate how gorgeous my girlfriend looks in those jeans." CeCe walked around Alexis. "Mmm, mmm, mmm. Would you look at those arms, tempting me in that sleeveless top." When she stopped in front of Alexis, CeCe gasped. "You curled your hair!"

"I wanted to look nice for you." It was Alexis's turn to give CeCe a shy smile, but she was thrilled CeCe noticed.

"Aww, Lex. You're beautiful anytime I look at you." CeCe leaned in and pressed their lips together in a sweet kiss. "Now I'm ready to go."

They walked to the car and Alexis drove them to the party. When she pulled to the curb at a house where the driveway was full of cars and several more were parked on the street, CeCe said, "Hey, this isn't far from your house."

"That's right," Alexis replied. "When Lana came to my house soon after I bought it, she liked the neighborhood so much she and Michael bought this place."

Alexis hurried out of the car and walked around to open CeCe's door.

"Babe, you didn't have to do that," CeCe said, taking Alexis's hand.

"I wanted to."

As they walked up to the front door, Alexis squeezed CeCe's hand. "Are you nervous?"

"I'm surprisingly not. I'm excited."

"Oh good." Alexis smiled over at her.

"It's because of this," CeCe said, holding their clasped hands up and kissing the back of Alexis's hand.

"I'll be right beside you all night long," Alexis promised.

"Oh, honey. We'll be fine," CeCe said, leaning over and kissing Alexis on the cheek.

"Oh my!" a woman said, opening the front door.

24

"Come right this way." The woman put her arm through CeCe's and pulled her inside the house. CeCe looked over her shoulder at Alexis and grinned as the woman jabbered.

She led her to a large kitchen/family room area where several women were gathered around a large island. CeCe glanced to the back of the room and through the double doors and windows she could see three men listening to another man, who she assumed was Michael, talking and pointing at something in the backyard.

"We are so glad you are here," the woman said, stopping at the end of the island.

"Oh no you don't," Alexis said, putting her arm around CeCe's waist. "You may be hosting us, Lana, but I will introduce my girlfriend."

CeCe looked over at Alexis with a wide smile and put her arm around Alexis's shoulders. She kind of liked this possessive little streak Alexis was showing.

"Yes, I did say girlfriend," Alexis said to the group. "CeCe knows that I rarely bring dates to these parties so please don't bore her with your stories."

Several of the women laughed.

"First, we have Donna Nall, who is the person that keeps our clinic running. Without her, all of us would be lost. Next is Mary Hiatt. She is a doctor in our clinic who specializes in obstetrics," Alexis said.

Both women nodded at CeCe as Alexis continued.

"This is Dawn and Tonya Castillo," Alexis said, nodding at the two women holding hands.

Alexis tightened her hold around CeCe's waist and pulled her a little closer. "I'm so happy to introduce all of you to this incredible woman." Alexis broadly grinned. "This is CeCe Sloan."

"Wow, honey." CeCe patted Alexis on the shoulder after that introduction. She looked around the island at the women and smiled. "I'm so happy to meet all of you. I'm sure y'all don't know how over-the-top Alexis can be at times."

All of the women had a comment and laughed.

"By the way," Lana said. "I don't know how she could leave me out. I'm Lana Pierce."

"I'm sorry, Lana. The way you whisked CeCe in here I thought you'd surely introduced yourself," Alexis said playfully.

"Very funny." Lana turned to CeCe and smiled. "You'll meet the guys later, but for now, what can I get you both to drink?"

Lana got them both a glass of wine and apologized for her overzealous greeting.

"You have to understand that we are all so happy Alexis is finally dating someone," Lana said.

CeCe Sloan is Swooning 209

"They don't seem to comprehend that you can be happy if you're single," Alexis pointed out.

"Is that right?" CeCe asked. She couldn't resist the opportunity to tease Alexis. "You seemed pretty happy introducing me as your girlfriend a few minutes ago."

Alexis gave her a faux menacing look. "You know what I mean."

CeCe laughed. "Of course I do. But let me tell you ladies, Lex would've probably kept our relationship casual if I hadn't made her change hairstylists."

"Is that how you met?" Dawn asked.

CeCe nodded. "I'd been doing your hair for about a year, I guess."

"My God, what took you so long!" Tonya exclaimed.

"She doesn't date her clients," Alexis replied. "Besides, I could tell something with CeCe wouldn't be casual for me."

CeCe looked at Alexis surprised. "You never told me that!"

Alexis shrugged.

"I hoped you would both finally figure it out," Donna said, smiling at CeCe. "I could tell every time she had an appointment with you because she came back to the office happier."

CeCe grinned at Alexis. "She wasn't the only one." CeCe turned to the group. "Enough about us, tell me the dirt on my girlfriend."

This brought another round of laughter.

"Sorry, babe. No dirt here." Alexis winked.

Lana led everyone over to the dining table where all sorts of snacks were laid out. As they noshed, Alexis looked on as CeCe had a moment to talk to each of Alexis's friends. She made eye contact with Alexis and gave her a smile to let her know she was okay.

When CeCe's glass was almost empty, she motioned to Alexis to meet her in the kitchen.

Alexis refilled both of their glasses and asked, "Is everything okay? They haven't bored you to tears yet?"

"No!" CeCe exclaimed. "They have all been so nice and welcoming. I can tell each one of them really likes you."

"Oh my God, CeCe. I'm so glad you're here," a voice said from behind them.

They both turned around to see two women smiling at them.

"Desi!" CeCe exclaimed. "Hi Erin, how are you?"

"How do you know the hospital administrator and her wife?" Alexis asked, her face full of confusion.

Erin chuckled. "I heard the famous Dr. Reed had a girlfriend."

"Will someone please explain what's going on?" Alexis said.

"Where do you think Desi gets this gorgeous haircut?" Erin said, reaching up and rubbing her fingers against the very short hairs on the side of her wife's head.

Desi had a sleek haircut with the sides short and the top longer. She had the top slicked back tonight, giving her an edgy look.

Desi smiled. "I see CeCe quite often because my wife loves to run her fingers over the short hairs on the side of my head."

"I don't know what I'll do if she ever wants to grow it out," Erin said with a grin.

"Oh!" Alexis said, realization dawning on her face.

"Desi and Erin have been clients of mine for a long time. Y'all have followed me from salon to salon all over town." CeCe laughed.

"Yep. But now that you own your own salon we expect

CeCe Sloan is Swooning   211

you to stay put," Erin said. "I'm so happy for you. I knew you'd have the best salon in our area if you ever got the chance."

"Aw, thanks, Erin," CeCe replied.

Erin looked at Alexis and grinned. "I not only heard you had a girlfriend, but the rumor is you actually smile and even laugh occasionally."

"Haha." Alexis smirked.

CeCe looked at Alexis and gave her the sweetest smile. She knew Alexis had a reputation at the hospital for being no-nonsense and expected the best from the people who worked with her, but to hear her demeanor was changing and others had noticed made CeCe's heart melt. Their relationship was making them both happy and it showed.

"If only they knew how sweet you really are," CeCe said, putting her arm around Alexis's shoulder. "I know you have to keep up your serious surgeon image, but Erin and Desi won't tell anyone, right?" CeCe gazed over at her friends and winked.

"Every hospital needs a brilliant, aloof surgeon," Erin said. "It would ruin our image if the public knew the soft side of your girlfriend."

"Soft side?" Alexis said, raising one eyebrow.

"I'm kind of your boss. Let me have this moment."

Alexis chuckled. "I don't know how long I'll be able to keep up this persona. When you're happy it shows, doesn't it?"

"I think you're right, babe," CeCe said. "These two smile a lot when I see them."

"I wonder if it could have anything to do with their sweet little girl?" Alexis asked.

Big smiles grew on both Erin and Desi's faces at the mention of their daughter.

"Lana didn't mention you would be here tonight," Alexis said.

"We weren't sure if we could make it, but our friends offered to babysit," Erin said. "CeCe, I saw that the spa day is coming up soon for the oncology department."

"It is. We have several special things planned for the women," CeCe said.

"You're the one who does the special event for my patients and nurses?" Dawn asked as she and Tonya joined them in the kitchen.

"She plans and organizes the entire event," Erin said.

"Thank you so much for doing that! I'm the oncologist at our clinic and my patients love the event! I thought the hospital did it for them. How did I not know it was you!"

"Oh no," Erin said. "CeCe came to us a few years ago with the idea and ran with it."

"It isn't just me. I have a lot of help," CeCe explained. She glanced over at Alexis and her face was full of delight. It made CeCe's heart skip a beat to see that look in Alexis's eyes.

"Your happiness is showing, Doc," Erin said to Alexis quietly as they both looked on while the other women asked CeCe about the day.

"CeCe Sloan is amazing. I don't know how in the world I got her to give me a chance, but I'm so glad she did."

"Desi knew it was serious when CeCe told her she made you get a new hairstylist," Erin said. "She had no idea it was you!"

"She did. The woman has boundaries and expects you to respect them."

"Hmm, that sounds like someone else I know. I'd love to hear that story." Erin chuckled.

CeCe Sloan is Swooning

"Everyone come in here and get something to eat," Michael said, walking in from the backyard.

Alexis grinned and shrugged.

* * *

After Alexis introduced CeCe to the guys it didn't take long for her to have them laughing.

Alexis looked on and smiled. If CeCe was nervous or apprehensive it didn't show. Occasionally, she'd look Alexis's way, smile then nod so Alexis knew she was okay. They didn't stay away from each other long. CeCe would move towards her or Alexis would walk over and grab her hand.

"This has been so much fun, babe," CeCe said walking up to Alexis. "Your friends are so nice."

"Don't forget how charming you are, Cecilia. You bring out the best in people," Alexis replied.

"I do? Is that what I've done with you?"

"You've brought out a part of me I didn't even know about. A very good part," Alexis said.

CeCe peeked around them then leaned in and kissed Alexis softly. "I like all the parts of you, Lex. I want it all."

Alexis smiled and took a deep breath. Her heart did that flutter-thing again that CeCe seemed to make it do whenever she felt like it.

"I need water. Do you want a glass?" CeCe asked.

"I can get it for you," Alexis protested.

"No, you've been getting me food and wine all night. It's my turn. I'll be right back."

Alexis watched CeCe walk away and smiled. CeCe turned and winked at her as she went into the kitchen.

"How about that story?" Erin said, sidling up next to Alexis.

"Story?"

"Yeah, the one about CeCe not dating her clients."

"There's no story. She said she didn't date clients and I told her I'd go to Ryan from then on." Alexis laughed.

"I think it says a lot that you were willing to change stylists," Erin commented.

"I really wanted to go out with her."

"It's obvious you make each other happy. Don't let that scare you, Alexis."

"Why do you say that?"

"I know you. Someone like you doesn't remain single unless they want to be," Erin stated.

Alexis nodded. She wasn't afraid, but she wasn't ready to proclaim her love either. She and CeCe both agreed this wasn't a fling, but they were dating. That was enough for now.

Alexis looked on and couldn't help feeling proud of her girlfriend. CeCe was such a wonderful person and her friends were finding it out.

CeCe walked up with a glass of water just as Desi joined Alexis and Erin.

"Hey, Desi, Cory mentioned she has volleyball practice tomorrow. Is the league starting back up?"

"Yep. Are you going to play this year?"

"Oh, I don't know about that. I fill in on her team occasionally when someone can't make it."

"Is the league at your fitness center, Desi?" Alexis asked. "I'm sorry, I can't remember the name of it."

Desi smiled at Alexis. "It's okay. If you'd come work out with us, you'd remember the name," she chuckled. "It's called Your Way."

"Hey!" Erin exclaimed. "You two should come do yoga with me. Stella is the best instructor!"

CeCe Sloan is Swooning 215

"Better than your wife?" Desi asked.

Erin smiled and put her arm around Desi. "Come on, babe. You know Stella is the best yoga teacher around. Your strengths are better in other areas."

"Would those other areas have anything to do with fitness?" CeCe teased.

"Hey now!" Desi exclaimed.

Alexis looked on and appreciated the banter between Erin and Desi. She realized that she and CeCe had that too. Alexis hadn't stopped to think about the fact that she now had a girlfriend. As surprising as it was to her friends, it still surprised Alexis at times. But she didn't just have a girlfriend, her girlfriend was an incredible woman who thought Alexis was incredible, too. Alexis never imagined she'd be in a relationship again, but here she was and she loved it.

25

A lexis pulled away from the curb and smiled at CeCe. "Did you have a good time?"

CeCe grinned. "I had a great time." She reached for Alexis's hand and held it in her lap. This had become the most natural thing for her to do when Alexis was driving.

"I was surprised that several of the guys were interested in me cutting their hair," CeCe said.

"Michael is very conscious of how he looks," Alexis commented.

"Kent—that's Mary's husband, right?"

"Right," Alexis replied.

"He took my number and so did Steve. He's one of the doctors in your clinic," CeCe stated.

"That's right. You remember everyone's names and their partners. Impressive," Alexis said. "Does it bother you that they asked about doing their hair?"

CeCe glanced over at Alexis. "Not at all. You'd be surprised how many clients I've gained from parties and events. Don't people ask doctors about their ailments when they see them in a social setting?"

Alexis nodded. "Yeah, I guess they do. I didn't want anyone to take advantage of the situation."

"Everyone was so nice. And several of the women wanted to help with the spa day event."

"How can they help?" Alexis asked.

"With donations for one. They also want to be there to help with the food and the patients," CeCe added.

"Thank you for going with me," Alexis said.

"I had a good time being there with you, babe," CeCe said, glancing at Alexis.

"And the rest of the weekend is ours," Alexis said happily. She flattened her hand against CeCe's thigh and began to slowly move it under CeCe's dress.

CeCe chuckled. "What do you think you're doing?"

"Getting the best part of the weekend started." Alexis grinned and winked at CeCe.

"Wait until we get home, honey. The last thing we want is to be in a car wreck."

"You're safe with me."

CeCe studied Alexis's profile as she kept her eyes on the road. She was falling in love with Alexis Reed and hoped Alexis would keep her heart safe. CeCe could feel Alexis's heart opening up. Alexis might want to think it was closed off and icy, but not anymore. CeCe wasn't sure Alexis realized it yet, but she would and CeCe planned on holding her tight. Alexis had made CeCe believe she belonged anywhere, especially when they were together.

But am I enough for Alexis? Sometimes the doubts still crept in.

* * *

It had been three weeks since the party at Michael and Lana's, and Alexis and CeCe had not only spent that weekend together, they hadn't spent even one night away from each other since. Sometimes they stayed at CeCe's and other times they stayed at Alexis's.

CeCe was thrilled when Alexis mentioned how her house felt more like a home now that CeCe had some of her things there. In turn, Alexis had several outfits and other things she would need to get ready for work in the mornings at CeCe's place. They had fallen into a routine that suited them both.

CeCe was staring out the window over her kitchen sink at her back yard. As she sipped her coffee she made a mental note to mow the lawn that weekend. Alexis had offered to pay her yard service to do it, but CeCe enjoyed taking care of her yard.

When she was growing up it was her responsibility to help her dad with the yard. She smiled, remembering the days she spent with him making their yard beautiful. He took such pride in having a manicured lawn and shrubs. CeCe wasn't quite as meticulous as her father was, but she did like to sit on her back patio and enjoy the shade from her trees and the scents and beauty of the flowers she planted.

"Your yard looks beautiful, babe," Alexis said, walking up behind her.

"Thanks, but it's time to mow again." CeCe turned around and poured Alexis a cup of coffee.

"Are you ready to treat the oncology patients and nurses to their spa day?" Alexis asked, taking a sip of coffee.

"Yep. I have to go by the salon and pick up all the supplies for me and Cory. She's going to mix tropical mocktails for everyone."

CeCe Sloan is Swooning

"Oh, that sounds like fun."

"Hey, I know you have surgery this morning, but do you think we could have lunch together?"

"Do you get a break from the event?"

"Oh yeah, we take turns and having lunch with you would be a treat for me." CeCe smiled at Alexis and gave her a hopeful look.

"I'll come by when I'm finished. Lunch with you would be a treat for me, too."

Alexis set her coffee cup down and eased CeCe against the sink. She reached down and began to run her hand up CeCe's thigh and under her dress.

CeCe set her cup down and giggled. "Of course you're going to do that since I'm wearing a dress."

Alexis grinned.

"I guess I'll know you're losing interest if you don't run your hand up my thigh when I'm wearing a dress," CeCe said, putting her arms around Alexis's shoulders.

Alexis gave her a sexy look. "How could I ever lose interest in you?"

CeCe giggled as Alexis's hand continued to stroke upward.

"I am performing surgery today and you know you take my stress away so I can concentrate on the patient."

"Hmm, of course I want to do what I can to help your patients," CeCe said, staring into Alexis's eyes. This woman could make her hot with a look. Add in that sultry voice and CeCe couldn't resist. Why would she want to!

CeCe put her arms on Alexis's shoulders and spread her legs a little wider as Alexis eased her hand into CeCe's panties.

"Mmm, I need one of your healing kisses, Dr. Reed," CeCe said breathlessly.

Alexis claimed CeCe's mouth with a searing kiss just as CeCe felt Alexis's fingers begin to roam through her wetness.

"You are amazing, babe," Alexis moaned as she kissed CeCe's neck.

"*You* are," CeCe replied. "Let's go."

With that bit of encouragement and the fact that they both had to leave soon, Alexis's finger circled CeCe's clit with deft precision.

"Oh yeah, baby. Just like that," CeCe groaned.

Alexis began with slow pressure then picked up her rhythm. CeCe squeezed Alexis tighter and held on as she matched Alexis's movements. Moments later CeCe bit down on Alexis's shoulder and could feel the orgasm racing through her. *What a way to start the day!*

CeCe shuddered one more time and looked up into Alexis's eyes. She wanted to tell Alexis she loved her, but CeCe wasn't sure Alexis was ready to hear it.

CeCe smiled and ran her thumb over Alexis's bottom lip. "Good God, doctor."

Alexis smiled. "Thank you for helping my patients."

CeCe smiled. "Anytime."

Alexis pressed her lips to CeCe's in a sweet kiss, but suddenly CeCe didn't want to let her go. She may not be able to say the words, but she could show how she felt in this kiss. CeCe held their lips together and let her tongue caress Alexis with her love.

When they both pulled away and took a deep breath, Alexis shook her head. "Wow, babe."

"You come find me at lunch," CeCe said and winked.

"You can count on it."

* * *

CeCe Sloan is Swooning   221

CeCe put another box into the back of her SUV.

"This should be the last one," Ryan said, sliding another box in the back.

"Thanks for taking care of the salon today, Ryan," CeCe said, closing the rear hatch.

"No problem. You have the cards I gave to you for the patients and nurses?"

CeCe nodded.

"Their hair will come back and I'm happy to give them a free wash, cut and style," Ryan said.

"You'd be surprised how many don't lose their hair anymore. Some chemo treatments don't cause that particular side effect."

"That's even better. I'd love to do their hair."

"You're a good guy." CeCe smiled.

"Hey, CeCe! Pull down here," Cory called from the back door of The Liquor Box.

"Good thing you put the rear seats down," Ryan said.

CeCe grinned. "That's what I love about this SUV. Plenty of room when you need it."

"Have fun. I'll see you when you get back."

CeCe drove the short distance to Cory's back door and opened the rear hatch. She pushed the boxes forward so Cory would have room for her drink supplies.

"I'll be there in a little while to start mixing the mocktails," Cory said, setting one of two boxes in the SUV.

"Okay. This is going to be so much fun."

"Wait," Cat said, wheeling a small dolly with a box on it towards them. "I have a box of books and magazines I thought the women would enjoy while they're getting their treatments."

"Oh, this is great," CeCe said, looking in the box.

"I also have several complementary codes for audiobooks. Maybe we can think of a cute way to raffle them off," Cat said.

"I'm sure we can come up with something."

"I'm waiting on Jessica to come in then I'll join you. I'll be there before lunch."

CeCe nodded. "Thank y'all for always pitching in to make this a special day," CeCe said, hugging each of her sisters.

"Hey, is someone helping you unload all this stuff?" Cat asked.

"Yes, two of Alexis's friends I met at the party will be there as well as Amber, Heather, and Nora from the salon. There's a maintenance man that has helped every year, too."

"Okay then. It looks like you're all set. We'll see you at the hospital," Cory said.

CeCe closed the hatch and headed to the hospital.

Once there her SUV was unloaded, the boxes whisked away to the treatment area of the oncology department, and Erin was waiting as CeCe made it to the space for all the festivities.

"Hi, CeCe," Erin said with a bright smile.

"Well, hey. I didn't expect for you to greet us," CeCe replied.

"I never know how busy my day might become and I wanted to welcome you and your team and thank you once again."

"Thanks, Erin. You know we love doing it. We get as much from the patients as they do from us, probably more. You know what I mean or you wouldn't be running this hospital," CeCe said.

"I see you recruited a few people from Lana's party," Erin said.

"Lana and Tonya were quick to volunteer their time as

CeCe Sloan is Swooning 223

well as money and Lana brought a few friends, too. Alexis's friends have really helped out."

"Aren't they your friends, too?"

CeCe raised her brows and grinned. "I think so."

Erin laughed. "I know exactly how you feel. When Desi and I got together I wasn't sure if her friends would accept me. I don't teach fitness or even work out regularly."

"I thought you wanted us to go to yoga with you?"

"I do, but that doesn't mean I go every week." Erin laughed. "Is Alexis coming by?"

"She's in surgery this morning, but she's coming by for lunch when she's finished," CeCe said with a lilt in her voice.

"And you are excited about it," Erin said.

"I am, but I'm sure you get excited when Desi comes by the hospital to see you."

"You're right. I love it when she pops in."

"I don't ever come to the hospital so it's special to see Alexis in her element," CeCe said.

"I'm sure she's looking forward to lunch with you."

CeCe grinned. "I think so."

"Okay, I'll let you get things set up. I'll try to come by again later," Erin said. "Thanks again."

"It's a joy for us, Erin. See you later."

CeCe helped the others get things set up and when the first patients arrived, Lana and her friends got them coffee while Amber, Heather, and Nora got to work on the manis and pedis. CeCe looked on with such joy. It was hectic getting everyone there with their supplies, but it was always worth it.

The stylists did the patients' nails while they were receiving their infusions, then CeCe had contacted a couple of massage therapists who took over after that. They didn't give complete massages, but they were able to work on calves, feet, and arms. The patients and nurses seemed to love it.

CeCe passed out magazines, puzzle books, and coloring books as well as novels to the patients who were interested. She told them about the mocktails Cory would be making and the food a local restaurant was providing for lunch.

Patients that weren't scheduled for treatment that day also came to enjoy the event. The nurses, staff, and even the doctors were all included.

CeCe breathed a sigh of relief as everything got started and she saw smiles on their faces and could hear the sweet sounds of laughter.

"Hey, CeCe," Heather said. "Have you seen the box with the nurses' gift baskets in them? I wanted to put a few nail coupons in them."

"It should be with the rest of the boxes. Let's look over here." CeCe and Heather walked over to the far side of the room where the boxes were stacked out of the way since they had been unloaded.

"I'm not finding it," Heather said.

CeCe quickly texted Ryan and a few moments later he replied. "It's on the table in the back room," CeCe said, reading the text out loud. "All the boxes were stacked by the back door when I got there this morning. I must have missed it. No problem. I'll run back and get it."

"Are you sure?"

"Yes! We were going to present them during lunch. I have plenty of time to get back before then. I'd ask Cory or Cat, but they just texted me that they're already here and on the way up. Show Cory where her make-shift bar is and I'll be back."

"Okay, I'll tell them."

26

CeCe hurried back to the salon and went in the back door. Sitting on the table was the missing box with the gift baskets inside. She shook her head and sighed. "Way to go, Cecilia. That's exactly where you left it last night when you finished packing it."

"Hey," Ryan said, coming in from the salon. "How are things going?"

"Great. Everything was just getting started when we realized this box was missing."

"There's someone out here that would love to say hello to you," Ryan said.

CeCe looked at her watch and quickly walked into the salon.

"There you are," Dottie Eubanks said with a smile.

"Well, hi, Dottie. We don't have an appointment today," CeCe said, hoping she hadn't misread her appointment book.

"No, honey. I came by to get a bottle of wine from your sister." Dottie giggled. "I giggle every time I say the name of her store."

CeCe chuckled. "It is funny."

"Anyway, I just wanted to come by to say hello and Ryan said you were gone to your spa day you do for the patients at the hospital."

"I was. I left something in the back and came to get it."

"That is such a good thing you do. Here," Dottie said, rummaging in her purse. She handed CeCe a one hundred dollar bill.

"Dottie!"

"You remind me next year when you're getting ready for it and I'll give you more," she said.

CeCe tilted her head then gave Dottie a hug. "Thank you."

"My daughter had cancer and I sat with her when she had her chemo treatments. You gave her the cutest style when her hair grew back."

"I remember that," CeCe said. "She was at the spa day and Nora did her nails."

"That's right. She still remembers your kindness."

CeCe smiled and nodded.

"Go on, now," Dottie said. "I didn't mean to hold you up. Those women are waiting on you."

"Thank you, Dottie," CeCe said. "I'll see you next week."

"You sure will."

CeCe smiled at Ryan as she left through the back of the salon. As she hurried back to the hospital, she wondered how many women had experienced the annual spa day. They had been doing it for eight years now and each year they tried to add something to make it even better.

With the donations from Alexis's friends, they were able to make sure each nurse in the department received a gift basket this year. The same gift baskets which were now in the back of her SUV. She glanced into the rearview mirror

CeCe Sloan is Swooning 227

and could see them stacked in the box. A quick glance at the clock on her dash and she knew she had plenty of time to get back to the event.

A smile grew on CeCe's face as she thought about having lunch with Alexis. She was looking forward to showing Alexis what the spa day was all about. Just then she heard an engine roar and looked in her rearview mirror then back to the front. Out of the corner of her eye she saw a blur.

"Oh shit!"

* * *

CeCe tried to open her eyes. She could hear beeping and someone talking. What was that pounding in her head? She was moving, but she wasn't driving. Then she remembered. Her eyes opened.

"Hey, just stay still. We're taking you to the hospital," a kind voice said.

CeCe looked around her then back to the paramedic who had spoken to her. *The hospital. Alexis!*

"M–m–my..." CeCe stuttered.

"It's okay. You've been in a car accident. Someone hit you," the paramedic said. "You've got a nasty bump on your head."

CeCe tried to nod, but the pain was excruciating and she winced.

"Easy, Ms. Sloan," the paramedic said.

"I'm CeCe," CeCe said hoarsely.

The paramedic smiled. "They're going to take good care of you at the hospital."

CeCe felt the ambulance stop then change direction. The doors opened and the kind paramedic began saying words that CeCe couldn't keep up with or quite comprehend.

They rolled her into the hospital and she closed her eyes at the bright lights. Suddenly they stopped and she opened her eyes and looked around. She was in a small room and people were busy hooking her up to things and examining her. CeCe reached out and grabbed one of their arms until they looked her in the eye.

"I need you to get Dr. Alexis Reed," CeCe said.

"Uh, we'll get Dr. Reed if it's necessary, but we need to finish examining you first," the woman said.

"She's my girlfriend," CeCe said, struggling to get the words out.

"Did you hear that?" the woman said to another person on the other side of CeCe. "She said she's Dr. Reed's girlfriend."

CeCe took a breath as a wave of pain washed over her. She opened her eyes and looked into a familiar face.

"CeCe," Erin said. "They're going to take good care of you. I'll get Alexis."

CeCe smiled. "Thank you." She closed her eyes and felt Erin grasp her hand.

"Page Dr. Reed and bring her to me," Erin said in a commanding voice. "You're going to be okay, CeCe," she said softly.

CeCe believed her. "I just want Alexis."

"We'll find her."

Suddenly the pain began to subside. CeCe opened her eyes and Erin was still there. "I feel better."

Erin smiled. "They gave you something for the pain."

"The baskets?" CeCe said, suddenly remembering why she was coming to the hospital. "The nurses' baskets were in the back of my car."

"We'll get the baskets. Don't worry about them."

CeCe nodded.

"I'm going to wait for Alexis while they get you ready to take upstairs. We need a CT scan of your head," Erin said. She bent down a little closer to CeCe and said softly, "I'm in the way, but I'll be right over there. I won't leave you."

"Thank you," CeCe said, not daring to move her head. "I want Lex," she said softly with tears in her eyes.

"I know." Erin smiled and backed away.

Alexis got off on the oncology floor still dressed in her scrubs. Her surgery had taken a little longer than she planned, but it went well and her patient should make a full recovery. The waiting area was full of activity as she looked for CeCe. Her beautiful red hair was easy to spot, but she wasn't anywhere in sight. She saw Cory mixing drinks at a little bar and Cat, Lana, and Tonya were passing them out.

There was a buffet line set up, ready for lunch to start. Alexis recognized a couple of nurses and continued to scan the room when the elevator opened. She turned around to find one of her co-workers smiling.

"Hi, Dawn," Alexis said. "I saw your wife over there."

"Hi, Alexis. I thought I'd come by and see how things were going and maybe help out."

Alexis saw Cory wave at her and started that way. "See you later, Dawn."

"Hey," Cory said. "Can I get you a mocktail? They are very tasty if I do say so myself."

Alexis chuckled. "I'm sure they are. Wow, y'all have really transformed this place. It looks great. You can't tell it's a hospital. Well, almost."

Cory laughed. "Yeah, it does look nice though. The patients and nurses are having a great time."

"Hey, Alexis," Cat said, walking over to them.

"Hi. I was just telling Cory how great this is."

"Yeah, everyone is smiling. Even patients that don't have treatment today are here. It's so cool," Cat said.

"Hey, where's my beautiful girlfriend? We're hoping to have lunch together."

"She ran back to the salon to get something that was left behind," Cory said.

"She should've been back by now," Cat added, looking at her watch.

"Here, Alexis. Try this," Cory said.

Alexis took a sip of the drink and nodded. "This is good."

"Told you!"

"There's Heather," Cory said, waving her over. "Maybe CeCe texted her."

"Hi," Alexis said to Heather. "Do you know where CeCe is?"

"She went back to the salon, but I haven't seen her since. Is she not back?" Heather asked.

"I'll go look in the treatment room. She could be with a patient," Cat said and walked away.

Alexis's heart began to beat a little faster. She took out her phone and called CeCe. It rang several times then went to voicemail. Alexis didn't bother leaving a message. She disconnected the call and quickly texted CeCe. No answer. Where could she be? Something didn't feel right. *Calm down. You're a doctor, remember? You don't get rattled.*

Cat came back from the treatment room and shook her head. "She wasn't in there."

Alexis wasn't sure what to do next when she heard her

CeCe Sloan is Swooning

231

name being called over the PA System. She was being paged to the emergency department.

"Go! They must need you," Cory said.

"We'll find her and I'll text you," Cat said.

Alexis gave them a forced smile and nodded then hurried to the elevator.

* * *

Alexis walked towards the desk in the ER, but before she reached it, Erin intersected her path.

"Hey," Alexis said, confused. What was the hospital administrator doing in the emergency department? "Are your kids all right?"

Erin nodded and pulled her towards one of the treatment rooms. "It's CeCe. She's been in a car wreck."

Alexis felt all the blood rush out of her body. Her heart began to pound. "Where is she!" Alexis demanded.

"Hold on," Erin said, grabbing Alexis's upper arms. "They are about to take her upstairs for a CT. She hit her head."

Alexis stared at Erin and listened to her words, but it sounded like she was far away. *Oh God! CeCe had to be all right.*

"Take a breath," Erin said in a low, tense voice. "You don't have to be a doctor at this moment. She needs her girlfriend."

Alexis did as Erin said and took a deep breath then let it out. "I'm okay, I'm okay."

Erin smiled. "Right this way."

Alexis walked into the exam room and all eyes turned to her. She didn't notice because all she could see was the woman she loved. Alexis grabbed CeCe's hand and bent down to look into her face.

CeCe slowly opened her eyes and when she saw Alexis she tried to smile. "Hi, baby. I'm so glad to see you."

Alexis gave CeCe her best smile. She hoped it gave CeCe a sense of relief and calm. "You're not supposed to *be* a patient. I thought we were having lunch," Alexis said, trying to ease the tension. "We're going up to radiology to do a scan of your head."

"We?" CeCe asked.

Alexis nodded. "You don't think I'm going to let someone else hold your hand, do you?"

CeCe smiled.

"We need to go, Dr. Reed," the attending doctor said.

Alexis nodded. She bent down and kissed CeCe gently on the lips.

"That's good medicine, Doc," CeCe said.

Alexis walked beside the gurney as they wheeled CeCe into the elevator. Erin stepped in and punched the button for the radiology floor.

"Why was the hospital administrator in the ER?" Alexis asked, looking at Erin.

"I happened to be doing a walk-through and I heard this woman say that Dr. Alexis Reed was her girlfriend," Erin said, smiling down at CeCe. "I had seen CeCe upstairs earlier at the spa event and I couldn't imagine it was her."

"How many girlfriends do you think I have?" Alexis asked.

"One!" CeCe spoke up. "Me!"

27

Alexis sat beside CeCe's bed and watched her sleep. She had been fooling herself about being in love with CeCe. When she couldn't find CeCe at the spa event an uneasy feeling ran through her. Alexis was rarely paged to the ER, so that added to her anxiety.

When she walked into the ER and Erin told her CeCe had been hurt, all her finely honed professionalism and mastered ability to remain calm flew away. All she could think about was getting to CeCe, seeing her with her own eyes, touching her, holding her...loving her. *I love CeCe Sloan.*

Alexis kissed the back of CeCe's hand and smiled at her sleeping face. "I love you so much, Cecilia," Alexis whispered softly.

CeCe stirred and moaned. Her eyelids fluttered open and when she found Alexis she smiled. "I fell asleep."

Alexis nodded and gave her a sweet smile. "How do you feel?"

"Have you been with me the entire time?"

"Where else would I be?"

Alexis watched as CeCe narrowed her eyes and she could see her wrestling with something.

"What is it, babe?" Alexis asked.

"I had the strangest dream just now," CeCe said. "You were telling me…"

Alexis smiled. She stood up and leaned over CeCe. "I didn't expect to tell you this for the first time while you're in a hospital, but—I love you, CeCe."

CeCe smirked. "You're saying that because I scared you."

Alexis looked at her wide-eyed then a slow smile grew on her face. She bent down and kissed CeCe tenderly. "I'm in love with you, CeCe Sloan. Believe it." Alexis had to chuckle inside. Not only did she believe she'd never utter those words to anyone again, but now that she'd said them, CeCe didn't believe her.

"This isn't a dream? Or these are very good pain meds they gave me, right?" CeCe said.

"No, baby. I've said it twice now."

"One more kiss and I might believe you," CeCe said.

Alexis grinned and softly kissed CeCe once again. When she pulled away CeCe was looking at her with such love.

CeCe cupped the side of Alexis's face with one hand. "I love you, too, Lex."

Before Alexis could say anything Cory and Cat came into the room.

"Hey sis, how are you feeling?" Cat asked.

"Better. What happened with the spa event? Did everything go okay?"

"Yes. After we went back upstairs and told everyone what happened, Lana and Tonya took over. They are a force," Cory said.

Alexis smiled. "I'm not surprised."

CeCe's CT scan showed she'd suffered a concussion.

CeCe Sloan is Swooning   235

When they went back to the ER Cory and Cat were waiting in her examination room. CeCe had given them instructions on what needed to be done then the medication they'd given her began to kick in. Cory and Cat had gone back to the spa event and Alexis stayed with CeCe.

"Are they going to let you go home?" Cat asked.

They all looked at Alexis. "I think so," she replied. "They wanted to keep you for a while for observation and your vitals have been good."

"Surely they'll let me go home with a doctor," CeCe said with a grin.

"I haven't been a doctor since I walked into the ER and saw you in this bed."

"I'm sorry I scared you, baby," CeCe said.

Alexis smiled and squeezed her hand.

"We haven't called Mom," Cory said. "She's going to be mad if we don't let her know what happened."

"I don't want her to worry," CeCe said. "I'll call her when we get home."

"We're going back upstairs to clean everything up. Heather said you brought all the boxes in your SUV," Cory said.

"I did."

"It's okay. Cory and I have plenty of room in my car," Cat said. "Text us when they release you."

"Okay. Sorry I messed all this up," CeCe said, smiling at her sisters.

"What! You didn't mess this up. The asshole that sped through that red light messed it up. Thank God you're all right," Cory said.

"I will be. I have a doctor who I'm sure will give me tender loving care." CeCe grinned at Alexis.

"Nope," Alexis replied, shaking her head. "You have a

girlfriend who loves you and will take very good care of you."

CeCe saw Cory and Cat share a surprised look.

CeCe chuckled. "Can you believe it, sisters! The hot Doc loves me."

Cory and Cat laughed. "Of course we can believe it. We didn't know y'all had finally figured it out," Cory said.

"At least something good came out of this," Cat said, elbowing Cory. "We'd better go. We'll talk to you later."

* * *

The ER doctor walked into CeCe's exam room. "Dr. Ames," Alexis said with a nod.

CeCe could tell from Alexis's body language that she didn't care for the doctor.

Dr. Ames studied his tablet then looked at CeCe. "How is your pain?"

"Much better."

"Your numbers look good, so I think it will be safe to send you home with your *girlfriend*," Dr. Ames said snobbishly.

"Surely, you're not disrespecting the renowned Dr. Alexis Reed," CeCe said. "You couldn't send me home with better care."

Dr. Ames bristled. "My apologies, Ms. Sloan." He turned to Alexis. "Sorry, Alexis. I didn't mean anything." He shrugged.

"Sure you did, Tom. I know my reputation around here," Alexis said.

"But not anymore," CeCe stated with a grin. "There are going to be a lot of sad doctors and nurses around here."

Alexis chuckled, still holding CeCe's hand.

CeCe Sloan is Swooning 237

Dr. Ames looked at them both and smiled. He went over CeCe's release instructions and answered their questions before leaving the room.

"You don't like him, do you?" CeCe said to Alexis.

"He's kind of arrogant."

"Really?" CeCe said playfully.

Alexis laughed. "I'm not *that* arrogant."

"Are they going to let you go home?" Erin asked, sticking her head in the room.

"Yes!" CeCe exclaimed.

A nurse came in to take CeCe's IV out and get her ready to go home so Alexis stepped outside the room with Erin.

"I'm glad she's okay," Erin said.

"Me too! That was scary," Alexis said. She put her hand on Erin's shoulder and earnestly said, "Thank you for calming me down. It was like all my training went right out the window when you told me CeCe was hurt."

"I could see it on your face."

"It certainly made me realize how deeply I've fallen for CeCe."

Erin smiled. "You haven't fallen all by yourself, pal. CeCe's in love with you, too."

Alexis grinned.

"Y'all are the talk of the ER," Erin said quietly.

"What?"

"CeCe asked for you by name and the nurse said they needed to examine you before a surgeon was called in." Erin chuckled. "Then she said you were her girlfriend. The nurse looked at her like that bump on the head had her dreaming."

"Aww, my poor baby," Alexis said.

"That's when I heard her and went into the room."

"So you had me paged?" Alexis asked.

Erin nodded. "She needed you."

Alexis smiled just as the nurse came out of her room.

"She's ready to go home," the nurse said.

* * *

CeCe reclined against the pillows Alexis had meticulously fluffed for her. She sighed. "Thank you, babe."

Alexis sat on the bed next to CeCe and smiled down at her. "Are you comfortable?"

"Yes, honey. Thank you for taking care of me."

Alexis tilted her head. "I love you. Of course I'm going to take care of you."

CeCe's phone rang and Alexis reached for it on the bed next to her.

"It's your mom," Alexis said as she looked at the caller ID then handed the phone to CeCe.

"Hi, Mom," CeCe said. "We just got home. I'm feeling much better."

While CeCe listened she ran her hand up and down Alexis's thigh. Having her near made CeCe feel better.

"Alexis is taking good care of me," CeCe said. "Sure, she's right here." CeCe put the phone on speaker. "We can both hear you, Mom."

"Do I need to bring you anything?" Christine's voice echoed from the phone.

"No ma'am. I'm taking good care of your daughter. I want you to know that I'm in love with her and I'm not going to leave her side."

CeCe's eyebrows flew up her forehead. She wasn't expecting Alexis to proclaim her love so publicly.

"Well, that's good to hear, but I'm still her momma and if you need me I can be there in five minutes," Christine said.

CeCe Sloan is Swooning

"I'll always need you, Mom. But don't worry, Alexis will take care of me tonight. I'll come see you tomorrow."

"Okay. Thank you, Alexis."

"See you tomorrow, Christine."

CeCe ended the call and stared at Alexis. "Are you telling everyone you're in love with me?"

Alexis grinned. "Is there something wrong with that?"

"No," CeCe replied. She smiled up at Alexis with sadness in her eyes.

"What's wrong?" Alexis asked concerned. "Don't you believe me?"

"Yes, babe. I believe you and I love you, too."

"But?"

"I worry that I won't be enough for you," CeCe said quietly.

"What!" Alexis exclaimed. "CeCe, you are so full of life. I'm not exciting and fun."

"That's not true, Lex. You may be the serious surgeon to everyone else, but I see you! I see the romantic woman who takes me on rooftop dates. I see the kid in you who loves to eat ice cream cones with me."

"I'm also the woman who loves you and is going to mow your lawn this weekend."

"What? You're a surgeon. You don't do lawns," CeCe said.

"I've never done it before, but you're going to sit on the back porch while I mow. I am a surgeon, but I'm your girlfriend and partner first. Don't you remember this morning?"

"My partner?" CeCe said softly. *This just keeps getting better,* she thought.

"We were looking out the kitchen window this morning and I told you how beautiful the backyard looks."

"Oh!" CeCe nodded. "Yeah, I remember that, but we can get someone to mow it."

"No, baby. I want to do it. I know why mowing the lawn and working in the yard is important to you. You used to do that with your dad and now I want to do it with you."

Tears pooled in CeCe's eyes. "How do you know that?"

"I knew there was something special about it when you wouldn't let me have my lawn service do your yard. So I asked Cory and she told me it was something you did with your dad."

"Lex..."

"You'll have to show me how to start the mower and what to do because I've never done something like that before. It could be fun and I'll be doing it with you," Alexis said.

"Mowing isn't really fun. Gazing at your beautiful lawn and flowers is fun when you know you've made it look like that."

"I want to do this with you, CeCe. It's a way to show my love."

"Alexis Reed!"

"Wait! Before you swoon, you need to realize you are now stuck with going to stuffy hospital galas with me."

CeCe smiled and shook her head. "Will Erin and Desi be there?"

Alexis nodded. "You'll be charming the board of directors and donors while I look at you with all my love."

CeCe laughed.

"You're so much more than enough, Cecilia. I've been in love with you since the day we started seriously flirting at your open house. No one tells me the conditions to go on a date. But you did and I knew right then I was falling for you. But..."

"But?"

"But I couldn't trust my heart because it had been closed

CeCe Sloan is Swooning 241

off for so long. How about we both stop being afraid and let our hearts love each other and see what happens."

"I want to show you how much I love you, Lex. But I can't right now," CeCe said.

Alexis gave her the biggest smile. "We're so much more than sex, babe. Tonight, we've got big plans."

"We do?"

Alexis nodded. "The restaurant at the spa event heard what happened to you and they're delivering food any minute," Alexis said, looking at her watch. "We're going to eat and laze in this bed and watch *Top Chef* and *Tournament of Champions* until you fall asleep in my arms."

"Lexie, you're going to make me cry. *Top Chef* and *Tournament of Champions*!"

"Oh baby," Alexis cooed. "I love you."

CeCe had never felt this loved. She couldn't believe she'd been run over by a truck and Alexis Reed had declared her love for her all in one day.

28

CeCe sat on the back porch and watched as Alexis grinned while she pushed the lawnmower from the back fence up to the patio. It was the last strip and Alexis had smiled and waved at CeCe the entire time. It had been two days since her car wreck and Alexis had been with her the whole time, rarely letting her out of her sight.

The surprising part was that CeCe didn't mind. She usually liked having a little time to herself, but that seemed to change since falling in love with Alexis Reed. They could spend the evening doing nothing, simply being together, and it made CeCe happy.

Alexis stopped the lawnmower and turned the engine off. "Wow!" she said loudly. "That was fun. I think next time I want to try and do a diagonal pattern."

"You're yelling, babe."

"Oh!" Alexis grinned.

"Do you smile while you're doing surgery?"

"What?"

"You were smiling the entire time you went up and down and around this yard," CeCe said.

CeCe Sloan is Swooning

"There is a sense of balance and precision to following the lines," Alexis replied. "It gives me a feeling of contentment. To answer your question, no, I am not always smiling while I'm doing surgery. I'm concentrating. It's like solving a puzzle."

"Or taking things apart and putting them back together again?" CeCe asked.

"Yeah, it's kind of like that." Alexis smiled.

CeCe reached for Alexis's hand and pulled her down into her lap.

"I'm all sweaty!" Alexis exclaimed.

"Do you know what else you take apart and put back together?"

"What?" Alexis replied, curling her arm around CeCe's shoulder.

"Me. That's kind of what it feels like when we make love. You take all the problems or the bad of the day away and there's only goodness. You make me a puddle of love in your arms then you put me back together," CeCe explained.

Alexis smiled. "We haven't done that in a few days, but seeing your smile can erase any bad part of my day. That's why I like to begin and end each day with you. I was so excited to have lunch with you the other day because I didn't have to wait until the end of the day to see you."

CeCe wrinkled her nose. "Sorry that didn't work out like we planned. I'll have lunch with you next week. I set my own schedule."

Alexis tilted her head. "I didn't think about that. We could have lunch every week."

CeCe nodded. The delight in Alexis's face made her heart melt.

"Our very own lunch date."

"Babe, it's just lunch. No rooftops. We have to go back to work after," CeCe pointed out.

Alexis chuckled. "Oh, now you really have my mind thinking."

"You know," CeCe said, raising one eyebrow, "when I was in the ER it didn't escape me that you could've snuck into the supply closet with any of those nurses or doctors. Maybe that's why the nurse was so surprised when I said you were my girlfriend."

Alexis tightened her hold on CeCe. "You know my past, but it has been a very long time since I did anything like that at the hospital. A very long time," Alexis repeated.

CeCe laughed. "It doesn't matter because you're mine now." CeCe pulled Alexis down into a firm kiss. "I'm feeling much better."

CeCe pushed Alexis up and she got out of her chair. She took Alexis's hand, led them into the house and to the bathroom. CeCe reached in and started the shower then turned to Alexis. She began to take her clothes off and threw the sweaty garments into a pile. "Let's get you nice and clean."

Alexis stepped into the shower and CeCe pulled off the T-shirt dress she was wearing and shimmied out of her undies. She walked into the shower and began to wash Alexis's hair.

"Ohhh, it's been so long since you washed my hair." Alexis groaned with pleasure.

"I can't tell you how much it means to me that you wanted to mow the yard and not pay someone to do it," CeCe said, continuing to massage Alexis's scalp. "Lean back and close your eyes."

While she rinsed Alexis's hair CeCe said, "I've been thinking, my dad is gone and I'd rather do something new with you. Would it be all right if you had your lawn people

CeCe Sloan is Swooning

mow and trim my lawn and we will take care of the flowers?"

Alexis raised her head and looked into CeCe's eyes. "Are you sure? I don't mind doing it with you."

"I know you don't, but it doesn't sit right with me to watch a person of your talents mow a frigging lawn. I'd rather us get our hands dirty together in the flower beds." CeCe took the bath sponge and squirted body wash on it and began to soap Alexis's skin. "These beautiful fingers and hands," she said, working the suds between them, "are for more important things than pushing a lawnmower."

Alexis grinned. "Let me show you what they love to do most." CeCe felt Alexis slide her soapy hands over her breasts.

"I know what they love," CeCe said. "Turn around."

Alexis stared at her.

"Please," CeCe said firmly.

Alexis pouted but did as she was told.

CeCe quickly ran the sponge over her back then washed a little lower. She slid her hand over Alexis's bare skin and moaned softly. "You are so fucking beautiful, babe."

Alexis leaned into CeCe's hand for a moment.

"Okay, rinse off," CeCe said, stepping out of the shower.

"Where are you going?"

Once she'd turned the water off, CeCe held a towel open for Alexis to step into.

"If you'll dry off a little, we're not going far," CeCe said.

Alexis took the towel and squeezed the excess water out of her hair then dried her body. CeCe had quickly dried herself and smiled as she watched Alexis.

"Now, let me show you just how much your kind gesture means to me, my love." CeCe took Alexis's hand and led them to the bed. She pushed Alexis down and stood above her.

CeCe's eyes roamed up and down Alexis's body. "Mmmm, you love me," she said with a hint of disbelief in her voice.

"I do," Alexis stated, "so much."

"I've been in love with you for a while, Lex, but I knew I had to be patient," CeCe said, crawling on the bed and straddling Alexis. "The day of the accident, that morning, at the kitchen sink..."

"I remember," Alexis said with a huskiness to her voice.

"I had to bite my tongue not to say 'I love you' after you kissed me."

Alexis smiled and ran her hands up and down CeCe's thighs.

"But now I can say it whenever I feel like it, which is all the time." CeCe smiled down at her beautiful girlfriend.

"I didn't think I could trust my heart, but I can. My heart is full of love for you and it keeps growing every day."

"Just because I can say the words doesn't mean I'm going to stop showing you." CeCe leaned over Alexis and gave her a sexy smile. "You mean everything to me, Lex. Let me show you how much I love you."

CeCe pressed her lips to Alexis's in a soft kiss that immediately grew in intensity. She pulled away, trying to get a breath. When she saw the look of concern in Alexis's eyes she smiled. "I'm fine. You take my breath away."

"I love you so much, Cecilia."

CeCe gazed down at the most beautiful woman she'd ever seen. The fresh fragrances from their shower mingled with the desire that permeated the room. Love was everywhere and CeCe wanted to bathe them in their love.

She started with kisses below Alexis's ear. CeCe knew

every inch of Alexis's body, but this was like discovering it all over again. She loved to hear the gasps and feel the goosebumps or shudders under her fingertips.

"I love you," Alexis whispered as CeCe continued with little kisses down her neck and across her chest.

CeCe could feel Alexis's chest rise and fall as she kissed lower. She cupped both of Alexis's breasts in her hands then moaned as her lips took one of Alexis's nipples into her mouth.

"Oh, God, baby," Alexis gasped. "Love me."

CeCe smiled as both of them kept saying the word over and over. Love here, love there, love me, love you, it was all love.

She continued to lavish both of Alexis's breasts with her mouth and tongue. Had they ever had this much fun making love? CeCe could feel Alexis's fingers combing through her wet hair and her lips kissed lower and lower still.

"I'm filling you with my love," she whispered across Alexis's stomach.

Alexis responded by raising her hips urging CeCe lower. "I love you," Alexis continued to whisper between moans and gasps.

CeCe inhaled deeply the scents of love emanating from them both. She peeked upward to catch a glimpse of her lover's euphoric face, but Alexis captured her gaze with the most sensual brown eyes full of love for her.

CeCe paused for a moment to answer Alexis's stare with her own intense look. She felt Alexis brush a strand of her hair from her face then they both slightly smiled. A moment later CeCe was running her tongue through the wettest, most luscious folds.

Alexis was a gorgeous woman, but when she groaned

with delight and urgency from a touch with CeCe's magical tongue she was beyond beautiful. CeCe loved how Alexis expressed herself with movement, touches, and sounds. They had never been tentative when it came to their bodies and CeCe was able to express her love openly and freely.

Now they both knew it wasn't just sex, and honestly it had been like that for some time. But today it was pure, open, exposed love.

CeCe ran her hands under Alexis's hips so Alexis's legs were on her shoulders. She caressed, kissed, and licked with her tongue until Alexis writhed underneath her. Then CeCe ran her hands around and held onto Alexis as she began to push with her shoulders and sucked Alexis into her mouth. They couldn't get close enough.

CeCe could feel Alexis's fingers in her hair as they tightened into a fist. She heard Alexis pound the bed with her other hand and shout, "Good God! I love you, CeCe!"

She held Alexis firm with both her hands and let her tongue lavish her clit as she sucked even harder.

The sound that came out of Alexis was the most bliss-filled moan CeCe had ever heard. It was like the most beautiful symphony, her favorite melody, and a heart piercing affirmation of love all rolled into one harmony only they could comprehend.

CeCe eased Alexis back down onto the bed and took a deep breath to enjoy the moment. Then she looked up to see Alexis, her half-dry dark hair fanned over the pillow. She took in this glorious sight as her eyes gazed at Alexis's parted luscious lips, her perfect nose, then rested on those dark brown eyes once again.

"I gave all I am to you," Alexis said softly with tears in her eyes.

CeCe nodded. "I've got you. I promise, you can trust me, Lex."

Alexis gave her the most beautiful smile. "I know." She reached up and cupped the side of CeCe's face with one hand.

"I love you, baby," CeCe murmured, sinking into Alexis's hand.

Alexis smiled, raised up and pushed CeCe onto her back. "I love you, Cecilia, and you're going to know it in every touch, every kiss, and every word."

CeCe smiled and opened her heart and her body. She wanted all of Alexis's love.

29

It had been a couple of months since CeCe's accident. She had a new SUV, there were no lasting effects from the concussion, and she'd welcomed several new clients from the hospital and even a couple of Alexis's friends.

They had been to two more of Michael and Lana's little get-togethers and CeCe was welcomed like she'd been there all along.

One evening she and Alexis were enjoying an ice cream cone on their bench, that's what they called it, at the diner next to the salon.

"I know it's boring, but vanilla is my favorite," Alexis said, taking another lick around the ice cream on her cone.

CeCe chuckled. "There is nothing boring about you, my love. Including your ice cream preference."

Alexis giggled. That little sound had become one of CeCe's favorites.

"Hey, babe. Have you noticed it has been over a month since we've stayed at your house?"

CeCe Sloan is Swooning 251

Alexis continued to lick her ice cream and shrugged. "I guess it has been a while."

"It leads me to the question: why do we have two houses?"

"Hmm, I don't know. I'll sell mine," Alexis said matter-of-factly.

"Whoa! Don't you like your house?"

"Not necessarily. I told you a long time ago it's just a house. Your place is home." She looked over at CeCe. "Our home."

CeCe smiled. "Are you sure? We could buy another house."

"You love your house and I do, too," Alexis said.

"But is it big enough?"

Alexis laughed. "We have been living in it."

"If you sell yours won't you be bringing more stuff to ours?"

"I suppose."

"What would you need if we made that our permanent home?"

"I have things in my office I need to bring. Would you share your office space with me?"

"All I need is a drawer. I don't really need an office. I just set that room up to look like an office because I didn't know what else to do with it. We have a spare bedroom if anyone comes to visit us."

Alexis chuckled. "Okay then, I'll make it my office because I do need more than a drawer."

"Perfect. We need more room for all your clothes," CeCe said, taking a bite of her cone.

"All *my* clothes? You have more clothes than I do," Alexis said.

CeCe laughed. "How about we buy new bedroom furniture? We'd have more room and we can clean out our closets. I want this to be our house, not you moving into my house."

"It can be your house until you're sure," Alexis said.

"What?"

"I know doubts still filter in sometimes. I'll sell my house so you don't have to worry about losing yours. And I will keep going to sleep every night with you in my arms and I'll wake up every morning in yours until the doubts go away. Just so you know, I'll be in your arms forever. I'm living our happily-ever-after."

CeCe nearly dropped what was left of her ice cream cone.

"It's okay, babe. I'm all yours. Forever." Alexis smiled.

CeCe grabbed Alexis behind the neck and pulled her lips to hers. She kissed Alexis with all the love, joy, and happiness they'd experienced together so far.

"Honey, I want what they're having," a woman said as she walked by.

CeCe and Alexis pulled apart in time for a man to grin at them as he held the door to the diner open for his wife.

They both giggled and licked their ice cream.

"Do you ever have doubts?" CeCe asked tentatively.

"About us? None," Alexis said, taking a bite of her cone. "We're going to be sitting on our bench eating ice cream cones when we're eighty, baby. Just you and me." Alexis winked and popped the last bite of her cone in her mouth.

Alexis was right. From time to time, rarely now, but occasionally, CeCe did doubt that she'd be enough for Alexis. Her old fear that she wouldn't fit in with Alexis's life was non-existent because they fit perfectly together. Their friends had meshed together and they were living a happy life together. CeCe realized Alexis was right, they were living their happily-ever-after.

How could she doubt that!

An idea began to take shape in the back of her mind.

"Let's go home, babe," Alexis said, standing up and reaching for CeCe's hand.

CeCe took it and followed Alexis back to the salon. *This was going to be fun!*

Selling Alexis's house not only consolidated their stuff, it expanded their friends circle.

CeCe enlisted her realtor friend, Marina Summit, from Make It Easy Designs to sell Alexis's house and Marina's business partner, Victoria Stratton, happened to be a friend of Alexis's.

Marina invited them to a pool party she had for the business and they became friends with the rest of the Make It Easy Designs' team. It turned out that CeCe had done several of the crew's hair and Alexis had been the surgeon for a few family members. What a small world.

It didn't take long to sell the house and CeCe and Alexis enjoyed creating their home together. They were both surprised when they agreed on furniture the first time they went shopping.

After they both went through their closets and donated the clothes they no longer wore, they had plenty of room at CeCe's. Alexis set up the office to her liking with a small desk for CeCe which was all she needed.

Once they were finished moving all of Alexis's stuff, arranging the new furniture, freshening up the living room, and planting fall flowers in the backyard, the transformation was complete. It didn't feel or look like CeCe's house any longer. It truly felt like their home.

"Do we have plans for tonight?" Alexis asked CeCe as they got in her SUV.

CeCe didn't think Saturday would ever get here. She had a surprise for Alexis that would take up their evening and night. "Uh, not really. Was there something you wanted to do after we finished with our errands?" CeCe cut her eyes toward Alexis.

Alexis reached over and grabbed CeCe's hand and held it in her lap.

CeCe smiled at the gesture. It didn't matter who was driving, most of the time one of them reached for the other's hand.

Alexis sighed. "I love our home and to me, the best nights are when we're together in our home sweet home."

"Wow, babe. When did you get so sentimental? I didn't think it mattered where we lived."

"It didn't until we made that *our* home together. Who knew!" Alexis exclaimed. "You have opened up all kinds of emotions in me and I love every one, even the ones where I miss you when I'm at work." Alexis paused. "Wait just a second while I throw up a little in my mouth because I can't believe I said something so frigging sappy."

CeCe burst out laughing. "Don't worry, I won't tell anyone. Besides, I like sappy Lex. She's all mine."

"All of me is yours. Are you sure you're still up for it?" Alexis teased.

CeCe kissed the back of Alexis's hand. "I'm all in, honey."

Alexis smiled and gazed out the window. CeCe glanced over at her and her heart skipped a beat. Her sisters were helping with this surprise and she hoped they were ready.

CeCe Sloan is Swooning

CeCe pulled into the Salon 411 parking lot and waited for Alexis to come to the front of her SUV.

"Let's go to Cory's store first. She ordered something for me," CeCe said, walking towards The Liquor Box.

"Ordered something? What'd you get? Wine?" Alexis asked.

"You'll see later."

"Oh, a surprise. I love your surprises," Alexis said, wiggling her eyebrows.

CeCe chuckled. Sometimes the little kid in Alexis came shining through.

Cory saw them enter the store and met them at the counter. She handed CeCe a bottle in a brown sack.

"Here you go, sis. Hi Alexis," Cory said in a playful voice.

"Hey, Cory. How's it going?"

"It's a good day!" Cory grinned.

CeCe widened her eyes at her sister's exuberance and shook her head as she grabbed the bottle.

"Okay." Alexis looked from Cory to CeCe. "It must be a Sloan sisters thing," she mumbled.

CeCe hurried them into the salon and out of the liquor store.

"That was kind of weird," Alexis said. "I wonder why she was so excited. Maybe she got that liquor sales person to back off."

"Who knows with Cory. Let's go see Cat. I heard there are new arrivals on The Bottom Shelf," CeCe said seductively, dragging Alexis to the bookstore.

"Wait, don't you want to check on the salon?" Alexis asked.

"Yeah, but let's do this first."

Alexis waved at Ryan and Heather as they walked by.

"Hey, sis," CeCe said, walking to the back of the bookstore.

"Hi, you two," Cat said happily. "Alexis, there are new toys." She pointed with her thumb to the back of the store.

"I heard." Alexis grinned.

"Maybe we should get something to go along with your cute little turquoise friend," CeCe suggested in a sexy voice.

Alexis grinned. "It never hurts to look."

"That's my girl," CeCe said.

They walked down the hall to the little room with the sex toys. "Do you remember the first time you took me back here?" Alexis asked as she opened the door.

"How can I forget?"

"That's kind of when we first started," Alexis said, putting her arm around CeCe's shoulder.

CeCe turned to look into Alexis's eyes. "Did you have any idea that night would lead us here?"

"I hoped."

CeCe rested her hands on Alexis's hips. "No way!"

"Yes, I did."

"When I gave you that little vibrator I couldn't get the image out of my head of you, naked, on a bed with that little toy in your hand. It still makes me hot just thinking about it," CeCe said, her eyes twinkling.

"Well then, let's see Cat's new arrivals," Alexis said.

They walked around the room looking at the vibrators. Some were small like the one Alexis had and others were larger.

"You know I don't have much experience with sex toys," Alexis said. "I'm not sure I know how to use some of these."

CeCe chuckled. "It still makes me giggle thinking about my quiet little sister ordering these and knowing how to use them."

CeCe Sloan is Swooning 257

"Do you think she's tried them out?"

"I want to say no, but..." CeCe shrugged.

They both giggled and continued to look at the toys.

"Look at this little finger vibrator. It's so tiny," CeCe said.

"It may be tiny, but if it's like the one you gave me it's mighty," Alexis said with a chuckle.

"Oh, I know how mighty our little friend is," CeCe said in a low voice.

"How about this?" Alexis said, holding up a wand vibrator. "According to the box it can be used in a multitude of ways, bringing the ultimate pleasure."

"*You* bring me ultimate pleasure, Lex," CeCe said as she put her arms around Alexis from behind and kissed just below her ear.

"Mmmm, and you know what that does to me," Alexis mumbled, leaning into CeCe.

"Okay, let's get that one," CeCe said, stepping back. "Cat would kill us if we got busy in her toy room."

"Oh my God! You don't think anyone has...you know," Alexis said, spinning around to face CeCe.

CeCe shrugged. "We should ask Cat sometime, but not today."

"Are you suddenly in a hurry to try this out?" Alexis asked as CeCe stuffed the toy in a bag and opened the door.

"No," CeCe scoffed. "I just remembered I left something in the back room of the salon."

"Okay, but don't we need to pay Cat?" Alexis asked as they hurriedly walked to the front of the bookstore.

CeCe waved at Cat who was with a customer and reached for Alexis's hand. "We'll pay her later."

"Where is everyone?" Alexis asked as they walked through the salon. "They were just here."

"I guess they're through for the day," CeCe said.

"Well, well, well," Alexis said. "Saturday night in the back room of the salon. I'm sure we could find something to do."

"Uh, I thought you wanted to be at our home sweet home," CeCe said as she stopped before opening the door to the back room of the salon.

Alexis grinned and raised one eyebrow. "You know how much I love this back room."

CeCe's heart began to pound in her chest and she gave Alexis the most beautiful smile. She opened the door and flipped the light switch.

30

"What's all this?" Alexis asked in a voice full of wonder.

The back room had been transformed into a romantic little alcove with strings of lights and soft music playing.

"When did you do this?"

"I did it yesterday. For you—well, us," CeCe said as they walked over to the table.

CeCe took the bottle out of the bag and showed it to Alexis.

"That's my favorite wine," Alexis exclaimed.

"It is and you are my favorite person," CeCe said with a loving smile. She opened the bottle of wine as her heart continued to race. Her hopes were to make this evening one of the happiest of Alexis's life.

"What's going on, babe? Why the special lighting and wine?"

"Oh, Lex. You should have everything special every day."

CeCe poured the wine into two glasses and handed Alexis one. "Did you know right before we had the open house, Cory, Cat and I raised a glass to toast the shopping center? Cory and Cat both said something about bringing joy to our part of town and then they looked at me."

Alexis waited. "And?"

"I wished that we'd all find our happily-ever-after." CeCe held up her glass. "You are happily-ever-after for me, Lex." CeCe smiled. "To our happily-ever-after."

Alexis clinked her glass to CeCe's and took a sip of the wine.

CeCe could see the delight in Alexis's face as the wine spread across her palate. Then CeCe set her glass down and took Alexis's as well and placed it on the table.

CeCe reached into her pocket and bent down on one knee. She reached for Alexis's hand and heard her gasp.

"CeCe," Alexis whispered.

CeCe looked up into Alexis's radiant face and smiled. "This is where our love began, so I thought it would be the perfect place to ask you something important. But first, you have given me the life I dreamed of. From when I was a little girl and imagined what true love would feel like to the woman I fantasized about who would whisk my heart away and make me swoon. You have done that every day since you walked into this salon all those months ago." CeCe paused and took a deep breath. "Alexis Reed, my beautiful Lex, will you marry me?"

Tears streamed down Alexis's face, so much so that she couldn't talk. She reached for CeCe and pulled her up until they were face to face.

"Oh baby," CeCe cooed, holding Alexis's face between her hands and wiping her tears with her thumbs.

"I never dreamed someone could love me the way you do." Alexis managed to get the words out between sobs. CeCe watched her take a deep breath and as she exhaled she shuddered. "Even more amazing to me is that I love you the same way. My heart wasn't made to love like this until I met you, CeCe Sloan. My heart was made to love you, Cecilia, and I will for all time."

CeCe smiled through the tears that were now streaming down her cheeks. "I didn't know we were going to cry. But, Lex...you didn't answer my question. Will you marry me?"

The brightest and most beautiful smile CeCe had ever seen graced Alexis's face. "Yes! Of course I'll marry you!"

Their lips met in a tear-soaked kiss. They couldn't stop smiling.

CeCe reached into her pocket and pulled out the ring. "Here," she said breathlessly.

Alexis held out her hand and CeCe slid the ring on her finger.

"Oh, baby. It's beautiful, it's perfect," Alexis exclaimed, looking at the band of diamonds with one larger diamond in the center.

"I know you don't wear jewelry much, especially when you're in surgery. The larger diamond is almost flush to the band because I knew you wouldn't want it sticking up too high."

"I love it," Alexis said, staring at the ring.

"That's not all," CeCe said, taking a small clear bag out of her pocket. Inside was a gold chain with a small circular hoop on it. "On days when you have surgery you can wear this necklace then when you get ready to scrub, the ring will clip into the circle right here and you can wear it around your neck."

"How ingenious," Alexis said. "Put it on me."

As CeCe clasped the gold chain around Alexis's neck she said, "I had a feeling you wouldn't want to take your rings off and I knew you couldn't perform surgery with them, so the jeweler showed me this."

Alexis turned around and faced CeCe with another bright smile. Her tears were gone and she stared at CeCe, shaking her head. "I love you so much. This is the biggest surprise of my life."

"I love you, Lex. I can't wait to be your wife. No more doubts."

Alexis smiled. "I knew the doubts were gone. I know you, babe. I have your heart."

CeCe brought their lips together in a tender kiss. This kiss promised a life of love and no more doubts.

They pulled apart and Alexis ran her hand over CeCe's hair. "This may top all those other nights in this room."

CeCe chuckled. "Up until now."

"Are we going to try out our new toy?"

"Not just yet, babe." CeCe grinned.

There was a knock on the door and Alexis furrowed her brow in confusion.

"Come on in!" CeCe yelled. "She said yes!"

The door opened and a group of people came streaming into the room with happy smiles and shouts of congratulations.

Cory and Cat were opening bottles of champagne as they quickly lined up glasses and began to pour. Someone turned up the music and the party started.

CeCe and Alexis stood arm in arm until Alexis had to keep her hand held out in front of her to show everyone her ring.

"The Lovers Landing ladies are here!" Alexis exclaimed.

"They're important in our story," CeCe said.

They both hugged Krista, Melanie, Tara, Lauren, Julia, and Heidi.

CeCe Sloan is Swooning 263

"Erin and Desi." Alexis grinned as they hugged her and looked at the ring.

Alexis's friends along with CeCe's co-workers and friends were all waiting their turn to hug the now engaged couple.

"Look, babe!" Alexis exclaimed. "There's Victoria with Shelby, Marina and Dru."

"I know, honey, I invited them, remember. Did you see Ella and Gia? They're here, too." CeCe laughed as Alexis continued to be awed by every person who came to celebrate with them. The stoic surgeon was nowhere to be found.

"Okay, I've waited long enough," Christine Sloan said, stepping in front of CeCe and Alexis.

"Look how beautiful the ring is on Lex's finger, Mom," CeCe said proudly.

"I knew it would be."

"You've already seen it," Alexis said with realization on her face.

Christine nodded. "You know she had to show it to her sisters as well."

Alexis grinned at CeCe. "They share almost everything, don't they?"

"Has she told you about the wedding yet?" Christine asked.

"Mom, we just got engaged," CeCe said with an edge to her voice.

"You should tell her, CeCe," Christine said firmly.

"Tell me what?"

CeCe sighed as Cory and Cat joined them. "Several years ago Mom entered us in this contest," CeCe began.

"And we won!" Christine exclaimed.

"Won?" Alexis looked at CeCe.

CeCe nodded. "We won an exclusive wedding."

Alexis's eyes widened. "Wow!"

"But it's for all three of us," Cory added.

"All three?" Alexis asked.

Cat nodded. "All three of us have to get married in one big wedding," Cat said with zero enthusiasm.

"Three sisters and their loves," Christine said, clapping her hands.

"CeCe is the first to get engaged." Cory grinned. "I'm so happy for you both. You are perfect together!"

"Thanks, Cory," Alexis said. "So we're all getting married together?" she asked with confusion on her face.

"We can talk about it later, babe," CeCe said.

"You'd better get busy finding Cory and Cat their soul-mates. Oh wait, you say the love of your life now, right?" Christine said dramatically, holding her hand to her chest.

"I'm sorry, CeCe," Cat said. "There's no way I'm getting married, so I guess none of us will get the fancy wedding."

"Hold on, Cat," Alexis said. She looked at CeCe and smiled. "I never thought I'd fall in love again. And there was no way I was ever getting married."

"That's right. Lex told me that from the beginning, but our hearts had a better idea."

"And here we are. I never imagined I'd ever be this happy," Alexis said, putting her arm around CeCe.

"Keep your heart open, Cat." CeCe smiled at Alexis. "You never know what can happen."

"What about Cory?" Cat said defensively. "She's not even dating anyone."

"More like I'm battling someone," Cory said.

CeCe gave her sister a strange look. "Is that who you were swearing about when I ordered our wine the other day?"

CeCe Sloan is Swooning   265

"It's nothing. I'm having an issue with a sales rep that keeps trying to steal my accounts. But I'm making progress and she and I are working on it," Cory said with a grin.

"You didn't look like enemies the other day when she was at your bar," Cat said.

"Hey, can we talk about this later? I'm engaged and I want to dance and celebrate with my fiancée, my family, and our friends."

"Yeah, we have plenty of time to figure out the wedding," Alexis said.

CeCe grabbed Alexis's hand and they danced into the middle of their friends.

"Hey!" Melanie shouted as she and Krista danced next to the brides-to-be.

"Have you met my fiancée?" Alexis said, putting her arms around CeCe.

Krista laughed and yelled over the music. "When you get ready to plan the wedding, call me. We could have a beautiful outdoor wedding at Lovers Landing."

CeCe looked at Alexis and nodded. "That's a great idea," she shouted back. "It's good to keep our options open."

After they'd danced and talked to a few more friends, Alexis grabbed CeCe's hand and pulled them away from the others. She stopped near the back door and turned to CeCe. "Look at all our friends," Alexis said, gazing back over the room.

"Are you having a good time?" CeCe asked. "I wanted tonight to be special."

"Every night is special with you, but this is wonderful. I'm so surprised."

"You keep saying that." CeCe grinned then her face turned serious. "I love you so much."

"I want to hear all about this wedding thing. I can tell it's bothering you," Alexis said.

CeCe draped her arms over Alexis's shoulders. "I don't want to wait forever to marry you, but this thing with my sisters could be a problem. Mom's right, neither one of them is even dating anyone."

"Babe," Alexis said. "We weren't dating anyone that long ago either. Love will find a way and we will get married when the time is right."

"You don't mind waiting?"

"It may not be as long as you think. Right now, can we go back to our engagement party and not worry about the wedding? Then later we'll go home and maybe we'll try out our new toy," Alexis said in a sultry voice.

"We don't need that toy tonight. It's you, me, and our love," CeCe replied.

Their lips met in a kiss that promised never-ending love. For a moment the world fell away and they were surrounded by the people they loved, sounds of joy, and the happiness their love had created. This was happily-ever-after.

SIX MONTHS LATER

"Knock, knock," CeCe said, slightly tapping on Erin's open door.

"Well, hey!" Erin exclaimed, getting up from behind her desk. "I figured you'd be off taking care of last minute wedding details."

"That's the beauty of winning an exclusive wedding. They take care of everything," CeCe said with a smile.

"Come sit," Erin said, indicating one of the chairs in front of her desk.

"I only have a few minutes," CeCe said. "I'm meeting Alexis upstairs. She was very vague. I know she didn't have surgery today, but she asked me to meet her at the nurse's station on the surgical floor. Maybe she's checking on a patient."

"Are you nervous about tomorrow?"

"Not really. I'm more excited than anything. Were you nervous at your wedding?"

"Oh, CeCe. My wedding was unbelievable. Desi and I got married at the courthouse in a rushed ceremony because there were complications with my pregnancy. We'd planned to get married after the baby got here."

"Oh wow."

"The unbelievable part is when we got home from the courthouse, Desi had planned this intimate wedding at our house with our close friends."

"Oh, Erin. That is unbelievably romantic."

Erin chuckled. "Desi still surprises me. You wouldn't believe the romantic streak my wife has."

"Oh, yes I would. Most people see the stoic surgeon in Alexis, but she is so romantic and sweet it would make your teeth hurt!"

Erin laughed. "And we're the lucky wives who get their attention."

"Almost wife," CeCe said.

"We will be there supporting you both tomorrow." Erin smiled.

"Thank you."

"I still can't believe you and your sisters are all getting married together," Erin said.

"I can't believe it either, but that's a story for another day." CeCe got up and walked to the door.

"All of Alexis's family is here?" Erin asked.

"Yes. It is the funniest thing. I have been to visit them several times since Lex and I were engaged and they have visited us here. But Lex's parents love my mom and she loves them!"

Erin chuckled.

"They are quiet, serious people, kind of like Alexis," CeCe said. "And my mom is rather loud and to the point, if you know what I mean."

"Why does it surprise you that they hit it off? Doesn't it remind you of someone else? Maybe we've seen this movie

CeCe Sloan is Swooning   269

before," Erin said, raising a brow.

CeCe laughed. "I guess so." She shook her head. "I never dreamed that forever could be like this. I can't believe it was only a year ago that I opened my own salon and when Lex walked in that door our hearts decided it was time for us to do something. We'd gotten to know each other through her hair appointments, but that day the serious flirting began and here we are. I love her so much."

"She loves you, too," Erin stated.

CeCe grinned. "I'd better go find my fiancée."

"Tomorrow you'll be calling her your wife," Erin said.

"I can't wait!"

* * *

Alexis was standing at the nurse's station chatting when she heard the elevator ding and the doors open. As CeCe stepped out Alexis strolled towards her.

"I will never get used to how hot you look in that white coat," CeCe said quietly as Alexis stopped in front of her.

"Remind me to wear this home," Alexis said and winked.

"I didn't think you had surgery today."

"I didn't." Alexis reached for CeCe's hand and intertwined their fingers.

"Then what are we doing here?"

"Do you remember when I came to your salon opening I couldn't wait to see your back room and find out if the stories I'd heard were true?" Alexis said as she began to lead them past the elevator and down the hall.

"Yes," CeCe replied, drawing the word out.

Alexis opened a door and quickly pulled them inside, closing and locking it.

"Babe!" CeCe squealed.

"Shhh." Alexis grinned, resting her hands on CeCe's hips and pulling her close.

CeCe quickly scanned her surroundings and saw shelves stacked with medical supplies. "This isn't..." She giggled.

Alexis nodded. "I thought since we started in your back room, we should end our last night as single women in my supply closet."

CeCe put her arms around Alexis's shoulders as a smile grew on her face. "Why Dr. Reed, you'd better make your last night worth it because tomorrow you become a married woman."

"I can't wait to be married to you," Alexis said. Her heart had never been this full and this happy. Alexis wasn't naïve though; she knew all relationships faced challenges at times, but she believed as long as she and CeCe were together they could take on the world.

"And eat ice cream when we're eighty?"

"Among other things." Alexis grinned. She pulled the little turquoise vibrator out of her pocket and held it where CeCe could see it. Alexis watched as CeCe's eyes widened.

"You are full of surprises, Alexis Reed!"

"All because of your love, Cecilia," Alexis said softly. "My heart may explode with joy after we get married tomorrow."

"I'll put it right back together," CeCe promised.

Alexis pressed her lips to CeCe's in a tender kiss. "I love you with all I am and will be. You've made me a better person, babe."

"Lex," CeCe gasped.

Alexis smiled. "CeCe Sloan is swooning."

"I love you, Alexis."

This time when Alexis touched her lips to CeCe's the softest moan escaped her throat. CeCe wasn't the only person swooning. If Alexis had learned anything in their time together she now knew swooning was the best feeling, second only to CeCe's love.

ABOUT THE AUTHOR

Jamey Moody writes heartwarming sapphic romance. Falling into a sapphic romance is an adventure. Her characters are strong women, living everyday lives with a few bumps in the road, but they get their happily ever afters. You can find her books on Amazon and on her website at jameymoody.com.

Emails are welcome at jameymoodyauthor@gmail.com

As an independent publisher a review is greatly appreciated and I would be grateful if you could take the time to write just a few words.

On the next page is a list of my books with links that will take you to their page.

After that I've included the first chapter of the next book in the continuing adventures of the Sloan sisters: Cory Sloan is Swearing.

Cory is having a battle with a sales rep from a discount liquor chain. Vi Valdez is simply trying to get enough accounts to move up the ladder and become the VP of Sales. Cory Sloan is swearing because Vi is making things hard on her in so many ways. I swear you're going to love these two as tensions build, but then Cory finds a way for them to be on the same team.

ALSO BY JAMEY MOODY

Stand Alones

Live This Love

One Little Yes

Who I Believe

What Now

The Your Way Series:

* Finding Home

*Finding Family

*Finding Forever

The Lovers Landing Series

*Where Secrets Are Safe

*No More Secrets

*And The Truth Is ...

*Instead Of Happy

The Second Chance Series

The Woman at the Top of the Stairs

The Woman Who Climbed A Mountain

The Woman I Found In Me

Christmas Novellas

*It Takes A Miracle

The Great Christmas Tree Mystery

With One Look

*Also available as an audiobook

CORY SLOAN IS SWEARING
CHAPTER 1

Cory Sloan walked back into The Liquor Box through the opening that adjoined her store to her sister CeCe's beauty salon, laughing boisterously.

"What's so funny?"

"Oh, Taylor," Cory snorted. "My sisters wanted to have a quick toast before we unlocked the doors for the open house and Cat made the nicest toast about spreading joy and when we looked at CeCe she said..." Cory paused and held up her champagne glass and chuckled.

"She said?"

"She said may we live happily-ever-after." Cory burst into laughter again.

"What's so funny about that?"

"It's kind of a strange toast to make when you're opening up a store, don't you think." Cory chuckled.

"I guess so since none of you have a girlfriend at the moment," Taylor said.

"Exactly!"

"Still, it was a nice thing to wish."

Cory quickly glanced around the store. "Are you ready?"

"Yes, boss. The samples are ready over there," Taylor gestured to a display in the middle of the store. "We have discount coupons for CeCe's salon and Cat's bookstore at the register.

"And the wheel is set up over here for prizes and discounts," Cory said, giving the wheel a spin.

"Like Wheel of Fortune!" Taylor said and laughed.

"Not exactly, Vanna."

Each store had been completed with the occupants in mind. Cory's had an open floor plan with rows of shelves for various liquors and wines. Refrigerated cases were along one wall that held cold beer, wine and a wide variety of hard seltzers. In the back Cory had set up a small bar where customers could get a quick drink on their way home from work.

There was a hallway in the back that led to the restrooms and then a storage room where Cory kept her inventory stocked. Her store was on the end and on the wall that she shared with CeCe's salon they'd made a large opening so customers could walk from one store to the other. They hoped to help drive customers to each other's businesses.

"Okay, let's do this." Cory unlocked the door and held it open to several people who were waiting outside. "Welcome!"

They had a steady stream of customers and Cory was having a good time helping people spin the wheel for prizes or assisting others looking for certain types of liquor or wine.

When she looked up a while later she saw Taylor waiting on a customer near the coolers and took a moment to catch her breath. Cory had been in marketing and retail

CeCe Sloan is Swooning

since she was a kid. Her first job had been as a salesperson at a local hardware store. She loved helping people. So when she went to college she majored in marketing and worked nights and weekends as a bartender. She loved creating drinks and introducing her regulars to new wines, beers and liquors.

This store would give her a better opportunity to spread her knowledge of spirits than owning a bar and the hours were a lot better.

She heard a jingling sound that indicated a customer had just walked into the store. Cory looked up to see a woman with very dark hair walk through the door. She gave Cory a measured look as Cory walked towards her.

Cory could feel the woman's eyes look her up and down then meet her gaze. The woman had dark brown eyes to match her dark hair and Cory felt her heart skip a beat. But then she heard warning bells go off in her brain: caution, caution, caution.

Cory called up her best smile and flashed it at the woman. "Hi, welcome to The Liquor Box. Can I help you find something?"

"Such an interesting name and the logo," the woman said with a hint of a smile.

Cory was proud to be a lesbian and wanted her store to be obviously welcoming to the LGBTQ community. Her logo which was part of the sign on the front of the store was a mouth with a tongue sticking out, much like the Rolling Stones iconic emblem. As a lesbian, with this logo, she thought The Liquor Box was the perfect name. It made her smile every time she thought about it, even though it might seem juvenile to some people. Cory had a good time wherever she went and wanted the same environment for her store.

"We like to have fun," Cory said with another charming smile.

The woman nodded and this time she smiled. "Do you also sell wholesale, or just retail?"

"We are happy to supply all your spirit needs. Whether it's an event or restaurant or something else we'd be happy to help."

Again the woman nodded and Cory couldn't help but feel like she was being sized-up in some way.

"I'll just look around," the woman said with a smile that didn't reach her eyes.

"Let me know if I can help."

A group of people came in from CeCe's salon taking Cory's attention away from the woman.

Several minutes later Cory finished with a customer and saw the woman walking towards the door. "Hey," Cory called to her.

She turned around just as she reached the door.

"Here's my card. Just give me a call if you need anything," Cory said.

The woman looked at the card. "Corrine Sloan."

"You can call me Cory."

The woman nodded and smiled at her again then walked out.

Cory felt a flutter of butterflies in her stomach for just an instant when the woman smiled. She was beautiful when she smiled, but there went those warming bells again.

"Hey, Cory," Taylor called. "Could you help me over here?"

Cory went back to her job, but couldn't shake the feeling that the woman was checking them out.

* * *

They had had a steady stream of customers, but things had quieted down.

"Taylor, I'm going to run next door and check on CeCe and Cat. Text me if you need help."

"Okay," Taylor said.

Cory walked through Salon 411, but didn't see CeCe so she kept going into the bookstore.

"Hey, Cory," Cat said, getting her attention.

"Hi," Cory said, walking over to where Cat stood with a customer.

"Cory, this is Elena Burkett. I was explaining to her that we're all in this together," Cat said.

"It's nice to meet you. I'm the oldest sister and The Liquor Box is my store," Cory said with a friendly smile.

"I love the name and logo." Elena grinned. "Cat was just telling me about the opening between the stores. That's a genius idea," Elena said.

"Thanks," Cory replied.

"I love the reading nook and plan to be here often," Elena said, smiling at Cat.

"That's why I created it," Cat said.

"Hey, I'm going to get something from the back," Cory said, giving Cat a knowing look.

"It's okay, Elena knows all about The Bottom Shelf," Cat said.

"Oh, okay." Cory chuckled.

"CeCe is in there with Alexis Reed," Cat said, raising her eyebrows.

A smile grew on Cory's face. Alexis Reed was an esteemed doctor who also happened to be CeCe's favorite client. Cory and Cat were certain they both had crushes on each other, but wouldn't admit it.

"I'll be right back," Cory said.

On her way to the back of the bookstore Cory muttered, "Alexis may not be CeCe's favorite client much longer." CeCe had a rule about not dating her clients and it wouldn't surprise Cory if Alexis had a new hair stylist soon.

A few minutes later Cory came back out of the room and stopped as she watched Cat giving Elena her purchases at the register. Cat and her longtime girlfriend had broken up a while back and Cory hadn't seen her smile at another woman quite like she was at Elena Burkett.

Maybe that happily-ever-after toast CeCe made earlier wasn't so funny after all.

"Did you get what you needed?" Cat said with an inquisitive stare. "You didn't embarrass CeCe did you?"

"No, I did not embarrass our sister and I didn't get anything for me."

"Oh?"

"Brandy asked me if you had a certain kind of vibrator," Cory said.

"Brandy? Why couldn't she ask me? We've all been friends forever."

"I don't know. You text her."

"Okay, I will."

"Gotta go, sis. Come see me when you close and we'll have a beer," Cory said as she left the bookstore. She waved at CeCe as she walked through the salon and into her store.

"Hey," Cory said to Taylor as she joined her at the register. "Everything okay?"

"Yep. I've made a few sales and oh— do you remember that woman who came in earlier with the dark hair," Taylor said.

"Uh, Taylor, a lot of women came in today with dark hair," Cory replied.

Taylor chuckled. "You didn't look at the other women the way you were looking at *this* woman."

Cory furrowed her brow. "Are you talking about the woman who walked through the store and looked at everything, but didn't buy anything. She was asking me about wholesale prices."

"That's the one." Taylor nodded.

"I was looking at her differently because something didn't seem quite right with her."

"Right?" Taylor said with a grin. "She came back and bought one of the expensive bottles of wine then asked me about wholesale prices for the wine on that display." Taylor pointed to a display near the front of the store.

"What did you tell her?"

"I told her she'd have to talk to you."

Cory nodded. "Hmm, I wonder who she is. Something seemed different about her."

Taylor shrugged.

"How did she pay? Did she use a credit card?" Cory asked.

"Yes," Taylor replied, opening the register and searching through the receipts. "Here it is."

They looked at the signature and the name above it.

"I knew it!" Cory exclaimed.

"What? I don't understand," Taylor said.

"It says her name is Violet Valdez, but below her name it says Spec's Wine and Spirits," Cory said.

"Spec's, the big discount liquor chain all over the metroplex?" Taylor said.

"Exactly!" Cory studied the receipt. "I wonder why she would be coming to our open house? We're just the neighborhood liquor store."

"I don't know." Taylor shrugged. "You're the marketing genius. I'm just your loyal manager."

Cory smiled. "You are and I plan to get you more help, too."

"I have a friend who needs a job. She's tired of the restaurant bar scene."

"Then why would she want to work in a liquor store?"

"She doesn't want to wait tables, but she knows her beer, wine, and liquor."

"Tell her to come by and talk to me."

Taylor grinned. "Would you look at that, she's walking in the store."

Cory laughed and after Taylor introduced them Cory took her to her office to fill out an application. Cory did a quick interview and was satisfied with her answers as they walked back to the front of the store.

"What's happening at The Liquor Box," CeCe asked as she walked into the store along with Cat.

"Let me introduce you to our new employee. This is Randi," Cory said.

"Really!" Randi exclaimed.

"The job is yours if you want it," Cory grinned.

"Thank you!"

"These are my sisters, CeCe and Cat. They own the other stores in the building."

"Oh, I know all about the Sloan sisters," Randi gushed.

'You do?" Cory asked.

"Oh yeah, the bar and restaurant scene has been buzzing about the Sloan Sisters Shopping Center," Randi said. "Say that fast."

Cory laughed. "I told y'all this was going to be fun!"

CeCe and Cat looked at each other and shook their heads.

CeCe Sloan is Swooning

"I know Dad is happy. We're working together. Sort of," Cory said with a big grin.

"Come on, let's break in that new happy hour bar of yours," CeCe said. "I'm buying."

Cory Sloan is Swearing will be available October 24th, 2023.

Printed in Great Britain
by Amazon